THE URBANA FREE LIBRARY

D0331043

The Urbana Free Library

DISCARDED BY
URBANA FREE LIBRARY

To renew materials call
217-367-4057

8-05

DATE DUE		
SEP 15 2005	NOV 0 4 2005	
9/29/05		
OCT 19 2005		
NOV 2 6 2005		
DEC 2 9 2005		
JAN 17 2006		
NOV 0 4 2006		

The MANIPULATED

WHAT THIS MYSTERY IS ABOUT...

... Sleeping with a surrogate daughter
... A Golden Globe
... Hockey at Staples Center
... The Velour Overground
... Black, green, and oolong tea
... Mao's Kitchen
... Alternate realities
... Zoloft
... Chicken marsala
... James Bond
... Johnny Depp
... Pink Pearls
... The use of light and shadow
... Fatherhood
... Stalking a former lover
... A head shop
... A time-traveling ninja master
... Iraq, because everything's about Iraq
... Beyoncé
... The Felonious Monks
... A little Taoism
... The Venice Riots
... A spate of epiphanies
... Tentacles

PEOPLE THIS MYSTERY IS ABOUT...

Joe Portugal
TV commercial actor
and perpetual stumbler over dead bodies

Gina Vela
Joe's wife, an interior designer by trade

Harold "The Horse" Portugal
Joe's father, a man feeling his oats

Ronnie McKenzie
She made it in Hollywood, but did she make it with Joe?

Mike Lennox
His troubles would kill a lesser man

Donna Lennox
His wife, a tea shop magnate, the subject of a fruitless search

Dennis Lennox
Their son, a Hollywood wunderkind and all-around bad guy

Carrie Fitzpatrick
Young enough to be everyone's daughter

Samantha Szydlo
She has paint on her nose,
but does she have blood on her hands?

Alberta Burns
She's off the force now, and she has a script to show you

John Santini
An import–export baron…and a whole lot more

Alma Rodriguez
Santini's right arm, a woman who brooks no nonsense

Trixie Trenton
She tried to be a bimbo and almost succeeded

Claudia Acuna
A television news reporter at a crossroads

Eric Stahl
One of Dennis Lennox's minions, a great father, but…

Sean McKay
A young man with a way with words
and with a bowling ball

Vikki Rodman
One of those people who's always looking for something

Ike Sunemori
L. Ron Hubbard wannabee, or true benefactor?

Emilio and His Uncle
One's fat, the other's a fathead

also by Nathan Walpow

THE
MANIPULATED

a Joe Portugal mystery

by Nathan Walpow

URBANA FREE LIBRARY

UGLYTOWN
Los Angeles

First Edition

Text copyright © 2005 by Nathan Walpow. All Rights Reserved.

This book is a work of fiction. Names, characters, places, and incidents are either the products of the author's imagination or are used fictitiously. Any resemblance to any persons living or deceased, events, or locales is entirely coincidental.

UGLYTOWN AND THE UGLYTOWN COIN LOGO SERVICEMARK REG. U.S. PAT. OFF.

Library of Congress Cataloging-in-Publication Data data on file.
ISBN: 0-9758503-2-6

Find out more of the mystery: uglytown.com/manipulated

Printed in Canada

10 9 8 7 6 5 4 3 2 1

Dedicated to the memory of William Relling Jr.

"The three most deplorable things in the world: the spoiling of fine youths through false education, the degradation of fine paintings through vulgar admiration, and the utter waste of fine tea through incompetent manipulation."

—Lichihlai, Sung Dynasty poet

one

Ronnie McKenzie shrieked, hurled off the bedding, and scrambled to her feet. She was naked. I'd seen her undressed before—sunbathing in the back yard next door to my house—but it still made a fine visual. Ronnie's in her early twenties, and gorgeous.

But, eye appeal aside, there was a problem. The bed she'd abandoned was still occupied. By me. And I was a married man. And Ronnie wasn't my wife.

I did a quick scan. The bed was unfamiliar and so was the room. My eyes went back to Ronnie. "You're naked," I said.

She looked down. Another screech scorched my ears. She tried to cover up, but given two hands, one crotch and two sizable breasts, something had to give. It was one of the breasts. The right one. It perched atop the arm attached to the hand more or less covering the other one, creamy, luxuriant—

I turned away. Had a thought. Was I naked too? If I wasn't, maybe nothing had—

I reached down. No underwear. Nothing down there but an erection. I willed it to go away. It ignored me. I looked at Ronnie again.

"What did you *do*?" she said.

"Me? There's two of us here. We both did it. Whatever *it* is."

A third shriek. This one from deep in her guts. Then she turned and ran out of the room. I got a great shot of her taut-yet-lush behind as she made her exit.

Three or four seconds later: "My panties!"

That was the last time I heard her voice until I got her fired.

My tongue was furry and so were my gums, and the wool went right up my nasal passages to my brain. My guts undulated. At least the erection was subsiding. A good thing, because I had to take a leak.

I extricated myself from the bedclothes and maneuvered to my feet. Turned out I wasn't naked. I had a sock on my left foot. Not mine, though.

A doorway led to a bathroom. I emptied my bladder, washed my hands, rinsed my mouth, looked in the mirror. I looked puffy. Also dissolute.

I left the bathroom and spotted my Jockeys under a chair in the corner. "My panties," I said, and went after them. I shook them and put them on and, as I got my balls arranged, stuff started coming back to me.

It wasn't enough stuff—it didn't explain why I'd slept, at the very least in the literal sense, with my barely-into-her-twenties protégé—but it was a start.

The night before ...

I'd been at the party an hour, most of which I'd spent wondering why I'd let Ronnie talk me into being her "date." Hollywood soirées are not my thing. But Gina—my wife—was out of town, and Ronnie didn't want to go solo. So there I was.

I wandered into the back yard and stumbled upon a guy smoking dope. He turned around and saw me and without a word held out a joint. Equally silently, I accepted it. I took a hit. I looked at the guy. "Keep it a while," he said. It was down to a roach before he'd take it again. By that time I was, well, you know.

We did what stoned boomers do: talked about music. He spent a good five minutes trying to convince me Foghat ought to be in the Rock and Roll Hall of Fame. At which point I announced I needed a bathroom and wandered inside. After I found one I took a wrong turn and came upon an open doorway. Beyond was a room with a wooden desk and a full complement of bookcases. An Oriental rug—*the colors, man, the colors*—overlaid most of the hardwood floor.

The light was dim. Just one small desk lamp. But it was enough to reveal something shiny on a shelf. I was curious. I walked in. Not the kind of thing I'd usually do. Blame the dope.

The shiny thing was a golden ball with a strip of film around it, atop a marble pedestal. A Golden Globe? I moved around and looked at it from various angles. "Neat," I said.

"Is it?"

I whirled around. Nearly fell down. The person who'd spoken was young, handsome, and confident. It was Dennis Lennox. Our host for the evening. He was a twenty-six-year-old wunderkind with a cop show and three sitcoms, including Ronnie's, on the air. The Brentwood mansion was his.

"Sorry," I said.

"For what?"

"I suppose I shouldn't have wandered in here."

"Not a problem." He gestured at the award. "I got that for *Protect and Serve*, you know. Everyone expected *The Sopranos* to win."

"I would've voted for *24*. I mean, if I had a vote. Which I don't. Being as I don't belong to—did I just say 'being as'?"

"You did. You're Joe, aren't you?"

"Yes."

"Ronnie's date."

"Not a date, really. Her—" I couldn't think of the right word. Finally, because I was loaded: "Her father figure."

He didn't say anything. Just came and stood beside me, regarding the Golden Globe. His nose twitched, and I knew he knew what I'd been up to outside. Finally he spoke. "It doesn't mean shit, you know."

"No?"

"It doesn't mean shit, and it's given out by a bunch of old men who can't find their dicks anymore." He positioned a hand behind my shoulder and hastened me to the door. "Nice talking to you." Then I was back in the hallway and the door was closing behind me.

I found my way outside. It was the front lawn this time, but my new friend was there anyway. He produced another joint, and I used it to combat the feeling of dread that had appeared out of nowhere. He started singing "While My Guitar Gently Weeps," and I joined him, both of us on air guitar. Then he ran into the house and came back with a beat-up Alvarez acoustic. I guess my air guitar was so phenomenal he could tell I actually played.

I didn't have a pick, so I used a quarter. The two of us sat on the grass and exhausted our repertoire of Beatles songs. The dread only surfaced once more. We were doing "Helter Skelter," and I thought of Charlie Manson and the Sharon Tate thing and how it happened in a house that was probably a lot like this one. I shivered once and grabbed another hit, and my mind jumped elsewhere.

Somewhere along the line I crashed right there on the lawn. It was that soft grass that pushes itself up into little pillowlike hillocks, and it called to me. I awoke once to the strains of "Why Don't We Do It in the Road." That was the last thing I remembered before waking up with Ronnie.

She'd come out from Arkansas a year or so back to chase down fame in Hollywood, and, against all odds, had found it. I helped some. I set her up with my cousin-slash-agent Elaine, who immediately got her onto the latest series of inane commercials for The Gap. Somebody casting a Dennis Lennox pilot saw her, the pilot made the fall schedule, and now she was on a better-than-mediocre sitcom called *The Galahad Sisters* that had just gotten picked up for a full season.

Ronnie's father died when she was two. A traffic accident. He got out of his car to fix a flat and got smashed to pulp by an errant semi. Her mother'd done a pretty good job raising her. But I knew she missed having a dad.

You see what's coming, right? She moves to L.A., there's this nice man next door who helps her get her acting career going, getting her to grow her hair out in its natural dark color, and to drop the cheap-sexy-gal stuff she was pushing in favor of her honest-to-God girl-next-door sex appeal. He's always there to offer support and advice, he's got a woman and clearly isn't trying to get her in the sack, and he genuinely seems to care about her welfare.

That's why I told Dennis Lennox I was Ronnie's father figure. In light of what followed, not the brightest thing I've ever done.

I went to the window. It was a gorgeous early November day.

The sun lit up the lawn. I was pretty sure it was the same one I'd been on the night before. I was still at Dennis's.

Two women were running across the lawn. The one bringing up the rear was wearing sweats and a baseball cap. The one in front was wearing a towel. Ronnie. She had her shoes in one hand and her purse in the other.

I entertained thoughts of going after her. Then she disappeared around a bend in the driveway. A few seconds later I heard the burble of the busted muffler on her Miata.

I turned from the window. Looked around the room. Found my shoes under the bed. One of my socks too. Maybe I'd traded the other one for the one I had on.

My pants were out in the hall. About, I estimated, where Ronnie'd found her underwear. I put them on, added my shoes and sock, found the stairs. Halfway down, I stopped. Sat on a step. The import of what I might have done swept in. Married less than a year, and already cheating. What kind of shit was I?

But maybe nothing had happened. Maybe there was a perfectly logical explanation for waking up naked with Ronnie. Maybe aliens had abducted us and dumped us in the bed when they were done sticking probes up our rectums.

Or it was all a psychological experiment. A woman I met the night before was with the psych department at UCLA. No, the philology department. Then maybe it was a philological experiment. Seeing how my language evolved when—

Or it was terrorists. Bed-putting, memory-sapping terrorists.

Or maybe we really had gotten it on.

The scene where I would tell Gina filled my head. It would be in the kitchen. Because being in the kitchen always gave you a lot to occupy your hands when undergoing psychological trauma. She'd be dicing onions. Gina, I would say, I'm afraid I slept with Ronnie. I don't know how it happened. I don't even remember it.

The chopping would falter. She wouldn't say anything, though, and I'd be dying there. I'd open the fridge, stare at the milk and eggs and Trader Joe's salads. Then Gina would come at me with the knife—

two

I heard a radio. I stood and followed its sound to a kitchen. It looked somewhat familiar. Another dim marijuana memory. If I could remember stuff like that, why didn't I remember getting into bed with Ronnie? Or what, if anything, happened after that?

One of the Sunday morning Beatles shows was on. "The Long and Winding Road" started up, the new-old version before Phil Spector got his hands on it and crapped it up with strings. The *Let It Be...Naked* album had come out that week, and a couple of days later Spector finally got charged with the murder of the woman who'd been shot at his house several months back. There was some kind of poetic justice there. Someday I'd be able to figure out what kind.

There were two people in the kitchen. One, who'd recently been spotted chasing Ronnie across the lawn, was loading the dishwasher. A tiny Asian woman I'd seen floating around the night before with trays of hors d'oeuvres. The baseball cap said *The Galahad Sisters* across the front.

The other person was the guy I'd been waxing nostalgic with the night before. His name was Mike. That was about all I remembered about him. That, and the fact that he had something to do with a head shop. Owned it, or worked at it, or just spent endless hours hanging out at it.

He was a few years older than me, a little shorter, gray-haired, with a bulbous nose and wire-rimmed glasses. He was wearing a black terrycloth robe and flip-flops, and holding a mug brimming with dark liquid.

"Hey," he said.

"Hey."

"You're up."

"Uh-huh," I said. "We woke up upstairs. I mean *I*. I woke up upstairs."

He and the woman exchanged glances. "Cool," he said.

Maybe he knew something. All I had to do was ask. I was afraid to. I did anyway.

"No idea," he said. "But right on, man."

"I'm sure nothing happened. Ronnie's a friend of mine."

"Wish I had friends like that."

"You're sure you have no idea how we ended up in bed up there?"

"I'm sure," he said. "Want tea?"

"Yeah, okay."

"What kind?"

"Hot."

"Black, green, oolong…"

"Black, I guess."

"Lu, could you make some of that nice Yunnan?"

"Of course, Mr. Lennox," the woman said.

"Thanks."

"'Mr. Lennox'?" I said.

"Yeah. Denny's dad."

"I didn't know."

"Well, there you go. By the way, I think your shirt's in a tree out front."

Half an hour later I had half a grapefruit and a couple of pancakes and two mugs of tea in my stomach. My shirt had indeed been found dangling from a palm tree in front of the house. Lu'd gotten it down with a fruit picker on a long pole.

She went off to do laundry. It was just Mike and me in the kitchen. I asked where Dennis was.

"Dunno. Maybe he went to the office."

"On a Sunday?"

"Hey, I did my best to drill my work ethic into him. Guess I didn't do so good. You got kids, Joe?"

"Nope."

"Want any?"

"Gina—that's my wife—is forty-eight."

"Your wife."

"Well, yeah."

He raised an eyebrow.

"I told you. Ronnie's just a friend. Besides, I'm old enough to be her father."

He frowned. "Sometimes I wonder."

"About what?"

"Nothing. Want to know the good thing about kids?"

Not particularly. "Sure."

"It's when you're older, like us, and you have this adult person who's the fruit of your looms."

"That's 'loins.'"

"Whatever," he said.

Soon as someone plays the *whatever* card, the conversation generally meanders to a halt. So it was that morning. Twenty minutes later a cab was whisking me home. The fare went on Dennis Lennox's tab. Mike insisted on it.

•

Gina was up in San Francisco visiting her old friend Annie. She was due back that night. I spent the rest of the day wondering what I was going to tell her. Hey, babe, funny thing happened this morning. I woke up in bed with Ronnie. I don't know if sex was involved, but if it was, I'm sorry. You want to go into the kitchen where the knives are?

Having a big hole in my memory worried me. What if the dope had been laced with something more potent? Ecstasy or horse tranquilizers or something I'd never heard of because I was so unhip.

Maybe Ronnie would know. Or if not, at least she could tell me why she ran off screaming. Whether she was embarrassed because we'd had sex. About the fact that we'd had it, or about my performance.

I went next door to see if she would talk to me. But Theta said she wasn't there. She's Ronnie's cousin, and she owns the house. I had no reason to believe Theta had ever lied to me, but blood is thicker, et cetera. I pointedly looked at Ronnie's Miata parked in the driveway, and Theta said she'd gone off shopping with Stephanie Urbano, the other Galahad Sister, and that she'd tell Ronnie I was looking for her.

Ronnie wasn't back by the time I had to leave for the airport to get Gina. Unless she'd been back all along and was hiding in her bedroom. Lacking any input from her, I decided to just tell Gina the truth. Plead that if anything had happened, if I was too out of it to remember, I probably wasn't responsible for my actions.

She came out of the terminal. Kiss-kiss, hug-hug. I weaved my way out to Sepulveda. We stopped at a light. I opened my mouth to confess. "How's Annie?" came out instead.

"An emotional wreck."

"How come?" I said, knowing what the answer would be.

"Guy she was seeing. She thought he was the one. Found out he was fucking his personal trainer."

"Oh."

"What an asshole."

I sat there, hands on the wheel.

"Guys are such jerks," she said.

"Not all."

"Most of them. Not you, of course. But most of them."

"Women too. Most of them are jerks."

"Agreed. Most people are jerks." One of our points of concurrence. A belief in the basic unworthiness of the majority of human beings.

The guy behind me honked. The light was green. I got moving. Gina told me some more about her friend Annie, then went off on an exhibit she'd seen at a gallery up there.

When we got home I decided to wait until bedtime to tell her my story. But when I came out from brushing my teeth she was already asleep.

When she woke up in the morning she jumped my bones. Afterward, I considered blurting out my sad tale. But I'd seen too many movies where the revelation that ended a relationship happened during the afterglow. People were particularly vulnerable then.

Gina went to see one of her interior design clients a little after noon. The minute she left I ran next door. Ronnie was probably on the set, but maybe she'd told Theta something.

Ronnie wasn't on the set. She wasn't even in Los Angeles. She'd gone to Hawaii to film a "very special episode" of *The Galahad Sisters*. She wouldn't be back for a week.

"I thought that was next week."

"It got moved up," Theta said. "Whole schedule got switched around. We just found out Friday. Didn't Ronnie tell you?"

"If she did, I don't remember."

"Is there more you don't remember?"

"I don't get you."

"Sure you do. Sunday morning. You. Ronnie. Between the sheets."

"What else did she tell you?"

"That she doesn't remember what happened with you two."

"Me neither. Nothing, I hope."

"So does she."

"Can't a woman tell?"

"Usually."

"Even if the guy uses a condom?"

"We have ways."

"So?"

"So she didn't get laid, if that's what you're getting at."

"So there's no problem."

"Not unless the two of you did something else. Us MacKenzie girls are very fond of, you know, mouth stuff."

"Oh."

"We're good at it too."

"This isn't helping."

"Sorry. Look, if anything happened between the two of you, since neither one of you can remember it, you probably had something in you that made it not be your fault. So I wouldn't worry about it."

"I'm married now. I have to worry about it."

"You haven't told Gina yet."

"No. I thought I could gather some more data first."

She shook her head. "Doesn't look like it's gonna happen, honey. Get your ass over there and tell her. Sooner the better."

But I didn't tell Gina. That night we went to my father's house, and we were there late, and I just chickened out. Tuesday morning Gina left early to have breakfast with another client. She had a professional society meeting Tuesday night. I resolved to confess when she got home. Longer it took before I told her, more it would look like I had something to hide.

Tuesday afternoon. The phone rang. "Hello?"

"It's Mike. Mike Lennox. You doing anything tonight?"

"Nothing in particular."

"You like hockey?"

"Sure." I did, more or less, though that whole offsides thing was too confusing. Not to mention icing.

"I got Denny's tickets for the box. Want to go?"

"You mean one of those luxury boxes?"

"Yeah," he said. "Sweet one, right at center ice. I'll pick you up at six-thirty. Give me your address."

"I didn't say I'd go."

"You didn't say you wouldn't."

I gave him my address.

"You idiot!"

This, strangely enough, was me. Jozef Stumpel had just blown a breakaway, the puck skittering off the end of his stick and dribbling harmlessly past the opposing goalie.

It was late in the third period. The score was tied. I understood offsides and was well on my way to comprehending icing too. The other people in the luxury box were entertainment industry types, but pleasant company nonetheless. A while back a prime-quality dessert cart had come around.

I turned to Mike. "Hey, man," I said, "Thanks for the ticket."

He put down his binoculars and said, "Any time, man. That's what friends are for." He turned back to the ice, jumped up, clapped his hand to his head, sank back into his seat.

Friends? We were friends already? After one dope-riddled evening, a kitchen conversation, and a hockey game? How could this have happened?

I'd spent my entire adult life without any close male friends. The only true friend I'd had since high school was Gina. Then, after nine years, things turned romantic. And while she was still my best friend, in that goopy way people speak of their mates, things were different. I didn't have that person anymore to hang with when I needed to hang and be rid of when I wanted to be alone.

The Kings lost on a last-minute goal. We walked over to the Pantry and had a bite. I got home after midnight. Gina was asleep. Another opportunity down the tubes. Or maybe I'd agreed to go to the game because I knew I'd be home too late to confess.

I got together with Mike three more times over the next week. We saw *Master and Commander*. The Russell Crowe character and the ship's doctor, they knew what it was like to be buddies. They blew up French sailors together, and when things quieted down they played duets on violin and cello. Things were so simple in those days.

Each time I saw Mike I asked him if he had a clue about what had happened with Ronnie and me. Each time he said no. The last time around he said blackouts were nothing to worry about. That they were nature's way of washing the bad stuff from your brain.

I found out some more about my new pal. He'd gone to work in a head shop in Venice as a kid in the sixties, bought the owner out in the early seventies, owned the place since. It was called Feed Your Head, and now he was happy to let the new generation run it. There wasn't much money to be made, but it stayed in the black, and that was enough for him. That, and hanging out there when he didn't have anything else to do. And being the nexus of a large colony of freaks and activists who lived and worked nearby.

He lived in an apartment above the shop, though he also made reference to a house and another source of income that had something to do with his wife. When I asked about the house and the wife he got vague on me. I got the feeling they were divorced but still friendly and that she had the house. When I went after more information he changed the subject.

The next time he called Gina picked up the phone. She listened a minute and said, "I'd love to. But I've got a meeting with one of my clients. Right, though actually we prefer 'designer.' But Joe's free. He's right here."

She pressed the mute button. "Your buddy. He called me an interior decorator."

I hadn't told her yet. The whole surrealistic Sunday morning experience was fading from memory. The longer I waited, the more I could convince myself that nothing sexual had happened with Ronnie. Our waking up naked together—except for that one sock, whose owner I never did discover—was the result of some drug-driven foolishness. Years in the future, we'd laugh about it.

Though Ronnie never did drugs. She hardly even drank.

And it didn't matter if nothing had happened. I still had to tell Gina.

And I was still being an asshole.

I resolved to tell her. Just as soon as I got off the phone.

three

We went to a club called Voom, Mike and I, where some friends of his were in a band called the Chickenfries. It was on Sunset, not far from the Whisky and the Roxy and the other rock and roll landmarks. It was dark and narrow, with a tiny stage at the end, a dozen Lilliputian tables, and a bar tended by one guy who was about six-ten and another who was a midget.

We ordered a couple of beers and talked about bands. I told him how I'd been in one called the Platypuses when I was a kid, how I'd gone in search of Toby Bonner, the lead guitarist who'd disappeared a couple of decades back, how the whole thing had deteriorated into a bunch of criminal activity. How I was still in touch with one of them, a guy named Frampton Washington. Frampton was foster-fathering a girl named Aricela, whose entrance into Gina's and my lives had exacerbated a round of midlife crises. We saw her once or twice a week, and that, I told Mike, was as close to parenthood as we were likely to get.

Which was a good thing, given how rotten a father I'd probably be. How could I teach my kids about honesty and all that if I couldn't even summon a little myself?

I seemed incapable of doing so. When I'd hung up with

Mike, Gina was on the other line, and by the time she got off, my resolve had melted.

When I get home, I promised myself. *No more excuses.*

The Chickenfries emerged. The drummer and the bass player were gray-haired twins. The guitarist was twenty years younger than the rest, with long blond hair and a baby-face. A heavyset woman was on vocals and keyboards, an earth mother type, hair in that twilight between auburn and gray, long muted Mama Cass dress. And beads. Remember beads?

They launched into Cream's "Strange Brew." The woman's voice was full of honey. They finished the song and moved on to "Red House." Then they played an original, something mean and slow. After that it was half covers, half originals.

They played for nearly an hour and took a break. Mike got us up and headed for the backstage area, a tiny room with two beat-up easy chairs and a miniature refrigerator. There was one dim naked bulb hanging from the ceiling and a subtle odor of old beer and new dope. I shook hands with the three men, turned to meet the singer. "Joe Portugal," Mike said, "Sarah Jennings."

She held onto my hand. "You don't remember, do you?"

"Should I?"

"The Velour Overground."

One of the many bands I'd been in after the demise of the Platypuses. I was twenty or so.

"I was Sarah Halliwell then. Tony's girlfriend."

Tony Jennings was our singer. I thought back ...

It was 1971, give or take a year. Tony and one of the other guys in the band lived in a trailer up in Newhall. We spent endless hours up there jamming and smoking dope. Sarah would sometimes noodle on the decrepit upright piano the guys had picked up in a garage sale.

One night between Christmas and New Year's we got hold of some mescaline. We were up all night, listening to Rotary Connection's first album over and over, looking for hidden meanings in the lyrics. Around five in the morning Tony suddenly announced he was going for a drive in his Alfa convertible. He wanted company. I decided to provide it. Somewhere between the sofa and the front door Sarah joined us.

She was a lot thinner in those days and could squeeze herself into the little area behind the seats. I rode shotgun. We kept the top up. We still had a little of our sanity. Tony drove well for someone tripping on mescaline.

We ended up at Pyramid Lake. We sat freezing our asses off on the shore, while the sun came up, discussing whatever kids that age think is deep. Tony sat with his arm around Sarah, with me a couple of feet away, the third wheel as usual. Then she looked at me, smiled, motioned me to come over. I did, and she put her arm around me. We sat like that, watching the colors. I felt good. I felt loved.

Then the cops came.

We weren't carrying, having used up our last joint half an hour before, smoking it down to the tiniest of roaches before Tony flicked it into the water. The cops dragged us down to the station anyway. They made us sit on hard wooden benches while they lectured us on the evils of drugs.

I was living with my cousin Elaine at the time, in my parents' Culver City house, the one I still live in. She had to drive up there and pick me up. Tony and Sarah were still there when I left. It was the last I ever saw of them. The

Velour Overground disintegrated and I went on to another lame band.

"Whatever happened to Tony?" I said.

"I married him."

"You still married?"

"Thirty-one years last March. Want to see pictures of my grandchildren?"

"Uh ..."

"I'm kidding. So. I'd ask what you've been up to, but I've seen your commercials. Also saw you on the news a couple of times."

The commercials were for Olsen's Natural Garden Solutions. The ongoing gig brought in a significant chunk of my income. My appearances on the news resulted from an accidental crimefighting career that had resulted in the apprehension of two murderers and the demise of two would-be ones. The last episode had been around the time of the Platypus reunion.

I told Sarah the only thing that had changed lately was my marital status. We shot the shit until the drummer said they ought to be getting back. After the second set Mike and I hung out with the band over a beer. When I left I traded phone numbers with Sarah.

Mike and I went outside and decided to get something to eat. We went to a coffee shop farther east on Sunset and grabbed an open table. The waitress came by, swept up the two quarters on the table, said, "Big spenders, that last crew."

"We'll do better," Mike said.

"See that you do," she said, handing us menus.

We ordered burgers, fries, Cokes. Then cherry pie for me, Jell-O for Mike. We yakked for a long time, until the waitress loomed over us. "Need the table."

Mike insisted on paying. He left a third of the bill as a tip. "Make up for the last prick," he said. We went outside, climbed into his ancient Mustang, drove north on Crescent Heights into Laurel Canyon.

"Where we headed?" I said.

"Take a ride with me."

"It's kind of late. Maybe I ought to be getting home."

"You really want to go home?"

There was something appealing about the prospect of gallivanting around all night. I'd done it regularly when I was young, on occasion in my theater years, not at all since. I remembered the first time I'd stayed out all night, winding up in San Pedro watching the ships as the sun came up. A treasured memory of my wasted youth.

And the later you get home, some voice in my head said, *the more likely Gina will be asleep.*

"Drive," I said.

We continued up the canyon and turned left onto Mulholland. Neither of us said much. The first Moby Grape album was in the stereo. You know you've found a kindred soul when they play Moby Grape in the car.

We passed Coldwater, then Beverly Glen. "Omaha" came on. *Listen, my friends,* the Grape insisted. We came around a curve, and Mike suddenly pulled the wheel to the right and skidded to a stop at an overlook. Down below the lights of the San Fernando Valley blossomed, myriad random pinpricks superimposed on a gridwork of streets and avenues.

"I got to tell you something," Mike said. "Do you want to hear it?"

"Depends on what it is."

"Nope," he said. "It doesn't."

This surrealistic exchange had me a little frightened,

especially when shared with someone who'd lured me to a deserted section of Mulholland Drive at two o'clock in the morning.

"Yeah," I said. "I do."

The dim light cast by the instrument panel revealed his nod. He turned off the lights and engine, rolled down his window. "Donna and I were married in 1975." Donna was his wife's name. That much I'd gotten out of him. "Denny came along a little after that. You're sure you want to hear this?"

"I said I did, didn't I?"

He paused, reached into a jacket pocket, and suddenly he had a lit cigarette. "You know DL Tea? On San Vicente in Brentwood?"

"I've seen it."

"DL's for Donna Lennox. She started the place in '83. A tearoom at first, but things changed. She kept the tearoom for the little old ladies, but mostly she sold loose tea. Turned out lots of people weren't happy with the crap they put in teabags." He took a hit off his cigarette, blew smoke out the window. "There's five DLs now. Besides the first one, there's Santa Barbara, Long Beach, South Coast Plaza, San Diego." Another pull on the cigarette, more smoke out the window. "Four and a half years ago, Donna went on a buying trip to China. I was gonna go with her, but the week before we were supposed to leave I broke my leg playing softball and the doctor wouldn't let me travel. So she went alone. She never came back."

The lights below fascinated me. I could spend hours just watching them. Counting the red ones down on Woodman Avenue, starting all over again every time one of them changed. Trying to figure out where there was a park, or a school, or anything at all that could occupy my mind.

Because I had a feeling, and I wanted it to disappear. Some people have feelings all the time. And if any of them ever pan out, you hear about it forever, no matter how low a percentage proves to be true. But I hardly ever get them. I had one the day I met Gina, knowing our lives would be intertwined somehow, and that's how things turned out, though we only knew each other a little while back then, and it was nine years until we got back together and things got interesting.

And now I had another feeling, and I was dead sure that unless I jumped out of the car, found my way down the hill and back home by myself, and never again had anything to do with Mike Lennox, from then on our lives would be connected.

I put my hand on the door handle . . . and remembered my recent midlife crisis. The one I was probably still going through. And how over and over I'd thought about my life likely being two-thirds over, and how many things I'd failed to appreciate, and how many things I'd avoided because of the possibility of pain or disappointment or even a little inconvenience.

My hand dropped from the door. "What happened?"

He snuffed his cigarette in the ashtray. "She had an appointment with someone at one of the plantations. He had a new oolong, and she wanted to bring it into the States. A driver picked her up at the hotel. They never made it."

"The driver?"

"Dead. Skull crushed. On the road a couple of miles from where they were going."

"I'm sorry."

"The Chinese government blamed bandits."

We sat quietly. Below, traffic lights traversed their endless cycle. Green, yellow, red. Green, yellow, red.

"You went over there," I said. Don't ask me how I knew. Like I said, connected.

"Broken leg and all. Spent five weeks in China. Went to the hotel, the tea plantation, the place they found the car, over and over. Found a guide, an old guy who got a kick out of bugging the officials, and he took me some places I wasn't supposed to go. But after all was said and done, nothing."

"What about our government? Couldn't they help?"

"I suppose they *could* have, and they did, as much as was convenient. But I always felt this pressure from them, like they wanted to tell me without actually saying the words to forget about her, it was over and done with, and in the long run things would be better if I just left it alone. I went through that whole five stages of grief business, but the whole thing was screwed up because I still wasn't convinced there was anything to feel grief about. So I spent a lot of time in denial, bounced back and forth between the others, ended up back in denial. Which is where I still am, basically."

He turned to me, tried a smile. "Been a long time since I've told anyone about this."

"Why me?"

"A vibe."

He started the car, checked the road. A motorcycle came whipping past, its rider wearing one of those silly little helmets like Arte Johnson's on *Laugh-In*. As the rumble faded we got back on Mulholland and drove west. Mike picked up the 405 and drove me home. Neither of us said another word except, "G'night, man."

I filled a water glass, brought it to my nightstand. I brushed my teeth. I got undressed, climbed into bed, and after a moment rolled over to nestle next to Gina. She stirred, said, "What time is it?"

"Three-something."

"You were with Mike the whole time?"

"No, I picked up a woman."

I'd made similar dumb jokes dozens of times. It just slipped out.

"Funny," she said. "You and another woman. Never happen."

Now's the time. Now or never. Come clean.

I gathered my thoughts. "Gi?" I said. "I have to tell you something."

four

No reply.

"Gi?"

Nothing. She was out again.

I lay there thinking about her, how for the first time in my life I was being dishonest with her, how I should just shake her, wake her, tell her the story. I put a hand on her arm, gave a jiggle. Not much of one. Not enough to awaken her. But I could tell myself I tried.

I thought about how devastated I'd be if she disappeared. How strong Mike Lennox was even to survive. Then I was out too.

Wednesday morning. I'd told Gina about the missing Donna Lennox. But not about the missing hours of my life. The optimum moment was gone. My resolve had been dashed.

I went into my parents' old bedroom to feed the canaries, a legacy from one of my murdered friends. All eight were glad to see me. At least I convinced myself they were. The telephone rang and the birds all provided harmony. I told them to shut up and went to get it. It was Elaine, with an audition late that afternoon for a new drug called Lidovec. I'd noticed more pharmaceutical commercials on TV lately, people high on Claritin cavorting in the fields, little oval entities pushing Zoloft, a guy who took some pill and suddenly found his aim so improved he could throw a football through a tire swinging at the end of a rope. With some of them, they never even said what the drug was for. If you had the affliction, they assumed, you'd know all about the possible treatments. If you didn't, they didn't care about you.

"What's this Lidovec stuff for, anyway?"

"Herpes."

The audition went okay. The casting director wanted to know if I'd ever had herpes. I told her you don't "ever have" it, you get it and have it forever. I didn't usually mouth off to casting people, but she looked barely out of her teens and she irritated me. I walked out figuring I'd blown it, and not caring. It surprised me when Elaine called in the morning with the callback. It surprised me more when, a day later, I got the job.

On Sunday night Mike took me to another hockey game. There'd been a ticket available for Gina too, but she had plans with her mother. "Basketball, I would blow her off," she said. "All those sweaty young black men. But not hockey."

This game was even tighter than the last, with the Kings and Rangers tied at the end of regulation. They went into overtime. With less than a minute left, with the whole crowd on its feet, a fight started on the ice, against the boards on the far side, right opposite us. Mike grabbed his binoculars and peered down at the action, as each combatant tried to pull the other's shirt over his head. Each one got a couple of good shots in; then the officials separated them and started doling out penalties.

I turned to Mike to say something. He was still staring

through his binoculars. He wasn't pointed at anything happening on the ice, as far as I could see, but was still focused on the area the fight had been in.

"What are you looking at?" I said.

He didn't say anything. His expression didn't change. But something about him did, like a load had been lifted and another dropped in to take its place.

He climbed past me, headed for the back of the box. The binocular strap dangled from his hand.

"Mike?" I said.

He kept going, ripped the door open, went flying out.

Whatever it was that got him going like that, he might need help.

I ran after him.

I spotted him at the end of the corridor, near the escalators, elbowing his way into the crush of people who couldn't bother to stick around for a couple more minutes to see how the game came out. Then I lost sight of him. I ran down there and inserted myself into the crowd, let the mass of people carry me to the top of the escalator. Halfway down I caught another glimpse of Mike. He'd made it to the bottom and was running along the concourse. When I got off I went the same way.

A big guy in a Kings jersey and Raiders cap stepped out in front of me. I crashed into him, bounced off, tripped over a little kid, hit the ground.

"What the fuck you think you're doin'?" the guy said.

A fair question. Helping a friend? Or simply running around mindlessly?

The kid was crying. His mother was calling me a son of a bitch.

"Sorry," I said, to anyone and everyone. I got up, took a

step. Didn't go anywhere. The iron grip on my arm saw to that. "Can you please let the fuck go of my arm?"

"Don't get smart with me."

"And watch your language," the mother contributed.

Jesus H.... Mike was probably halfway to San Pedro.

I bent back one of the guy's fingers. He yelped, let go, took a step back. Right into the kid and his mother. All three went down in a clump. More wailing. I got moving.

After five or six more sections a stitch in my side slowed me to a walk. I passed one of the TVs they have mounted up high, so you can follow the game in the concession lines, and heard that the Rangers had scored. A massive grumble arose. A wave of disappointed fans erupted into the concourse.

I kept going. Wherever Mike was headed, it had something to do with what he'd seen in the binoculars. The spot was almost directly opposite us. I checked the section numbers, did a calculation, walked a few more yards. Then slipped through one of the entryways.

Nearly everyone was on their way out, except a few diehards staring numbly at the ice. The PA guy was announcing the three stars of the game. I looked across the way, tried to spot our box. Thought I had it, worked out the geometry. Where Mike had been looking should have been right... about...

There. Two sections away.

He was standing in the aisle, a couple of rows up from the ice. He scanned his immediate area, and upward toward the exit. The binoculars were gone. His hands clenched and unclenched. He started up the aisle.

I met him halfway. "Hey," I said.

He kept going. "Hey."

"What's happening?"

He said nothing, continuing toward the exit. When he reached the walkway that circles the lower stands, he stopped, again looking around.

"Tell me what's going on," I said.

He surveyed the scene again, then turned to me. His eyes were wide. "Sitting there in the second row," he said. "It was her."

five

I walked with him as he wandered the arena, and when it was virtually empty, in the concourse, and when that was nearly deserted, in a couple of parking lots. I didn't say anything, other than, "Watch it," when he was about to step off the curb in front of a car.

Finally he stopped, standing among a slowly clearing mass of vehicles. "You think I'm crazy," he said.

I shrugged. "What are the chances?"

"It was her."

"Mike." I moved closer. "You were a hundred yards away."

"The binocs are really powerful. It was her."

I didn't bother mentioning that somewhere in his mad dash he'd lost those powerful binoculars.

"I mean, her hair was different. But it was her."

"It was someone who looked like her."

"How do you know? You've never seen her."

"True enough. But answer me this. If it was her—if she somehow got out of China after four-plus years and has returned to L.A.—why didn't you know about it?"

"I don't know. Maybe she lost her memory."

"You really believe that?"

He turned away, seeming to study the oversized paintings

of Shaq and Kobe and another African-American giant that graced the side of a nearby building.

"Mike?"

He took a couple of deep breaths. "Old guy like me shouldn't be running around like that."

"Answer the question."

"I saw her. I know I did." His attention swung back to me. "Help me find her."

"If she was here, she's probably—"

"She was here."

"*If* she was here, she's on the freeway by now."

"I know. I didn't mean, help me find her here. I meant, help me find out where she is."

"But—"

"You're good at that kind of thing. You found Toby Bonner."

I had, in the version he heard. "Actually, I didn't."

"You said—"

"I know what I said."

"Anyway, it doesn't matter. You're good at looking."

"Mike—"

"Come on, man. Do a friend a favor."

This, I thought, could lead to nothing but trouble. And trouble wasn't supposed to be my business.

I looked in his eyes. They reminded me of a basset hound I once knew. "Okay, man," I said. "I'll help you look."

Gina was asleep when I got in, and I had to get up early in the morning to shoot the herpes commercial, so I didn't get to tell her about the excitement at Staples.

Or, of course, about anything else. It was getting easier by the day to believe I'd imagined the scene at Dennis Lennox's place.

The commercial shoot was way up I-5, off the Grapevine in a meadow only yards from land scalded during the big fires in October. It consisted of shots of three women and three men, individually at the beginning before they knew about Lidovec, in couples after they'd made the wonderful discovery. There was a pretty young white couple, a pretty young black couple, and an older pair, to cover the audience who'd gotten herpes back in the free love days.

My fake wife was named Roberta Salkind. I'd worked with her before. She was one of those people who join each new human-potential movement, convinced they've finally found the thing that will turn their lives around. Her latest discovery was something called Ambiance. As far as I could tell it wasn't any different from est or Lifespring or Scientology or any of the others. It was led, she told me, by a man named Ike Sunemori, and to hear her tell it he was God's gift to the human race. I got this picture of a bald old general in my head, and after that I took her even less seriously. Finally I got fed up and asked, if Ambiance was turning her life around like she said, why was she shooting a commercial for herpes medicine? Which really didn't make much sense, but it shut her up long enough for me to escape. I wandered over to the two younger actors and listened to them dissect the Lakers.

It was nearly bedtime when I recounted Mike's sighting to Gina.

"Not this again," she said.

"It's different."

"How?"

I was sure it was, but when I considered the two situations, they sounded a lot alike. Toby Bonner hadn't been seen in years. Neither had Donna Lennox, though in her case the number of years was far fewer. Nobody knew if Toby was even alive. Same with Donna. Toby'd supposedly been sighted around L.A. As of approximately twenty-four hours ago, so had Donna.

"And you never found Toby," Gina said. She was the only one who knew this. I'd admitted it to Mike outside Staples, but I doubted he'd remember it, the state he was in. And if he did I could just say he misunderstood me. As far as everyone else who cared was concerned, I'd seen Toby's remains.

"What harm can it do to look? I'll just poke around a little, satisfy Mike that he was wrong, be done with it."

She adjusted one of the pillows propping her up in bed. "You'll call Burns, no doubt." Alberta Burns was a police detective I'd known since the first of my friends was murdered. She'd just left the force, after getting shot by a gangbanger made her reevaluate her life. But she still had contacts.

"I hadn't thought about exactly what I was going to do, but yes, that would be an excellent place to start."

"And you'll ask her to find out who has those seats."

"How come you're coming up with all the ideas here? It sounds like you're more into this hunting-down-the-missing stuff than I am."

"Just helping my little hubby."

I went in and brushed my teeth, came to bed, picked up the Jefferson Airplane biography I'd slowly been working my way through.

Gina looked over at me. "What's going on with Ronnie?" she said.

six

Things whirled around in my guts. Finally I managed, "What do you mean?"

"I haven't seen her in a while."

My intestines ground to a halt. "She's in Hawaii. Didn't you know?"

"I thought that was next week."

"It got moved up. I haven't seen her since the party."

"How was that, anyway? You never said anything."

My perfect chance, right? If ever I was going to spill, this was the time, yes?

Evidently not. "It was okay. You know, one of those Hollywood things. I spent most of my time on the lawn getting loaded with Mike."

"Think there's any hope?"

"Hope?"

"You know. You. Me. Ronnie."

Have I mentioned that Gina's bisexual? This particular *ménage* had come up several times before. "Sometimes I think you're serious about you-me-Ronnie."

She took my hand. "You know I'm not. But if I were unattached, I'd be all over her like flies on honey."

"That's flies on shit. Honey is bees."

"Whatever. Wouldn't you? Oh, right. You think you're her father figure. That nasty incest taboo. Has she ever actually said that? That she sees you as the father she never had?"

"No."

"It's probably just a fantasy of yours."

Last chance, Portugal. Speak now, or forever hold your peace.

I put down my book. And turned off the light. "I'm going to sleep," I said.

A couple of men were out back, working on our remodel. They had a radio going, a Spanish station, playing mariachi music. It was way too loud, but if that was the price I had to pay for a smidgen of progress, I was more than willing.

The first contractor we hired overcharged us, used miserable materials, and caused a gas leak that brought out the fire department. Then he threatened to sue us for non-payment. When we finally got rid of him—Gina knew someone at City Hall who put on pressure—we found another guy. Sweetest man in the world, came highly recommended, seemed to understand our concerns. For two weeks everything was perfect. Then people stopped showing up, and for the last two months it had been a constant game of will-they-won't-they. We were considering firing the new guy too. But what guarantee did we have that anyone else would be better?

I endured the music until a quarter to ten, when I left for the library. I ran into Theta on the way out. She said Ronnie'd called, and they'd decided to extend the Hawaii shoot a couple of days. She'd be back on Friday.

When I reached the library I took a chair and sat staring at a computer screen. I'd been dragged kicking and screaming into the information age, finally making the grudging admission that using the Internet didn't mean I was giving up all that was good and true about my life.

That didn't mean I had to enjoy it.

I clicked and typed and found the Staples Center site. Went to the seating chart, printed it out, marked where the Lennox Productions box was and approximately where Mike thought he'd seen his long-lost wife. Then I got a page of contact information.

Next I went after Donna. Found a couple of references to her disappearance. Nothing I didn't know. They mentioned DL Tea. I clicked my way to its website.

I drink tea because I don't like the taste of coffee. Most of the time, whatever bags they happen to have at Trader Joe's. I'd never visited the big wide wonderful world of loose tea. So the DL site was a revelation. I went to the Darjeelings because that was what was in my current TJ's bags. They had fifteen of them. They compared them to apricot, cinnamon, and muscatel. They talked about the scent and the briskness and the fullness.

There were other black teas, and green, and white. But I went next to the oolongs. It was an oolong, Mike had said, that Donna was after when she vanished. Oolongs, I discovered, were partially fermented. Sure to come in handy if I ever went on *Jeopardy!*

There were eight of them, four from Taiwan, three from mainland China, one Darjeeling oolong just to confuse me. I moved in on the mainland ones. Each had a Chinese name and an English one. Ti Kuan Yin, for instance, was Iron Goddess of Mercy. Was one of these the one Donna'd been after on the trip she never came back from?

I printed the oolong page and wandered some more. There were pages about tea history, preparation, equipment.

I went back to the home page and spotted a link I hadn't noticed. Donna Lennox. Our Founder. *Click*. Donna was a brunet, her hair to her shoulders, her eyes very dark. She was smiling like she had a secret, standing in front of a rack of copper-colored tins. The photo didn't look like a portrait. The focus was soft, like it was a snapshot that should have ended up in a shoebox in Mike's closet.

The text underneath didn't address her disappearance. It was written so, if you didn't know what had happened, you'd get the feeling she wasn't around anymore. But you wouldn't be sure.

I'd promised to help out at the Kawamura Conservatory, repotting plants that had outgrown their pots. This killed the rest of the morning, and I made it kill the afternoon too. Later Gina and I went to Red Moon for Vietnamese. When we got home Mike was on the machine. I didn't have anything to tell him about what I'd found out or what I was going to do. But I did have a question. I called him and we worked over the seating chart and pinpointed the exact location he'd "seen" Donna. He said I was a good guy.

I hung up. Something was bothering me. That web page from the tea shop. If it had been a handsome studio portrait of Donna Lennox, I don't think it would have come up. But that snapshot, taken in an unguarded moment, with Donna doing what she loved, expecting to go on doing it for who knew how many more years…

I'd picked up a copy of *National Geographic* because there was an article about plant life in Madagascar, a significant element in a couple of my murder escapades. Leafing through, I'd come across a piece on cosmology, replete with theories about the universe and how it started and how it would end.

It said there might be an infinite number of universes, each varying from the next by one little event or condition...

Maybe there was one where Donna's trip to China had gone exactly as planned. And maybe if I messed with the one I was in, somehow I'd screw up that other one and make things worse there.

I'd had enough trouble dealing with one universe. Now I had billions to obsess about. Good going, Portugal.

Next morning when I called, Alberta Burns was home, and she had a craving for pancakes.

We met at the IHOP on Manchester Boulevard in Inglewood. They seated us at a corner table. Burns let the waitress pour coffee. I asked for tea. I received a pot of tepid water and a basket of teabags. I picked out an English Breakfast, removed it from its packet, started examining it.

"What the hell are you doing?" Burns said.

"Looking at the leaves."

"You're supposed to get them wet before you tell fortunes."

I dropped the bag in my cup. I made sure the coast was clear, unpacketed another bag, ripped it open. "This stuff is like powder," I said.

"So?"

"It's the dregs of the dregs."

"Have coffee, then."

The waitress passed by, saw what I was doing, shook her head. *White people.*

"Portugal," Burns said.

"Hmm?" I'd dumped the tea into my saucer and was poking it with my fork.

"Does whatever you want from me have anything to do with your science project?"

I pushed the whole thing aside and launched into the Donna Lennox story. By the time I was done, our food was there. When I finished, Burns told me—for the third or fourth time—that I was out of my mind.

"Probably," I said.

"People misidentify people," she said. "Trust me on this. I've interviewed dozens, probably hundreds of witnesses who swore they saw someone somewhere and turned out to be wrong. And ninety-nine percent of them were a lot closer than all the way across Staples Center."

"You're probably right."

"Will you stop saying 'probably'? Next time I'm going to whack you one."

"So you're not going to help me."

She took a sip of coffee, made a face, put the cup down. "Even if you weren't chasing wild geese here, you're forgetting that I don't work for LAPD anymore."

"And the minute you left the force, all your contacts there went up in smoke."

"A lot of them did."

"Fine."

"Fine?"

"Yeah, fine. I just thought I'd ask."

"You have something up your sleeve, don't you?"

"Who, me?"

"I can read you like a book, Portugal."

"Let's change the subject. Tell me about your script."

"Why do I have the feeling I'm about to be manipulated here?"

"Go ahead. Tell me. Last I heard, you and your partner, what was his name?"

"Paul Witten."

"Right, you and Paul Witten, you had this idea for a TV show. All about a woman on the police force, written with all the authority a veteran of... how many years was it?"

"Twelve."

"All the authority a twelve-year veteran of the force can muster. This Paul Witten guy, he's pretty good, is he?"

"Yeah. Hell of a writer. Portugal—"

"But never had anything produced. Which means he doesn't have any more contacts in Hollywood than you do."

"You shithead."

"You know, they could use a show like that. I mean, what was the last show about a lady cop on the streets? Sure, they have women on *NYPD Blue*, but everyone knows it's really about Sipowicz and whoever his partner happens to be that season. No, there hasn't been anything like that since that Angie Dickinson thing *Police Woman*, has there? And I always had the feeling it wasn't exactly realistic."

"I say again: you shithead."

"Have I mentioned Donna Lennox's son is Dennis Lennox? TV's flavor of the month?"

"This is blackmail."

"No, blackmail is when you've done something wrong and someone wants money to keep it quiet. Off the force a couple of months, and already you've forgotten simple stuff like that? Actually this is closer to extortion, though that doesn't quite cut it either. Hmm. The term *quid pro quo* comes to mind, and I'm sure if I thought about it a little more I'd come up with—"

"Shut up."

I did.

"You know," Burns said, "I'm going to come out of this a lot better than you are."

"Probably. Oops. Please don't whack me one."

"I'm not going to find anything out."

"But not for lack of trying, right?"

"Right. And when I'm done finding out nothing—"

"I'll set you and your writer friend up with a meeting with Denny Lennox. And, hey, he'll be extra receptive, because you'll have gone out of your way to help him find out whatever happened to his mother. Give him some closure." I'd stopped to Xerox the marked-up seating chart on the way over, and I handed over a copy. I stood, pushed my chair under the table, said, "Thanks for breakfast." I walked outside, got in the truck, and drove away, wondering how many pieces of my soul I'd be willing to trade away for my new friend's sake.

It was a permit parking area, and I had to drive three blocks from DL Tea, finally finding a spot under a big ficus. The sidewalk was root-raised and cracked and covered with dozens of figlets crushed by passersby. Someday a senior citizen would trip and break his or her neck, and then the city would get around to fixing the sidewalk and putting a root guard around the tree. Maybe if I stuck around long enough I'd see it happen.

Instead I walked back to San Vicente and stood across the street from the tea shop. It was between a flower stand and a hat store. The first person in was a little old lady. So was the first one out. Aha. Just as I suspected.

The next person in was a tall young man with spiky hair and a leather jacket. The next person out was a stunning young woman in the miniest of skirts.

Thus assured I wouldn't be the only non-little old lady present, I crossed San Vicente and sauntered in. I recognized the grid of tea tins from the photo on the Internet. There were six shelves, each with roughly twenty tins. The leather-jacketed guy stood by a bunch of tea paraphernalia, deep in discussion with a short round man in a fez. There were more tins at the far end, next to a door leading to a room with tables and chairs and lots of hanging ferns.

"Hi. May I help you?"

She looked about sixteen, a strawberry blond. Her shirt was covered with pictures of little bowls of green stuff. Across her perky bosom it said TEA SHIRT.

"Not quite yet," I said. "I'm going to browse a while."

"Let me know if I can help, okay?" She motioned with her hands, taking the room in. "This can be a little intimidating the first time."

"How do you know it's my first time?"

"Isn't it?"

"Yes, but how'd you know?"

A minute shrug, so cute I wanted to take her home and set her up as Ronnie's little sister. "You have the look."

I eavesdropped on the leather jacket and the fez while checking out some squat metal pots on the wall opposite the big display. They were discussing Assams. I picked up a pot. It was heavier than it looked. It cost seventy bucks. A placard said it was a *tetsubin*, from Japan. Others were stoneware, fanciful shapes like frogs and dragons and little old fishermen. Yixing, from China. The card provided the proper pronunciation. *Yee-zhing*.

I wandered, seeing but not really registering the pots and filters, cups and mugs, jars and cans. I looked through the door at the end, into the tearoom. Bright and airy and civilized. There was a small open kitchen and a patio in back with a few more tables, one of them occupied by the senior

I'd seen go in when I was spying on the place. A woman all in white saw me, smiled, offered me a table.

I shook my head, turned from the tearoom, saw the memorial. It was along the wall, near the corner. The centerpiece was a color eight-by-ten of Donna Lennox. There was an engraved name plaque below it. Next down was a wooden shelf bearing several white porcelain bowls of tea, a lit candle spewing a vaguely soapy smell, a couple of carved soapstone animals. One was a frog and the other could have been nearly anything with four legs. A couple of wall vases flanked the photo, one with dried lavender and the other with cut orchids. Dendrobiums, I thought, but my knowledge of orchids was rusty and I intended to keep it that way.

"Sometimes I think she's still here." The young woman was at my shoulder. Up close, she looked older, though not much. "I mean, I'm not a spiritual person, but sometimes at night, when I'm the only one here, I can feel her around, watching over the place."

"Did you know her?"

"Only for a few days. I came to work here right before she went to China and ... well, you know."

"I do?"

"I knew you'd be coming in."

"Okay, I'm confused."

"Mike told me about seeing her the other night. And about you."

Soon the entire tea fraternity would expect me to work a miracle. "How'd you know I was me?"

"Those bug ads on TV. I'm Carrie, by the way. Carrie Fitzpatrick."

She held out a hand. It was small, delicate, warm. I told

her my name, she said she knew, I said of course she did. "So what do you think, Carrie? Did he see her?"

"Of course not."

"You seem pretty sure."

"She's dead."

"You seem pretty sure of that too."

"Or she's in white slavery in China somewhere, so she might as well be. I try not to think about it, but when I do, that's what I come up with."

"So you think I'm wasting my time."

"No."

"I don't get you."

"I don't think you're wasting your time if you manage somehow to make Mike feel better. Excuse me a sec."

The two customers were at the counter. The younger one had Carrie fill three bags from the bins. The fez bought one of the Yixing pots. A dragon. When they left Carrie came back over. I said, "Tell me what you meant. About making Mike feel better."

"He has to let her go."

"Why?"

"To move on with his life."

"You seem to care about him a lot."

"I do."

Silence. I remembered Mike's frown, his unfinished thought, when I said I was old enough to be Ronnie's father.

"You and him," I said.

"Me and him," Carrie said.

seven

She turned to the shrine, back to me.

"How long?" I said.

"A little over a year."

"You're …" I stopped because I knew she'd heard it a thousand times.

"Young enough to be his daughter? I know. Believe me, I know."

"I didn't know he was involved with anyone."

"Yeah, well … he's very conflicted about it."

"I guess he must be."

"But what's he supposed to do? He's never going to have proof she's dead, unless some Chinese peasant stumbles across her skeleton sometime. Is he supposed to spend the rest of his life alone?"

"No one said that."

The door opened. Another young man came in. His shopping bag banged against the door frame and metal clinked inside. "Hey, Carrie," he said.

"Hey. Be with you in a minute." To me: "Hang on, okay?" She went behind the counter, scribbled something on a slip of paper, then crossed to a display near the door and pulled out a white cardboard box, a foot square, six inches high.

She came back and handed me the note. "Call me. We'll talk some more. I think we can help each other." She gave me the box. "And this is for you. Mike said you needed one."

"What is it?"

"Starter kit." She smiled. "What we call in the catalogue, An Introduction to the World of Fine Tea."

"How much?"

"A gift."

"Thanks."

"You're very welcome. Oh, and if when you call you get my roommate ... she's lousy with messages. So try again."

"Will do." I took my prize and left.

When I got home Mike Lennox was staring at my front door. He turned, saw me, stood by the driveway as I pulled in. I got out, carrying the tea kit. "You've been to the shop," he said.

"Uh-huh."

"And met Carrie."

"Right again."

"And now you think I'm a dick."

"Actually, *prick* was the word that came to mind, though I admit they're similar in both sound and meaning. But I think women tend to use *dick* more than men do."

"Let me explain."

"No need to. I said the word came to mind. But it left as quickly as it came. It's your business. You want to come in?"

"Okay."

I unlocked the door. We went inside. I put the box on the dining room table.

"Aren't you going to open it?" Mike said.

"Not now," I said. "I want to do it alone. Some kind of voyage of discovery thing."

"Gotcha."

I went in the living room, stuck *After the Gold Rush* on the turntable, got it going. I sat on the couch. *My* couch. There were two of them jammed into the room, my crappy old one and Gina's designer version, awaiting the day when the addition was finally done and we could figure out what to do with two homes' worth of furniture.

I was vaguely aware I should be offering Mike refreshment of some type. He sat on Gina's sofa, kept the beat to "Tell Me Why" with his hand on the arm. When the chorus came he sang along. When the song was over he said, "Here's the thing. Donna is still the biggest thing in my life, but a guy's got to move on and—"

"That's exactly what Carrie said. 'Move on.' Look. I can't say this for sure, but if Gina disappeared for four years and change, I could see myself hooking up with someone else—"

Or even if she just went to San Francisco for the weekend.

"—even while I still hoped and prayed every day that the doorbell would ring and she'd be standing out there. So it's okay if you do the same."

He nodded slowly. His mouth clenched, and I was afraid he was going to go weepy on me, but he forced a smile. "So you really don't think I'm a dick? Or a prick?"

"I think you're both those things, but it has nothing to do with your love life."

Nothing.

"That was a little guy humor. I'm sorry, I don't have a lot of experience with this kind of thing."

"Oh. Funny."

Guy silence, until:

"I mean, after all," he said, "didn't you ball that Ronnie chick, and your wife's not even—"

"Jesus, Mike, nothing happened with me and Ronnie. Get that through your thick head, will you?"

"Sorry, man. Don't get all irate."

"Yeah, well, I'm sorry too."

"Did you tell her?"

"Tell who what?"

"Your wife. About—"

"Yeah. Everything's cool. Just drop it, okay?"

"Okay."

A car pulled into the driveway, and in a moment Gina came in. "Company. You Mike?" He nodded. She looked down at the coffee table. "Not surprisingly, my husband hasn't offered you anything to drink." You could see the instant of unfamiliarity when she said "husband." We were still getting used to the *h* and *w* words.

"S'okay, I'm fine," Mike said.

"No, you're not. Beer? Juice? I think we have a couple of Cokes."

"A Coke's fine."

"It'll just be a second." She went in the kitchen.

Mike came closer. Sotto voce: "Your wife's a babe."

"Goes without saying."

"Great ass."

Gina came in with Cokes and glasses. "I'll just leave you boys to your … whatever it is boys do." She picked up her purse and walked into the bedroom. Then she popped back out. "Mike?"

"Uh-huh?"

"You might want to work on your stage whisper. At least, if you're planning on continuing your anatomy critiques." She went into the bedroom again.

"She hates me," Mike said.

"No."

"You sure?"

"I'm sure," I said. "She was smiling when she said it. Drink your Coke."

The next morning I called the number Carrie at the tea shop had given me. She wasn't there, according to her roommate. I asked if I could reach her at work. She said no, that Carrie was taking a class at Santa Monica College, and that was where she was. Then she asked if I was trying to go out with Carrie. I said no, that I understood she had a boyfriend. The roommate said, oh, that old fart, he's just using her for sex. I said I'd call back later. She asked if I wanted to leave a message, but remembering Carrie's warning I said no.

I heard noise out back and went to see what was going on. There was a lone workman out there, futzing with some insulation. I said hello. He said the same. I asked what he was doing. He said, "Insulation," and it was clear that if I asked for further explanation it would be in a language I didn't understand. I nodded, went back in the house, turned on the TV. On the Channel 6 morning news ace reporter Claudia Acuna was discussing liposuction. Sweeps month, I thought. They always hauled out the cosmetic surgery stories.

I flipped the channel and found a James Bond movie. Part of a marathon on Spike TV. Jack Lord came onscreen, the first in a long line of Felix Leiters. It was *Dr. No*, Bond's filmic debut. I'd missed the beginning, but no matter. Ursula Andress would be showing up soon. I sunk onto the couch and watched the rest of the movie. And the one after. *Moonraker*. I'd forgotten how bad it was.

When it was over I went to Trader Joe's. When I got home there were two calls on the machine. The first was Carrie.

"Samantha said someone called but didn't leave his name. I thought it might be you. I looked you up in the book. Hope that's okay."

The second: "Portugal. Burns. I have something for you. You'll like it."

I called Burns back. "It's Joe."

"The tickets belong to a man named John Santini."

"That was easy."

"No, it wasn't, but I won't bore you with the details. You want his number?"

I took it down.

"When do I get to see Dennis Lennox?" she said.

"Soon."

"Don't screw with me, Portugal."

"Hey, you're going to hang with us Hollywood types, you have to expect to get screwed with."

"Don't give me—"

"I need a little time, okay? Let me straighten Mike out, then I'll see what I can do."

"It better be good."

"It will be," I said. "I guarantee it."

I went out back. The workman was still there. He was sitting exactly where I'd seen him earlier, holding a piece of insulation that looked suspiciously like the one he'd had before. I said, Insulation, he said, Insulation, I went back inside and called Carrie.

Samantha the roommate answered and passed the phone on. "Hi," Carrie said.

"There you were all worried that if I left my name Samantha wouldn't give you the message, and I didn't leave my name and you got the message anyway."

"Life's funny that way."

"You want to talk some more?"

"Sure. Want to come over for tea?"

"To the shop?"

"To my house. Actually, it's Samantha's house, but you know what I mean."

"And where would that be?"

"Venice. Near the beach."

"Okay."

She gave me the address. Said parking was terrible, but she'd pull the cars up so there was room for me in the driveway.

Fifteen minutes later I was there. A block from the traffic circle, near Mao's Kitchen and Aaardvark. I turned into the driveway and parked behind a gray Civic. In front of it was a VW Thing in military green. It had a WAR IS NOT THE ANSWER sticker in the back window and a Jack in the Box antenna ball.

The cottage was pale blue and white, with hibiscus in the tiny front yard and an arbor overgrown with dead wisteria above the gate. A couple of sets of wind chimes jingle-jangled overhead. As I stepped onto the porch the door opened. The woman standing there was wearing a Che sweatshirt and cutoffs and a dab of green paint on her nose. Her black hair was piled on top of her head, held in place by a red, white, and blue ribbon. "I'm Samantha," she said. "Which you probably figured out. Come on in."

The windows were arched and there was stained wood trim around them and bordering the doors. There were a couple of bookcases and some art on the walls and magazines scattered all over. Something sweet was or had been baking.

"How come there's paint on your nose?" I said.

"I'm an artist."

"Do all artists have paint on their noses?"

"At some point, yeah, all of us do."

Carrie popped out of the kitchen, said tea and scones would be ready soon, retreated.

"Let's go out back," Samantha said.

"Lead the way."

I followed her toward the back. Near the end of the hall were two doors, one on each side, with a tiny bedroom beyond each. The one on the left was a mess. Samantha's, I guessed. The one on the right was in perfect order. Carrie's.

Another door in the back, and we were through it and in the yard. It was a little bigger than the front one, but still miniscule, and most of it was filled with a rundown gazebo. Several paper Japanese lanterns hung down. There was a table with four chairs, and sitting in one of the chairs was Dennis Lennox.

eight

"Hi," Dennis said. "Surprised to see me?"

"I guess I am."

He came down the two steps to ground level, walked over, shook my hand. "I thought it was time we talked."

"You could have had your girl call my girl. We could have taken a meeting."

He smiled. Real? Maybe. "Dad said you had a good sense of humor."

"What else did Dad say about me?"

"That you're a hell of a guy. Sam?"

"Hmm?" she said.

"Could you give us a little time alone?"

"Sure, Sweetie." She stepped over, kissed his nose, went back in the house.

"Let's sit," Dennis said.

We took over a couple of chairs in the gazebo. The table was set for four. The plates and cups had a steel gray under-coat, a green iridescent glaze. The flatware looked vaguely Asian.

"Let me see," I said. "Your father's involved with Carrie, who lives with Samantha, whom you met and are now seeing."

"Very good."

"How do you feel about your father and Carrie?"

"Fine. Shouldn't I?"

"You don't think he's being—"

"Unfaithful? Let's face it. My mother's dead."

"You seem pretty sure of that."

"I am."

"Your father's not."

"No."

"This person he saw at Staples. The one he has me looking for. You do know about that."

He was nodding. "Someone who looked a little like my mother. Or even a lot. Come on. They keep her in captivity for four-plus years, she escapes, comes back to L.A., doesn't tell my dad?"

"Amnesia."

"If one of my writers on *Protect and Serve* came up with that ... well, I'd probably let them run with it. But this is real life."

"What did you want to talk about?"

"I want you to tell Dad you found the woman."

"Oh?"

"And that it wasn't my mother."

"I see. And why would I do that?"

"How does a recurring part on *The Galahad Sisters* sound?"

"Like a bribe."

He smiled, looked at the house. The light had gone on in Samantha's bedroom. She was watching us and gave a little wave. He blew her a kiss, she moved from the window, he turned back to me. "That's exactly what it is."

"Look, kid, I don't even care about my commercials. Being on a sitcom isn't much of an inducement for me."

"On *Protect and Serve* then."

"Neither is being on a cop show."

He sighed. "Thought I'd give it a shot."

"So what comes next? I'll never work in this town again?"

"No. I may have more power in this town than anyone my age should ever have—did you know I was number forty-two on *Entertainment Weekly*'s list of the most powerful people in Hollywood?—but my tentacles don't reach commercials."

"Why are you so set on your father forgetting about this woman?"

"He's in a kind of purgatory. On the one hand, he's capable of having a relationship with another woman. On the other, he still thinks my mother's going to come waltzing back some day. I just want him to get this behind him." A pause. "Did you know Ronnie's contract is for one year?"

"So?"

"Come on. Do I have to spell it out?"

He didn't have to. But I wanted him to. I wanted to hear it from his own lips. "Go ahead and spell."

"*Eight Simple Rules* is going on without John Ritter. They killed off his character when he died."

I said nothing.

"And going back to your day, they killed off McLean Stevenson on *MASH*."

My day. The little shit.

"My point being, no one on a sitcom's ever not expendable."

"You do anything to hurt Ronnie, I will—"

"You'll what? Hunt me down to the ends of the earth? Stick a cactus down my throat?"

It wasn't a cactus, you little fuck, it was a euphorbia that killed my friend Brenda Belinski, but it sure is nice to know you've done your homework on me.

"Think about it," he said. "That's all I ask."

I stood up. My fists, I realized, were clenched. I wondered what I could do to this creep's face with them.

"Think about this too," he said. "You and Ronnie. In bed together at my house. Have you told your wife?"

I surprised myself, how fast I moved. Within two seconds the front of his shirt was in my hand and I had him suspended several inches above his chair. "Tell me what you know," I said. "Or I'll break your neck."

nine

"Let go of me," Dennis Lennox said.

"What do you—"

"Let go of me, or I'll have you arrested for assault."

I looked in his eyes. Clear and green, they said *and I can do it too.*

I let him go. Didn't step back, though. "Tell me what you know."

"Think about what I said. That's all I ask."

"Tell—"

"Asking me again is going to get you nowhere. You know that, don't you?"

Yeah, I knew it. The prick wasn't going to say anything, not without some bodily harm involved, and the time wasn't right for that. Not yet, anyway.

And with no information coming, what I needed more than anything was to be away from there. To be well clear of this worm.

I turned and made my way inside. I told Carrie, "Sorry, change of plans," and went out the front. I got in my truck and drove away.

I told Gina the story—less the part about Ronnie and me—

when she got home. "It's impressive," she said, "that he's gotten to be such a jerk at such a young age."

"Being such a jerk is probably how he got where he is. Screw it. I'm going to call this Santini guy."

"Who's he?"

"Right, I didn't tell you. Burns called this afternoon. She found out who had the tickets for those seats. A man named John Santini."

"Call him."

"What if Dennis finds out and cans Ronnie?"

"Don't call him."

"Then I'm letting Mike down."

"I hate when you dither."

"I hate when I dither too."

"Speaking of Ronnie—and of producers—did you know she has a boyfriend?"

"She does?"

"Name's Eric something. He works on your friend Dennis's cop show."

"*Protect and Serve.* How'd you find this out?"

"Theta and I were talking. She's not fucking him yet, though. I asked."

"Well, *that's* a relief."

"I know. You want your surrogate daughter to stay a virgin all her life. Why the face?"

"What face?"

"The face on your face. Sour. Like you got some bad yogurt."

"Heartburn."

"You never get heartburn."

"Well, I've got some now. We got any Tums?" I headed for the bathroom.

•

The supermarket strike led off the late news. It had been going on longer than anyone expected. If it didn't end soon—and there was little indication it would—it was going to affect Thanksgiving shopping. Though more people were crossing the picket lines. Channel 6 showed an interview with a picketer. They were in it till the end. Then one with a line-crosser. She supported them at first but, you know, I've got five kids and it's too much trouble.

Gina pressed the mute. "Which reminds me," she said. "Catherine called. We've got vegetable duty."

Catherine was one of my father's housemates. Gina and I were going to their place for Thanksgiving.

"I was thinking," she said, "that we ought to invite Mike."

"Why would you think that?"

"I get the feeling he's the kind of guy who might end up alone on Thanksgiving."

"He's probably doing something with his asshole son. Or the freaks from Venice. He's evidently a pillar of their community."

"Ask him anyway."

"Okay."

We went to bed. In due course, we woke up. Gina headed for the Design Center. I wandered around the house all morning. I played both my guitars, the SG and the acoustic. My playing sucked more than usual. Eventually I gravitated to my refuge by the TV. The Bond marathon was up to *Goldfinger*. It was the big climax, where Bond and Oddjob struggle in the Fort Knox vault, and the counter on the nuclear device counts down. Bond electrocutes Oddjob, stops the timer at 007. The world is saved again.

When the movie was over I found the number Burns had

given me for John Santini. I stood over the phone with it for several minutes. Finally I dialed.

A gruff male voice answered. "Santini Imports." I told him my name and what I wanted.

"Hang on." He came back on the line in a minute. "Three o'clock."

"I don't really need to see him. I can just talk to him on the phone."

"Mr. Santini doesn't like doing business on the phone."

"It's not exactly business."

"Is three good or not?"

"It's good."

"Here's the address. Write it down."

I did.

"Don't be late," the man said, and hung up.

I sat down to return to my Bondfest, but they were running *Moonraker* again. I didn't get the scheduling, but then I didn't get a lot about the entertainment industry. Like how a twenty-six-year-old shit like Dennis Lennox got to where he was. I flipped channels for a while, came to the Channel 6 noontime news, put down the clicker. Kobe Bryant's rape case, Michael Jackson's freak show antics, young Americans getting blown up in Iraq. A two-year-old had been killed in gang crossfire in South-Central. Only they weren't calling it South-Central anymore. Now it was South Los Angeles, like changing the name was going to take away the bad taste.

There was good news too. A profitable Christmas shopping season was projected. Whoopee.

Claudia Acuna came on to tell us more about the new cosmetic surgery. This segment concentrated on buttocks implants for women and pectoral ones for men. I tried to decide if Claudia Acuna's breasts were real.

At two I got in the truck, paged through the Thomas Guide, figured out where I was going. I reached the address southeast of downtown early and lucked into a spot around the corner. It was a part of the city that resembles other cities more than most of L.A. does. Warehouses and whole-sale houses, establishments with signs in languages I couldn't read. Vans and pickups double-parked, people pushing metal carts small and large, others standing in doorways smoking cigarettes, staring out at infinity.

I negotiated the corner and continued to Santini Imports. It was a three-story building. The top one had two windows; the next one down, a row of them. There was vague move-ment behind a couple. The ground floor's dingy concrete wall was unbroken except for a sign that said the loading dock was in the back and a door that looked like it could keep out Godzilla. Next to it was a buzzer. I hit it. Someone said something that could have been a request for me to identify myself. I said who I was and that I had an appoint-ment with Mr. Santini. No reply. I waited. The door opened. The guy who opened up was roughly my age. That was all we had in common. He was tall and muscular and was wearing a stained undershirt and work pants that were somewhere between green and brown. "Yo," he said. The voice I'd heard on the phone.

"Hi. I have—"

"I know. Come on."

I walked in. He slammed the door behind me, checked that it was locked. The interior was lit by a few dull overhead fixtures. It was gray and damp and depressing. I followed him to and up a staircase. The second floor hall was marginally brighter. The walls were studded with office doors straight out of a Bogart movie. Battered wood with frosted glass windows. Remnants of gold lettering decorated a few of them. As we passed one on the left, I heard someone say, "Tell that son of a bitch..." but I never found out what the SOB was going to be told because we kept going. We stopped at the last door on the right.

"In here," said my escort, knocking.

"Yeah?" said a voice inside.

"The Portugal guy."

"Send him."

The muscular man turned the knob, pushed the door open, waited until I went in, retreated. The office I was in kept up the Bogie look. One wall was lined with filing cabinets that had been around since the Hoover administration. There was a black leather couch, cracked and sagging, the kind you usually find in the waiting room at your mechanic's. A bare yellow bulb burned overhead; the light it provided was lost in what came in through the windows. The wall opposite the filing cabinets had a calendar that featured a coquettish young woman clad in very short shorts and a strategically-placed newspaper. Next to it were a bunch of framed photos. I recognized Sam Yorty in one, Duke Snider in another, Warren Beatty in a third. All three were doing the staged handshake thing with a man who was a younger and thinner version of the one who came out from behind a worn wood desk to greet me. He was my father's age and a couple of inches shorter than me. He had glasses with the thickest black frames I'd ever seen. He wore a navy cardigan over a white shirt and a cleaner version of the pants the guy who brought me up there was wearing.

"John Santini," he said. He took my hand, held it with a strong grip. With his opposite hand he clapped me on the shoulder, and held that one there too. "So," he said. "Here you are."

"Yes."

A broad smile revealed an even set of teeth. "You were looking at the pictures."

"You know a lot of people."

"You live long enough, it happens." He let go of me, gestured toward the couch. "Sit." He went to the Yorty photo. "This was back in, what was it, '66? Testimonial dinner for Pony Petrelli." He dragged an ancient wood-and-leather chair from behind his desk, positioned it and himself in front of me. "Poor old Pony. A week after that, they found lung cancer. He was dead in a month."

"I'm sorry to hear that."

"Could've expected it, the way he smoked. Like a fucking chimney. Pardon my French."

"Pardoned."

"Hey. Excuse me. You want something to drink?"

"I'm fine."

"One thing my wife Gloria taught me, God rest her soul. Always offer your guests something to drink."

"It's a wife thing. Mine taught me that too."

"How long?"

"Less than a year."

"You held out a while, huh? I mean, no offense, but you're no spring chicken."

"Waited till the right woman came along."

"Me and Gloria, we were together forty ... ah, you don't want to hear that. So. I hear I can help you out somehow. What do you need?"

"It's about your season tickets to Staples Center."

"You need tickets?"

I smiled and shook my head. "This is about a game that already happened. Last Sunday night. The thing is...well, this is going to sound stupid."

"Kid."

Before I was no spring chicken. Now I was a kid. "Uh-huh?"

"Don't ever say anything you're gonna say's gonna sound stupid. Puts you at a disadvantage. You got something stupid to say, be proud of it."

I smiled. I liked this guy. Kind of like my father, but without the familial baggage. "Good advice. I'll try to remember."

"Good. Go ahead."

"This friend of mine...his wife disappeared four years and some ago on a trip to China. She's never been found. Sunday night, we were at Staples together, and he was looking though his binoculars, and he happened to see someone he was convinced was his wife."

"Guy needs to let go."

"I agree. But I've gotten involved in a couple of things in the last couple of years that made him think I could find this woman, and either it would be his wife or it wouldn't, but at least he'd know. So I pulled a couple of strings and found out—"

"That they're my tickets, where she was sitting."

"That's it."

"And you want to know who was using them that night."

"I know, it's—"

He gave me a look. Don't be ashamed of your stupidity. I shut my yap.

"You're a good friend," he said.

I shrugged.

"And kind of a good detective too."

"I suppose."

John Santini was watching me, and again I was reminded of my father, and how when he inspects me I feel like a teenager.

"My assistant," he said.

"I don't get you."

"My assistant, her name's Alma Rodriguez. It was her I gave the tickets to. I mean usually they go to customers, you know, that's mostly what they're for, but her brother was in town from New York. Big Rangers fan, so I gave her the tickets for her and her husband and him and his wife."

"I see. Any way I could—"

"Sure. She's up on the third floor. Fucking place is a mess up there, we got a crew cleaning up, she's making sure they do the job right. I'll get her down here." He got up, picked up the phone, punched three keys. "It's me. Come on down a minute. I got someone I need you to meet." He hung up. "On her way."

"I really appreciate this, Mr.—"

"John."

"John. I really do appreciate it."

He waved my thanks away. "Nothing. It's nothing. Hmm. Portugal. Hey, you wouldn't happen to be related to Harold Portugal, would you?"

Where had this come from? "As a matter of fact, he's my father."

"You're Harold the Horse's kid?"

"Sure am."

"How the hell is he?"

"He's fine. How—"

A knock at the door.

"Alma? Come on in."

The door swung open. A dark-haired woman stood there. I found myself on my feet.

ten

It wasn't her.

There was some resemblance, general size and shape, hair color, something about the contours of the face. But Alma Rodriguez's eyes were closer together than Donna's. And she was at least five years older than Donna would be, and her face was much harder.

But across an arena through a pair of binoculars, with everyone on their feet and jumping around at the end of a game, when you're still pining for the woman you lost four years ago? I supposed someone could make that mistake.

I walked forward, shook her hand. "Ms. Rodriguez."

"Mrs. It was good enough when Mario and I got married, it's good enough now."

"Thank you for coming down. I …" I didn't know what to say. I turned to John Santini for help.

"The other night, at Staples," he said, "this friend of his thought he recognized you. There's more than that, but you probably don't care."

"If you say so, John."

"You done with her, Joe? 'Cause she's got a lot to do, and with her down here the idiots upstairs are probably goofing off."

84   •   The Manipulated

"Yeah," I said. "I'm done." I turned back to her. "Thanks for ... well, just thanks. From me, and from my friend."

"You're welcome." She left the room, flicking the light switch off on her way out. The useless overhead bulb went dark.

I returned to the couch, sat, got up again. "I shouldn't take up any more of your time."

"Wasn't her."

"No. But I see how my friend could have made the mistake. She looks kind of like his wife."

"Glad I could help."

"So I'll be getting out of your—"

"And you can help me sometime."

"I don't know how, but, yeah, if I can ever do you a favor ..."

"That's the way of the world, isn't it?"

"I suppose." His world, maybe.

"Good. I'll call Vito. He'll let you out."

Vito? A name you don't hear too often. Unless you're watching a gangster movie.

And speaking of gangsters ... "How do you know my father?"

He smiled, like we were sharing a secret. "Long time ago, we were business associates."

"How long ago?"

"Jeez, let me think. Early, mid-sixties, I guess."

"Business associates, huh?"

"Well, yeah. I'm taking from the look on your face that you know what kind of business your old man was in back in those days."

"I do."

"Well, me too."

"Back in those days."

"Yeah. Back in those days."

He seemed to be daring me to push it. Idiot that I am, I did. "What about these days?"

He took off those bulky glasses, squinted through them at the window, went to his desk and jerked a tissue from its box. Rubbing the glasses without looking at them, he said, "I'm a legitimate businessman."

"No one says they're a legitimate businessman unless they're something else."

"You're a pretty brave little shit, aren't you?"

Sanity kicked in. I pictured myself at the bottom of the Los Angeles River, wearing a pair of concrete overshoes. Given the average depth of the L.A. River, I'd be more likely to die of sunstroke than to drown, but still...

"Look," I said. "This conversation is going somewhere it doesn't need to. If I've said anything to offend you, I apologize."

He took a step toward me. I flinched. Then we were back like we'd been when I first came in, right hands clasped, his left on my shoulder. "Nothing to worry about, kid."

"That's good."

"Course it is."

The door opened. There stood Vito. Santini hadn't called him, had he?

"Say hello to your old man for me," Santini said. "Tell him to give me a call sometime. Tell him I'll treat him to lunch at Phil's. He'll know."

"I'll do that."

I'd been maneuvered into the hall. The door closed and Santini was gone. I followed Vito down the hall, down the stairs, to the front door. He opened it.

"I didn't hear him call you," I said.

"No," Vito said. "You didn't." He gestured with his chin. Outside. I took his suggestion.

That night. I sat on the bed. Tried to remember Mike's number. Couldn't. Looked it up. Dialed.

"Hello?"

"It's Joe."

"Hey. How you doin'?"

"Good. You?"

"You know." So far, a typical guy conversation.

But not for long.

"Find anything out?" he said.

"As a matter of fact, I did."

"You found out who has those tickets?"

"Better than that."

"What do you mean?"

"I met her. I met the woman."

Nothing.

"It's not her. It's a woman named Alma Rodriguez. She looks a little like Donna. Across Staples, yeah, you could have thought it was her."

"You sure?"

"Positive."

A sigh, loud enough to hear over the phone. "It was worth a shot."

"Sure it was."

Another sigh.

"Mike?"

"Yeah?"

"You okay?"

"Sure. Hey, thanks, Joe. Thanks for checking it out for

me. You're a hell of a friend. If I can ever do anything for you—"

"Then you will. That's what friends do. It doesn't need to be said." Unless the person saying it was, quite possibly, a gangster. *And you can help me sometime.* "Hey, you got plans for Thanksgiving?"

"Huh? No. I was just gonna rent a couple videos and watch football."

"You want to come to my father's?"

"Thanks, Joe, but—"

"Plenty of room, plenty of food. My dad's a kick. You'll like him."

"Some other time. I'm just going to hang by myself, okay?"

"Okay. If you change your mind, call me. Or even later, in the afternoon, give a call at his place. Harold Portugal. He's in the book."

"Yeah. Cool. Listen, I got things to do, so I'll be going. See you." The phone went dead.

I spotted Ronnie a couple of times over the weekend. She had a nice tan. I supposed that with her back from Hawaii, sooner or later we'd have to talk over what happened at Dennis's. I hoped I could avoid it. Like I'd avoided talking to Gina.

Monday night. After eight. Rain outside. The doorbell rang.

It was Ronnie. She had red splotches on her face and her eyes were a mess. She saw me and burst into tears. I shuffled us inside and kicked the door closed. Gina was in the kitchen, watching with a what-the-hell expression. I let Ronnie wail for a while, then maneuvered her to the couch.

Gina brought her a glass of water. Ronnie reached for it. It slipped through her fingers, bounced off my knee, fell to the carpet. No breakage, water everywhere.

"Tell me what happened," I said.

"They fired me."

"They what?"

"They *fired* me. They said they're not gonna renew my contract for next year, assuming the show's picked up, which it sure as hell is gonna be with our ratings and everything."

She rubbed her eyes. A bubble grew from one nostril and burst. Gina handed her a tissue. Then another. Then the whole box.

"They said they'd decided to go in another direction."

"Who said?"

"Joanie Phillips."

"Who's she?"

"One of the producers. But it didn't come from her. It came from Dennis."

"You know this for sure?"

"I asked Joanie, and she said it was a hard decision but one everyone'd agreed was for the best, but I asked her was it from Dennis and she didn't answer me and I knew it was."

Fresh tears, fresh snot, fresh tissues.

"I think I must have done something, and I don't know what it is. And I don't know how to make it right."

"Everyone loves you, Ronnie," Gina said. "Everyone thinks you're adorable. If these idiots are dumb enough to drop you, someone will pick you up for something else."

"I don't *want* something else. I want my job back." She drew back far enough to look me in the eye. "What could I have done?"

"You didn't do anything," I said.

"I must have. I—"

"No. *I* did something."

"What? What are you talking about? How could you have—"

"That son of a bitch."

"Who? You're not making any sense, Joe." She looked at Gina. "What's he talking about?"

"Tell her," Gina said.

"Tell me what?" Ronnie said. She stood, looked down at me. There was anger mixed into the dejection. "Will you please tell me what the fuck you two are talking about?"

She was pissed, all right. That "hell" a minute ago was as far as her profanity generally went.

My turn to look at Gina. She shook her head. I had to do it.

"You know about his mother," I said to Ronnie.

"How she disappeared? Sure. What's that got to do with me?"

"Dennis's father asked me to track down a woman he saw who looked like her. Like Dennis's mother. Dennis found out about this and told me not to do it. He tried to bribe me at first, and when that didn't work he threatened you. Threatened to do exactly what he just did."

"That's crazy? What's one thing got to do with the other?"

"Nothing."

"But you kept looking for her? Why?"

"I guess I didn't think he'd go through with it."

"This is your fault, then?"

"No, it's Dennis's fault, but—"

"What, you're getting back at me for what happened at the party?"

"Why would I do that? I don't even know what happened at the ..."

I didn't have to turn around. I knew Gina was looking at me in a way she'd seldom, if ever, done before. I knew I'd fucked up royally, and that she knew it and was just waiting for Ronnie to get her cute little ass out of there to find out what I'd been covering up all this time.

"Oh, yeah, right," Ronnie said, "You *bastard*." She ran to the door, flung it open, slammed it shut behind her. I followed, opened it again, ran outside in time to see her disappear into her Miata and peel away into the rain. She'd gotten the muffler fixed.

I stood there getting soaked until it was time to face the music.

eleven

"You've been off since I came back from San Francisco."

"I have?"

"Don't act dumb," Gina said. "I hate when you act dumb. Tell me what happened."

"I kept meaning to tell you. I just never found the right—"

"Tell me what happened, please."

How to put it? As simply as possible. "The morning after that party—and I have to preface this by saying I have absolutely no memory of what happened after I blacked out on the lawn—I woke up in bed with Ronnie."

I could see her processing the information. Trying to fit it into her reality. Deciding she needed more.

"We were naked," I said.

"You shithead."

I almost added "except for a sock." Decided we could do without that detail.

"Why didn't you tell me?"

"Like I said, I was going to, but I was afraid to, and then I thought I'd wait until I figured out what really happened, and Ronnie was in Hawaii…" It sounded feeble even to me.

"I don't care what happened," she said.

"You don't?"

"Oh, on some level I do, I mean, yeah, I'd like to know if my husband is screwing our next-door neighbor, but you know what? I know if you did that, there'd be a decent enough reason. Like you were under the influence of some kind of drug. Which you clearly were, since you don't remember anything. Unless you're lying about that. And I don't think you are. Are you?"

"No. I don't remember a thing."

She pulled out one of the dining room chairs and sat in it and stared at the vase full of tired flowers sitting on the table. She got up again, picked up the vase, dumped the flowers, ran water in the vase. Then she leaned against the sink. "I can't believe you didn't tell me."

"I was afraid."

"Of what?"

"Of what it might do to our marriage."

"You think a roll in the hay with Ronnie's worse for our marriage then you not telling me about it?"

"I never thought about it that way."

"Before we got involved—when we were just friends—would you have told me?"

"Of course. We told each other everything."

"So why is now different?"

"Because it might change things."

"Jesus." She looked in the sink, at the vase, then at me. "Go away."

"You want me to leave? You want to split up?"

"I want you out of my sight."

"I'm sorry."

"Just go."

I watched her, some part of me clinging to the hope that she'd take pity, hold out her arms, say all was forgiven.

There wasn't a chance.

I went outside.

Next door at the Clement house, the sprinklers were going. They came on every night, rain or shine, a little after midnight. They'd run for twenty minutes and shut themselves off. Depending on the wind they'd sometimes get my truck or Gina's Volvo wet. Bill Clement would apologize profusely and swear he was going to get them fixed. I didn't think he ever would, and I didn't care.

On the other side, at the house occupied by Ronnie and her cousin Theta, there were two cars in the driveway. Ronnie'd come back after an hour and run inside. I didn't think she saw me lurking in the shadows on my front porch. The rain was still coming down hard then, though it had stopped since.

Lights were on in there. I could go over and try to make things right. Or at least see if she could come up with a clue or two about what had happened that night.

Instead I sat in one of the wicker chairs and thought about Dennis Lennox. And once I started thinking about him, I realized what I should have realized the minute he tried to bribe me into dropping the search for the woman at Staples. And if not then, the second he threatened to reveal what he knew about Ronnie and me.

He'd done something to the two of us that morning. Dropped a roofie in our drinks, maybe. If I'd even had a drink. I couldn't remember.

I had to get back at him. Everything was his fault.

Except you not telling your wife what you should have told her the minute you saw her.

I wouldn't have had to if it weren't for him.

Right. Blame your moral failings on a virtual stranger.

Thoughts collided, combined, escaped. One thing was clear. I didn't know where to start with Gina. I'd have to give it a little time, let her cool off, work my way back into her good graces. Just like any sitcom dad would do.

Meanwhile, I initiated a vendetta against Dennis Lennox.

It was stupid. I knew it from the onset. Me trying to bring him down for what I'd wrought through my own cowardice was like … it was sort of like the war in Iraq. Osama blew up the Twin Towers, can't find him, let's knock the shit out of Iraq. Worked for the president, might work for me.

I could put some private eye to work. "Dig up the dirt," I would tell him, and he'd sit on a park bench somewhere and watch Dennis selling crack to middle-school kids or going down on a priest or taking a meeting with the afore-said Osama. And I would calmly saunter up to Dennis's office with photos and tape recordings. "Give my surrogate daughter back her job, creep," I would cry, and he would capitulate immediately, and as a bonus would reveal to Gina that he'd given me a drug that not only blanked me out, but also broke some connection in my brain, making me incapable of admitting what little I knew about what had happened.

Or, there was my new friend. John Santini. "John, baby, I know you're retired from the kneecap-breaking game, but there's this guy who's pissed me off, and would you be so kind as to take care of it?" And one day Dennis would wake up with a horse's head in his bed, and after he finished his screaming and weeping he would capitulate immediately, et cetera, et cetera.

Or I could slip us all off to one of those alternate universes, one where whatever had turned Dennis into such a slimeball had never happened, and we all lived happily ever after.

Next door, the sprinklers flicked off. A few final droplets fell and the night was silent. I sat a couple of minutes more and went in to sleep on the couch.

Gina and I acted coldly civil in the morning. There was a big dead moose in our lives, and we were carefully avoiding talking about it. She got out of the house as soon as she could.

Noonish. *Rinnnnng.*

"Hello?"

"Joe?"

"Uh-huh. Who's this?"

"It's Samantha Szydlo."

"The woman with the paint on her nose."

"That's me."

"What's up?"

"I heard what happened to your friend Ronnie."

"News travels fast."

"I got my oil changed. They had a copy of *Variety* at the garage."

"Very L.A."

"Dennis was responsible, wasn't he? It has his stink all over it. There's no way in hell that chick should have been let go. Look, I think we should get together."

"What for?"

"To plot our revenge," she said.

twelve

"*Our* revenge?" I said.

"The fucker dumped me."

"What? When?"

"Saturday."

"Sorry to hear it. No, I'm not. You're better off. He's a real asshole."

"I know I'm better off. I still want revenge."

I met her at Mao's Kitchen for lunch. Brick walls covered in Chinese propaganda posters. Chairman Mao and various loyal communists staring proudly out at whatever it is people in those posters always find so fascinating off in the distance. A long communal table in the middle of the floor, surrounded by young men in wool hats and young women in piercings.

The waiter brought crispy noodles and dipping sauce. He went away, he came back, we placed our orders, he went away again.

"Okay," I said. "What kind of revenge were you thinking of?"

"Something involving honey and an anthill."

"Pretty traditional."

"And a feather. How about you?"

"I don't want revenge. I just want to get Ronnie her job back. It was my fault she lost it."

"It's that fuckhead Dennis's fault."

"I was the catalyst. Tell me what you really have in mind."

She'd unwrapped and split a pair of chopsticks. Rubbed them together to remove the splinters. "I was thinking we could shoot someone and make it look like he did it. His father, maybe. Or the housekeeper."

"You don't like Mike."

"Why do you say that?"

"Suggesting shooting him for one thing, plus what you said the first time I spoke to you on the phone. That he was only seeing Carrie for sex."

"I was being dramatic. He's okay. As far as shooting him … can you see the headlines? *Young TV Genius Guns Down Father*. It's perfect. Like Marvin Gaye in reverse."

I dipped a noodle in sauce, wolfed it down. "What about serious ideas?"

"None, really. That's why I wanted to get together. See if we could come up with something."

"People get dumped all the time," I said. "Average person probably gets dumped at least half a dozen times in their life."

"Where'd you get that figure?"

"Same reliable source that said there were weapons of mass destruction in Iraq."

"We get this revenge stuff nailed down, maybe we can go after those fascists in Washington."

I took a quick count. "I can give you eight times I was unceremoniously dumped before I—"

"Settled down?"

I smiled, nodded. "My experience is, sooner you get thoughts of them out of your head, the better off you are."

"You ever been betrayed? Not just dumped, but betrayed."

"Please. I know enough actresses. I don't need drama from you too."

"The whole time we were seeing each other he gave me this line about how happy he was that he met me, and he'd never been with anyone like me, and all that crap. And how he'd hardly ever wanted to be with one woman before, but he did with me. And all the while he was seeing other women, and mostly this one named Trixie. Trixie, for God's sake, and what kind of name is that for a grown woman?"

"And you fell for it."

"I was such a fucking idiot. Listen to this. He told me he was going to New York for a meeting and came back with a tan. Which of course I commented on, and he told me they moved the meeting to Miami at the last minute. And fucking idiot me believed him." She shook her head. "I've done some checking since Saturday. He was in Cozumel with Trixie the slut."

The waiter came by with our soup and tea. He heard the last bit. He wanted to stick around for more, but Samantha kept her mouth shut.

I stuck my spoon into the soup, looked at the bits of tofu and scallion swimming around the broth. "Love makes us stupid. Infatuation makes us even stupider. But, if I may be excused a when-you've-been-around-as-long-as-I-have moment, sometimes you have to learn stuff about relationships the hard way."

"You never answered my question."

"Which was?"

"Have you ever been betrayed?"

Sure I had. The Samoan Boyfriend Episode. "Once."

"And you didn't want to get back at her?"

"Of course I did. I even had a plan. This guy I was in a theater company with, he was an Adonis, smart, funny, the whole package. If I were gay I would have totally been in love with him. And I was going to pay him off to seduce this woman, and lead her on, and then crush her."

"Did you do it?"

"I actually got as far as broaching the subject to him, but he wanted too much money. And I went away from that conversation and went home and realized how out of my mind I was to even think of such a thing."

"Who gets the Mao's Hometown?" said the waiter.

"I do," I said, pushing my soup aside to make room. He left off Samantha's Long March Camp-Fry, gave us each a quizzical look, marched off.

"Do you have a thing for this Ronnie chick?" Samantha said.

"Not at all. It's more of a father-daughter thing. Or mentor-mentee, protégor-protégé, whatever you want to call it."

I dug into the entrée, ate a few bites, said, "This is going to lead nowhere. Number of people he's done wrong, you have to think if there were a way at him, someone would have found it by now."

"Maybe they have. Maybe someone found out a deep dark secret about him and he paid them off to keep it quiet."

I shoveled in another mouthful, followed it with a sip of tea. An oolong I never would have ordered in the pre-Mike days. "Samantha."

Around a mouthful of vegetables she said, "Hmm?"

"I want you to forget about this."

"You *want* me?"

"It's bound to lead to more trouble."

She poked her food with a chopstick. "Hey, I know. We could get him busted for drugs."

Drugs? Wait a minute... "Were you at that party at his place, about three weeks ago?"

"No. I was in San Diego. A friend had an opening. But I'll bet there was lots of coke around. There always is. If we knew a cop, we could set him up."

"I know a cop. Well, an ex-cop."

"What are we waiting for?"

"Getting him busted does nothing for Ronnie."

"Oh. Her."

"Here's the problem. What you want to do is hurt Dennis. What I want to do is just threaten him with something that will compel him to give Ronnie her job back. We're at cross purposes."

"There's got to be something we can come up with that'll do both."

"If there is, it's going to take a more Machiavellian mind than mine to come up with it."

"You think we're wasting our time."

"If you consider having a nice talk and a good meal wasting our time, then yeah. Though we're not really doing justice to the meal. Samantha, this is stupid. We're good people, you and me. We're not the kind of people who pull stunts like what we've been talking about. So why don't we just forget about it?"

"Okay. We'll forget about it."

A little later. Outside Mao's. "Guess I'll get going," I said.

"And I guess I'll get back to fooling with my paintings."

We looked at each other. I said, "You're not really giving up on Dennis, are you?"

"Of course not. You?"

"No," I said. "But it was a nice little facade while it lasted."

•

After dinner—leftover Thai—the phone rang. I stood there.

"Going to answer it?" Gina said. It was the most she'd spoken to me since she got home.

"I suppose." I stepped over and picked it up. "Hello?"

"Joe?"

"This is him. He."

"It's Dennis Lennox."

"What do you want?"

"To straighten things out."

"Really."

"Look, I know some things have gone wrong, and they're all my fault, and, like I said, I want to straighten them out."

"Give Ronnie her part back, everything's straightened, as far as I'm concerned."

"There's more to it than that."

Now we were getting somewhere. "About what you did to her and me at your party?"

"That too. Look, I'd like to see you. Talk face to face. Explain my actions. Can you come to my house tonight at ten?"

"I'll be there." I hung up on him.

thirteen

I told Gina where I was going. She grunted. I told her not to stay up. She said there wasn't much chance of that.

I reached Dennis's at ten to ten. I rang the bell. No one answered. Rang it again. Nothing.

"What a schmuck," I said.

Another car arrived. A Miata. Ronnie stepped out of it. She came closer, cast a glare my way. "What are you doing here?"

"It's good to see you too."

She brushed past me, rang the doorbell, waited, pushed the button again.

I came up behind her. "I tried that already."

She stared at the door. "You think he's having fun with us?"

"I wouldn't put it past him. He's probably watching from upstairs with night vision goggles. Hey! Dennis! You in there, you prick?"

Still no response. I banged on the door with my fist. Kicked it. Kicked it again.

"That's probably not going to help," Ronnie said.

"Testosterone."

Another car came up the driveway. A VW Thing. It stopped and someone got out and the door slammed. The driver approached. Samantha. She was wearing a short red dress with trim that reflected the floodlights. It seemed too festive for the occasion. "Joe. And Ronnie, we met once, remember, Dennis had a—"

"I remember," Ronnie said.

"Why are the two of you standing around out here?"

"Shithead's not answering," I said.

"That bastard." She peered at the door like she was trying to open it through mind power. "He called you?"

"Yeah."

"Me too," Ronnie said.

We heard yet another car. In a few seconds a small sedan pulled in behind the Thing. A dome light went on, another door slammed, someone came near.

"I don't fucking believe it," Samantha said.

"What?" I said.

"It's that Trixie bitch."

That Trixie bitch was pretty, in a girlie-calendar way. Blond hair that, even in the dim light on Dennis Lennox's front stoop, had clearly suffered from too many dye jobs. Slim, but with oversized breasts overflowing her hoochie-mama dress. She hadn't mastered the art of walking on four-inch heels. At every step one or the other ankle threatened to buckle and drop her to the ground. The overall effect made me think of Ronnie before I remolded her. Though I'd never seen Ronnie carrying a shih tzu.

Trixie flounced up. "Why doesn't someone ring the bell?" she said. Her voice was high, piercing, grating.

"We did," Samantha said, with "you moronic bimbo" clearly implied.

"Oh." She checked Samantha out. "I bet I know who you are."

"Do you, now?"

"Uh-huh, and honey, if it makes you feel any better, he gave me the same treatment."

"What? When?"

"Saturday."

"That fucker. Same day he dumped me." She thought a second. "Know what? It doesn't make me feel any better."

"Don't take it out on me, okay? I had a root canal today and I feel like doggie doo." She held the dog out in front of her. Its rear legs dangled. It looked bored, like it was used to such treatment. "Not that there's anything wrong with doggie doo, Snoogums."

Another car in the driveway. Another engine silenced. Dome light, door slam, footsteps. This time it was a young man. Medium height, thin face, good-looking in a delicate way. Dressed in shirt, sport jacket, jeans.

He came into the dull circle of light, took us all in, seemed about to say something. Then his hands went up in an I-give-up gesture and he shook his head.

"Yeah," I said. "We all feel pretty much the same way."

He looked us over, one by one. "He shit on all of you?"

"You got it."

"What a dick." He stepped toward the door, stopped, turned around. "You tried it, didn't you? Which is why you're all standing around out here." He came closer, held out a hand. "Sean McKay."

I shook with him and told him my name. He made the rounds, came back to me. It was clear he'd put me in charge. "So what do we do now?"

"See who else shows up. What'd he do to you?"

"Stole my script. You?"

"Fucked over someone I care about." I glanced at Ronnie. She turned the other way.

"The bastard," Sean McKay said.

"Seems to be the conventional wisdom."

Everyone waited around until ten-fifteen. A consensus was reached: Dennis had staged a prank at our expense. He wasn't even there.

Trixie and Sean McKay headed for their cars. She laughed too loud at something he said. She was resilient. I had to give her that.

"Everyone," Ronnie said. "I heard something. Inside the door."

I went over. Scratching sounds. Like an animal. And something that could have been a voice.

I said, "Somebody go after those two who're leaving." Samantha ran to retrieve them.

More noises inside. It sounded like someone was clawing their way up the door. Then the sound of a deadbolt being undone. A doorknob being turned.

The door popped ajar. I heard the muffled thud as whoever was on the other side crumpled back to the floor. I pushed the door, felt the resistance as I slowly shoved them aside. When the opening was wide enough I squeezed in and saw who was lying there. It was Dennis's housekeeper Lu.

fourteen

I knew Ronnie had a cell phone. I told her to call 911. I appropriated Sean McKay's jacket for a pillow. The others made their way inside.

There wasn't a whole lot of blood. Just enough to scare us. It was mostly on the back of Lu's head. I found it when I tucked the jacket-pillow beneath it. A glance at the floor showed a trail of spots leading away.

Trixie was treating us all to a freak-out. She kept uttering little theatrical screams, muttering, "She's all bloody," over and over. She'd lost one of her shoes and listed dangerously to the left. She dropped Snoogums, and he ran in circles, yapping his head off.

Ronnie knelt beside me. "Got an ambulance on the way," she said. She took a long look at Lu. "She going to be okay?"

"I have no idea."

"Is she going into shock?" Sean McKay said. "People always go into shock when they've been hit in the head."

I knew what had happened. Young Mister McKay had done this. He clobbered Lu and drove away and came back to mingle with the rest of us outside. Else how would he know she was hit in the head? I had him arrested, convicted, and executed before I remembered he could see the blood as well as I could.

Lu was breathing. Shallowly, but enough. Her eyes fluttered. "I think she's coming around," I said. "Someone get her some water. But don't touch anything. If you have to, use gloves."

Ronnie gave me a look. Like, do you see any gloves around here?

Lu's eyes were open most of the time now. Just the occasional series of blinks. They were directed at the ceiling, though. Not on anything going on around her.

Sean came running up. He had a glass of water. He wore yellow rubber dishwashing gloves. He saw me looking. "Under the sink," he said. "Seemed like a good place to check."

"Good job," I said.

Some spark of awareness came to Lu's eyes. She said something I couldn't make out.

"Don't try to talk," I said.

More malformed words.

"Don't—"

The word she interrupted me with was clear as a bell. "Dennis."

"Dennis did this?"

Something that could have been a shake of her head. "In den. Dennis in den." And she was out again.

Ronnie's eyes caught mine. Then Sean McKay's. Dumb, dumb, dumb. Everyone's mindset was that Dennis was playing a trick on us all. He was out partying with his latest girlfriend while we were standing around like befuddled sheep.

But we were all wrong. He was right there.

I got up, left Lu in Ronnie's charge. Followed the spots of blood. They went across the big entrance hall, into the rooms beyond. Sean McKay—still wearing his Playtex gloves—was behind me.

The spots continued down the hall. Joe Portugal, ace detective, followed the trail of blood.

One of the doors was open. The drops led right to it. It was a familiar room. The one where I'd met Dennis Lennox. The one with the Golden Globe. The den.

No light inside. I stuck my head in. There was nothing. No sound, no movement. I reached inside for the light switch, snatched my hand back. "Sean."

"Uh-huh?"

"Give me one of your gloves."

He handed over the left one. I pulled it on. It was snug. Designed for a hand smaller than mine.

Again I went for the light. Found it, toggled it upward. It controlled a floor lamp by the desk.

What I saw didn't surprise me. But it still startled me. No matter how many dead bodies I encounter, each one brings a new variety of shock.

Dennis Lennox lay on the Oriental rug. He wore khaki pants, a dark green Izod shirt, a pair of deck shoes. Several feet away, his Golden Globe lay on its side. There was blood on it. Not a lot. Not enough to explain the kind of damage that Dennis's face had suffered. There was just enough of his features left to tell it was him. The rest was a mass of blood and flesh and bone and other body parts I couldn't identify.

I stepped closer. Then back again. There was an awful lot of blood around. In the age of AIDS, I didn't want to go near the blood of someone who slept with as many women as Dennis evidently did.

Then what I was seeing truly registered.

I hadn't tossed my cookies in several years. I guess I was due.

fifteen

"So much," I said, "for not messing up the crime scene." I was dizzy and I tasted bile. I'd managed not to get any puke on the body or the Golden Globe. Just all over the rug.

"Phew," Sean McKay said. He'd backed out of the room. I joined him in the hall. We met Samantha halfway back to the front door and turned her around. I sent the two of them to gather the others back where Lu lay. There were enough people to tend her. I could spare a moment for myself.

I found a bathroom. I used my still-gloved hand on the light switch and the faucets, washed out my mouth, put water on my face. When I was done I went up front. Everyone was huddled just inside. Lu was awake and leaning against the wall, attended by Sean, Trixie, and Snoogums. "Ronnie?"

"Yes?"

"When you called 911—"

"Police are coming too."

"Thanks. Everyone know what we found?"

A round of nods. Sean looked up at me. "I told them. I hope that was okay."

"It was fine." I looked at Lu. Her eyes were open and something was going on there.

Things were momentarily calm. An opportunity to take inventory of what I knew. The trail of blood. The Golden Globe. That was Lu. Whoever offed Dennis clobbered her with the award. That much seemed clear.

Another thing: she knew Dennis was in the den. Had she seen him there? I'd had to turn on the light before I spotted his carcass. Did that mean the light was on when she went in? Then who turned it off? Lu? Highly unlikely. The killer? Possible, I supposed. Or maybe Lu didn't have to see Dennis to know he was lying there. Some connection they'd built up through living in the same house for however long.

I stepped away, far enough to watch them all. "Everyone. Please give me your attention."

Four pairs of eyes came my way. Lu's stayed where they were.

"Which of you killed Dennis?"

A round of protest. Everyone asserted their innocence. Samantha rolled her eyes. No one did anything that made them look guilty.

"We were all out there with you," Sean McKay said.

"Any one of you could have been inside, gone out the back or something, run to your car, and come back."

"Please," Sean said. "That kind of thing only happens on *Murder, She Wrote*. Next thing, you're going to gather us all in the drawing room and reveal what actually happened."

I heard a siren outside. "It was worth a shot," I said. The siren came closer. Then there were door slams and running feet and two young men in uniforms. One dropped down next to Lu and opened his kit while the other herded the rest of us outside. Two minutes later the first police car showed up.

After that, things went pretty much as they had every

other time I'd uncovered a violent death. Lots of cops, a bunch of techs, a couple of men in jackets and ties to order everyone else around.

Fifteen minutes after the paramedics showed up they carried Lu out, stuck her in the ambulance, sped off. Someone asked the uniformed officer guarding us whether she would be all right. She didn't know, the officer said, and the way she said it made me think she didn't much care.

Sometime after that they began questioning us, one at a time. They did all the women first, then Sean, then me. They brought me to a game room where I sat randomly moving marbles around a Chinese checkers board. If it was me in charge, I wouldn't have let me touch the marbles. Maybe they'd already dusted them for prints.

I answered all the standard questions. In your own words, Mr. Portugal, what happened here tonight? What was your relationship with the deceased? Do you know anyone who would have had a reason to want him dead? Is there anything else that you can tell us that might help with our investigation? I answered everything as truthfully as I could. Though they didn't need my help to figure out that everyone on the scene with the possible exception of Lu had a reason to want Dennis Lennox dead.

Mike showed up while they were talking to me. I saw him go by. He looked tired and small.

They finished with me and sent me back to the holding area. By this time it was past one-thirty. I asked to call Gina. They didn't want to let me, but I made a pest of myself, and they relented. I told her where I was and what was going on and said I'd be home as soon as I could. She was concerned, but underneath that, she was still pissed. I asked her to go next door and let Theta know Ronnie was fine.

At a quarter to three they let us go. I asked if I could see Mike. They wouldn't let me.

Ronnie got home a little before me. As I pulled up she was unlocking her front door. I was sure she saw and heard me. She didn't wait around for me. By the time I got out of the truck her door was shut.

Gina was asleep on the more comfortable of the sofas. The TV was on, its sound down low. It was tuned to an infomercial, some cream that would make you look twenty years younger.

I went in the bathroom, shut the door, took a long hot shower. When I came out I turned off the TV, woke Gina, led her to the bedroom. Said I'd tell her everything in the morning. I poured her into bed. Went to join her.

"I still want you on the couch," she said.

I awoke a little after seven and turned on the TV. The Channel 6 morning show found the Dennis Lennox "slaying" made to order. But with all the babbling, there were but two pieces of information that were new to me. The first was that Lu, last name Tom, was critical but stable. The other was that Dennis's mess of a face was caused by the exit of a high-caliber bullet. He'd been shot from behind. The high-caliber part was the news. I'd figured out the rest.

Gina wandered in just when they were saying the scene was soaked in blood. "Oh, please," she said.

"It was. Worse than you can imagine. Made me sick. I threw up."

That was where she was supposed to say, "Oh, babe, I'm sorry." No such luck. Just a look of disgust.

I watched them blather on, anchors Jim and Tabitha, ace field reporters Claudia Acuna and Terry Takamura, pundit

Peter Saint Fontaine with a hard-hitting commentary on violence and movie ratings and video games. Entertainment reporter Timmy Gold came on with a report about Dennis's short but prolific career. There were clips from all his shows, including *The Galahad Sisters*. Ronnie and Stephanie Urbano were discussing some guy's buns. Ronnie thought they were tens. Stephanie had seen better.

There was a bit about Ronnie getting fired from the show "under mysterious circumstances" and a reminder that she was one of the people on the scene. "So there are questions to be answered about that," Timmy Gold said, before turning things back to Jim and Tabitha.

They finally moved on to the next story—the upcoming Mars landings—and I shut off the sound. The doorbell rang. Theta. I ushered her in and asked how Ronnie was. She pointed to the TV. "You saw a minute ago?"

"About the questions to be answered?"

"Uh-huh. Makes it sound like Ronnie had something to do with it."

"How is she?"

"As good as you could expect. Still mad at you. We're out of coffee. Can I get a cup?"

"Coming up," Gina said.

The bell dinged again. I went for the door. Mike Lennox stood outside.

sixteen

"Hey," he said.

"Hey," I said. "Come on in."

If he'd gotten any sleep, it wasn't much. He was pale, almost ghostly. Under his eyes were flabby patches of skin. His hair stuck up at odd angles. He had on the same clothes he'd been wearing the night before. "You got any tea?" he said.

"I'll make some."

His nose twitched. "Don't go to any trouble. I'll have some of that coffee."

"It's no trouble," Gina said. She opened the cupboard where we kept the teabags, shut it, went for the tea starter kit, opened it, began sorting through the contents.

Mike sat at the table across from Theta. She gathered who he was. "I'm sorry about your son," she said. Then she got up, went around the table, knelt, put an arm around him. "It's okay." They stayed like that while Gina announced the coffee was ready and poured some for Theta and for herself.

Mike patted the hand Theta had on his shoulder. "You're very nice, whoever you are."

Theta got up and went into the kitchen. I took her seat. Gina brought in two mugs and placed them in front of Mike and me. He took a sip and almost smiled. "Yunnan," he said.

Gina nodded, went back to what she was doing. Mike looked at me. "Who do you think did it?"

"I haven't the foggiest. I really don't."

"Probably wasn't anyone there last night, huh?"

"You mean, that was waiting outside with Ronnie and me? I doubt it. But I don't know."

"Could've been a lot of people."

"Mike, I—"

"Hey, kid's dead, we don't have to gild his lily. Kid was a real shit. I raised a real shit."

"No, I—"

"I was a lousy dad. Spent too much time loaded, never had time for—"

"Stop it!"

We both turned toward the kitchen. Theta stood there, spatula in hand, a red Bristol Farms apron wrapped around her. "If your son was a shit," she said, "he would've been one no matter what you did. You got plenty to feel bad about. You don't need to go inventing more. Okay?"

"Okay," he murmured.

"Good." She returned to her skillet.

Everyone gobbled their food, like we were in a hurry to be done with it so we could go our separate ways. But when we were finished we all sat around staring at each other. No one wanted to go out and face the big wide rotten world. Finally Mike stood and began clearing the table. He got all the dishes, loaded the dishwasher, washed the stuff that wouldn't fit. The rest of us continued to gape at one another.

When he was done with the dishes Mike found the Comet and began to clean the sink. He scrubbed it way more than it needed. Way more than Gina or I had ever scrubbed. I was about to get up to stop him when he put down the sponge and began spraying rinse water. Then he turned from the sink, looking for some other chore to keep at least a little of his mind occupied. That was when I went after him. I led him out of the kitchen and out the front door.

We walked up to Culver Boulevard and began a circumnavigation of Sony Studios, not saying much, just putting one foot in front of the other. Somewhere along the way Mike produced a cigarette, and somewhere beyond that he threw the butt into the gutter. We were almost all the way around when he stopped, stared, said, "Wasn't there a Trader Joe's here?"

"Moved. Down the block, to that new downtown development."

"Everything changes."

"Eventually, yeah, everything does."

"Everything changes, and everyone dies."

"Sooner or later."

He crossed the street, I followed, he peered into the front window of the former market, looking for all the world like we was willing the store to reappear. Maybe if it did, time would reverse itself. Dennis would still be alive.

My thoughts, of course, not his. I was projecting them on him. That alternate reality crap again.

"I feel like Job, you know?" He was still staring into the dark interior. When he finally turned back to me he said, "I'm on antidepressants, did you know that?"

"No."

"Been on them since the first time I came back from China. Zoloft."

All I knew about Zoloft was the commercials with the little oval entities. "I didn't know people stayed on them for so long."

"Some people, yeah, they do. It's got its upsides and its downsides."

"Side effects?"

"Not what I meant, but, yeah, those too. Like, it makes it harder to come."

"I didn't know that."

"Sometimes I can't at all. When you're a kid, you see a bra strap and your pants are wet. Then you end up so it takes you all night. What a life."

"We should probably—"

"But the side effects, those I can deal with. But you know what else about Zoloft?"

"What else?"

"It takes the edge off."

"How do you mean?"

"It's kind of like ... okay, life's got its ups and downs." He was drawing a wave in the air, a big one reaching from above his head to his knees. "But once the pills get a hold on you, it's like this." The wave was smaller now, from his neck down to his hips. "You lose the lows, sure. But you lose the highs too. Sometimes I miss those highs. I've been smoking a lot more dope, trying to find the highs."

"Does it work?"

"Not really. But see, the highs aren't all of it. Sometimes I miss the lows too."

"Like now?"

"Yeah, like now. I want to really feel what I ought to be feeling with my son dead, and I just don't. I mean, yeah, I feel terrible, and nothing else matters right now, not even Donna. But I don't really *feel* it. You know what I mean?"

"I think so."

He took another look inside the dead market, turned

to me. "Shit, man, I shouldn't be dragging you down with this."

"What friends are for. Speaking of which ... that Thanksgiving invitation to my father's still stands." *Nice segue, Portugal.*

He shook his head absentmindedly. A thought had come into his head. It was a big one. He started walking east and I went with him. He worked on the thought for two blocks, stopped in front of the soon-to-be Kirk Douglas Theatre. "Went to the movies here when I was a kid."

"Me too," I said.

"You know what I've been thinking?"

"I'm pretty sure."

"You do?"

"Yeah. I think we might have some low-grade telepathy going."

"What do you think about it?"

"I think we ought to let the police handle it."

"You did know."

"See? Telepathy."

"But I mean, in case they don't."

"They will."

"'Cause you did such a good job the other time."

"That was easy. Finding someone who didn't know I was looking for her."

"You're saying it would be harder to find someone who knows you're looking for them?"

"I'm saying it's more dangerous looking for someone who's already killed someone."

"You're scared."

"Damned right, I'm scared. You didn't see what I saw in the den ... oh. You did."

"I made them show me." He started walking again. After another block I managed to get him turned toward my house. After one more he said, "What could it hurt to poke around a little?"

A question, I was irritated to realize, I'd already been asking myself. "Let's see what the police come up with. They'll probably have somebody in custody by tonight."

"And if they don't, you'll take a shot at it?"

"No."

"Well, how long does it have to be before you'll take a shot at it?"

"I don't know. I—"

"Two days? Three?"

"This is—"

"How about a week? If they haven't found the guy in a week, will you take a shot at it?"

"I don't—"

"Come on. A week. Humor me. They've got to find this guy in a week, don't they?"

"Is another side effect of the Zoloft that it makes you a huge pain in the ass?"

He forced a smile. "That sounds like a yes to me."

"Yet another side effect. Your hearing's all screwy."

"A week. Then you'll start."

Mostly, I said it to get him off my back. Mostly. "Okay, Mike. After a week, if the police haven't found the guy, I'll start poking around."

"Good man." He stuck out his hand. I put out mine. We sealed the deal.

We continued back toward my place. Just after we turned down Madison he said, "That's a week from last night, when it happened, right? Not a week from right now."

"Don't push it, man," I said.

seventeen

That night. Guess whose *punim* was up there on the screen?

Right. An ages-old head shot that they used whenever they chose to embarrass me by playing up one of my brushes with crime.

It was Channel 6's lead female anchor, Jessica or Jennifer or whatever she was called. "We now have new information on the Dennis Lennox story. Present on the scene was this man, fifty-year-old Joseph Portugal of Culver City, who has been instrumental on several occasions in aiding the police with difficult cases. It is understood that Mr. Portugal was among those who discovered the victim's body. It is not known what his further involvement in the case is or whether he is assisting authorities with their inquiries. Or…" Dramatic pause. "Whether he is a suspect in this killing. More when we have it. Ted?"

Anchor Ted—blond, but otherwise a dead ringer for morning anchor Jim—started in on an update on the Phil Spector business—the murder, not the Beatles album—and I muted him.

Ring.

I picked up the phone. "Hi, Dad."

"How did you know it was me?"

"Wild guess."

"Again you get involved with killing."

"I didn't exactly have a choice. Had I known he was going to be dead, I wouldn't have gone up to his house."

"This man. This Lummox."

"Lennox. You knew that. Don't make yourself sound like a dope."

"You shouldn't hang around with people like that."

"What am I, sixteen? You can't tell me who I can and can't hang around with." Though he didn't do it when I was sixteen either, since he was away at San Quentin.

"Advice I can give, though."

"I assure you, I did nothing to bring this on. Anyway, I've gone a whole year and a half without any violence. Doesn't that count for something?"

Nothing.

"Dad?"

"That was supposed to be a joke, yes? Tell me that was supposed to be a joke."

"Dad, I know I worry you, and I don't mean to."

"You're all I have left."

"Stop that. You have Catherine and Leonard." The other housemate. "And Elaine and Wayne and the kids. And you have Mary Elizabeth." The woman he'd been keeping company with.

"But you're my only son. My only child."

"I've always been your only son. How come now it's suddenly worth mentioning?"

"I'm getting old, Joseph."

"What's with you? You're especially morbid today. Did one of your old gang buddies die?"

"Heinie Silverberg."

"Heinie the Hanky?"

"Him."

"Wasn't he, like, ninety-five?"

"Ninety-six."

"That's twenty years older than you. Not worth this they're-dropping-like-flies routine you're laying on me."

"How close do they have to be for me to lay?"

That was a tough one. I didn't have an answer.

Nor did he expect one. "See, I can make a joke too. You're right. I should snap out of it. You're fine, right? That's all I care about."

"I'm fine."

"Good. Let me say hello to that gorgeous wife of yours."

I turned over the phone and looked at the TV. Sometime during my conversation my gorgeous wife had changed the channel to the James Bond marathon on Spike TV. It was *A View to a Kill*, the one with Patrick Macnee, and I knew he was going to get knocked off and that made me sad. Then I thought of *The Avengers*, and how Mrs. Peel was in her sixties now, and how did that happen? And how old did that make Patrick Macnee, if he was even still alive?

I knew something then. I knew that the worries about aging and mortality and the big sleep I thought I'd worked my way through back during the Platypus reunion were still with me. They were as profound as ever, and they'd be there until the day I died.

Eventually I went to sleep. Still on the couch. I kept waking from dreams where I was being chased by gangsters. Or maybe they were aliens. They had characteristics of both. Sometime after two in the morning they showed up again and I discovered they were from Homeland Security. I awoke yelling and kicking and fell off the couch.

I sat in the living room with the TV on and the sound down low. The Bond movie was a Timothy Dalton one that had nothing to do with anything Ian Fleming ever thought of. After twenty minutes I began surfing. I stopped on an infomercial where a woman with canyonlike cleavage asserted that size did matter. I thought of fixing her up with Vito until I realized the whole thing was about penis enhancement. You took one of their pills every day, and in three weeks you'd be longer and bigger around. After six weeks you'd have grown a full three inches. How did they get away with advertising this stuff?

At some point I dropped off again. When I got up the shower was going. I went in the bedroom and undressed and looked at myself in the mirror covering the sliding closet door. I imagined what I would look like if I were a full three inches longer. And bigger around.

"What the hell are you doing?"

Gina was standing in the doorway. She was wrapped in a ratty robe and had a towel on her head.

"Do you think I'm adequate?" I said. "Penis-wise, I mean."

"Of course you are. What a dumb thing to say."

"I saw this ad on TV last night. For enhancement."

"Your dick is just fine."

"Remember in *Boogie Nights*, where Marky Mark had that foot-long schlong?"

"It was prosthetic."

"I *know* it was prosthetic, but still."

"Still what?"

"Still, a guy wonders what it would be like."

"You know what it would be like? Painful."

"You've been with a guy like that?"

"Jesus. No. I'm just conjecturing. Now stop. It's not appropriate to talk about penises on Thanksgiving."

She seemed to have called a truce. But maybe it was just for the holiday. Like that Christmas during World War One where the French and the Germans took the day off from fighting and celebrated together. If that were the case, my respite would be short-lived. The next day they were back to shooting each other's heads off.

We had a baker's dozen for Thanksgiving. Me, Gina, my father and his girlfriend Mary Elizabeth, Leonard, Catherine. Elaine and Wayne and their twentyish daughter Lauren and their seven-year-old Miles. Gina's mother and the mariachi she was seeing. And my father's friend Sonny Patronella, recently widowed, who I'd last seen five years back, during my first murder extravaganza, when my father called in a favor and had Sonny follow me around to make sure I didn't get myself killed.

I managed a few minutes alone with my father. He asked advice about his posies, which to him meant any flowering plant smaller than a rosebush. I told him what I could. He treated me as his own personal gardening expert, though my expertise never went far beyond succulent plants, and even that knowledge was fading.

We sat down to dinner at three o'clock. My father and Leonard wanted to do it later, "like Jews do," but Catherine said if and when they ever did the cooking, they could set the time. There was enough food to feed Albania. We went through it like a pack of starved hyenas. By four-thirty all the men were arrayed in the living room, rubbing their stomachs, watching an Animal Planet show about sharks. By five the women, a traditionalist lot who did all the cleaning up, had joined them.

I got tired of the talk about Kobe and Michael and the war and wandered into my father's bedroom. Miles was in there with his dinosaurs. He knew all the names, and proudly told me each one. I played dinosaurs with him for a while, until he asked if I wanted to play chess. I said I didn't know how. He said he'd teach me. He beat me three straight games.

Sometime around nine, in the midst of my father's recitation of our family history, I realized I hadn't thought of Mike Lennox or his recently deceased son Dennis for a couple of hours. I wanted my father to continue. I wanted him to keep spinning yarns, like an old gray Scheherazade, for hours and days and weeks, until all the Lennoxes and their troubles and foibles and demises were just a dim memory.

I didn't hear from Mike, and I didn't call him. I'd let him phone me when he was ready. If after a month or two he didn't, maybe I'd give him a call. Or maybe I wouldn't. Maybe I'd never talk to him again, yet another person I didn't care enough about to keep track of.

The airwaves and the newsstands were still filled with Dennis Lennox's sudden end. The media frenzy rivaled the one when Nicole and Ron were killed. Michael and Kobe were relegated to the inside pages. Iraq and the Mars landers didn't get the attention they deserved. The earthquake in Iran registered less on the Richter scale than the killing did.

After a few days Lu was upgraded from critical to serious. She was able to give the police a statement. She'd been upstairs in her room watching TV, had heard odd noises, and gone downstairs and into the den to find the same thing I had, less the Golden Globe. She heard a sound behind her, but got clobbered before she could see who it was. She lost consciousness briefly, came to, heard the doorbell and banging, made it out front and let us in. The police didn't know how the killer had gotten in, but he or she had probably escaped through a side door, which was found unlocked.

The story the papers got said we had all gathered there for "a meeting." Nothing about him righting any wrongs, nothing about him screwing everyone over. During my interview with the police I'd simply told them we'd had a disagreement to work out. Theta said Ronnie'd told them much the same. Ronnie was still making herself scarce, and I didn't have any contact with any of the others. I didn't know if the cops had put together what a creep Dennis was, or if they'd already known, and I didn't much care. I just wanted them to find whoever offed him and be done with it.

Everyone who'd been at Dennis's house had an alibi covering the time just before they got there. Most of them involved watching TV. Ronnie with Theta, Samantha with Carrie, Sean McKay with his father. Trixie, last name Trenton, was the exception. She had spent the evening at Ambiance, the est-like group my fake wife in the anti-herpes commercial frequented, leaving only when Dennis called on her cell phone. She had a dozen witnesses to her whereabouts.

The *Times* ran a sidebar with a paragraph about everyone who was there that night, along with a photo of each of us. They too had discovered my crimefighting exploits and ran a shot left over from one. Sean McKay, who had "worked with the victim on a project that never came to fruition," was represented by a fuzzy portrait. Ronnie got a glamour shot, as did Trixie Trenton. It turned out Trixie'd done a couple of soft-core porn flicks, the kind they ran on the Playboy Channel. And yes, that was her real first name. Her sister was Alice, her brothers Ralph and Ed. Her father was a big *Honeymooners* fan.

Channel 6 was running a special at nine every night,

pre-empting the usual *Hunter* reruns. Claudia Acuna hosted. A segment on Trixie Trenton was the highlight. They'd gotten hold of one of her soft-core films and ran a couple of minutes of the most revealing footage, smudging the picture anytime a nipple or any pubic hair threatened to make an appearance. Then they had her on live. She sat there wearing a dress cut up to here and down to there and said, no, she didn't regret for one minute doing those movies, that there was nothing shameful about the human body, and that she'd had very special feelings for Dennis and hoped his killer was found "like, tonight."

Claudia Acuna called one evening and asked for an interview. I turned her down. Then I ranted about how this was a perfect example of how loathsome local television news was. She waited until I was done and said I was absolutely right. My opinion of her went up a degree. Maybe two.

They did a piece on me anyway, and thirty-seven seconds after it finished, my father called with another of his patented watch-out-for-danger speeches. I'd spoken to him a half-dozen times since the Lummox conversation. The exchanges varied little. Again, you get mixed up with bad people. It's not like I planned it, Dad. You'll be careful? I'll be careful.

He asked to speak to Gina. I made an excuse. Two days after Thanksgiving, she'd said she needed some space, and gone to stay at her mother's.

As the week went on I was vaguely aware of the promise I'd made to Mike. I really did think the cops, with their ace investigators, database networks, and microanalysis equipment, were going to nab whoever did it. As each day passed, the conversation outside the Kirk Douglas Theatre grew dimmer and less real. By the weekend I was convinced that Mike, with all he'd been going through that day, wouldn't even remember it.

Tuesday morning, ten or so. I'd been sleeping alone, living alone, for three days. The phone rang. I picked it up. "Hello?"

"That you, Portugal?"

I recognized the voice. I wished I didn't.

eighteen

"It's me," I said.

"This is Vito. Mr. Santini wants you to have lunch with him tomorrow."

Oh, boy, I thought. It didn't take him long. He was going to call in his favor and have me … have me what? Rub out some Mafia rival? Carry drugs across the border in my underwear?

"Um …"

"He'll pay."

"That wasn't why I was hesitating. I've just got a lot to do tomorrow." Very convincing, I was sure.

"He'd really appreciate it if you could fit him in. He has to talk about something with you, and he doesn't want to do it on the phone."

"He doesn't like to do business on the phone."

"Now you're catchin' on. So how about it?"

Did I have a choice? "Where should I meet him and when?"

"Noon at Valencio's."

"I don't know where that is."

"Find it."

"I'll find it," I told the dead phone.

•

I called Alberta Burns and offered to buy her lunch. We decided on the Thai Dishes on Manchester. It had a big fish tank near the front door. A blue-and-white specimen swam in our direction and seemed to be watching us. As the hostess led us to a table, I felt it was following our progress. But when we were seated and I looked up front, it was just disappearing behind a fake castle.

You're going psycho, Portugal.

Clearly it was a possibility. Just as clearly, there was nothing I could do about it, so I turned my attention to the menu. We ordered lunch specials. The waitress walked away and came back not thirty seconds later with a couple of Asian-restaurant salads. Some bits of pale lettuce, a sliver each of cucumber and tomato, dressing that resembled semen.

When she was gone, Burns said, "I guess you didn't get a chance to talk to Dennis Lennox about my project."

"Well, I did, the minute I saw him. Right after I threw up. Except for being dead, he was very responsive."

"Ass."

"No. I didn't get a chance."

"Probably wouldn't have liked it anyway. Not enough T&A. Okay, what do you want from me today?"

"You ever hear of a guy named John Santini?"

"Sure. You're not a cop in L.A. long without knowing about John Santini."

"What is he?"

"Why do you want to know?"

"I've gotten mixed up with him."

"Now you've done it."

"He's in the Mafia, isn't he?"

"Not exactly."

"What's that mean?"

"It means there's other organized crime besides the Mafia."

"But he is in organized crime."

"Was."

"He's not active anymore?"

"Not exactly."

"I know how that works. The ones who are really in charge act all retired, hang out with their grandchildren, and tend their grapes. Then when something important's going down, they suddenly show up again, and everyone you thought was in power kneels down and kisses their ring."

"I think that's the pope."

"Their cheek. Their shoe. Something. Why isn't he in jail?"

"He still has his hand in a lot of pies."

"Thus reinforcing the idea that he ought to be in jail."

"Some of those pies have other hands in them. And those hands belong to people in high places."

"Politicians?"

"Look, Portugal. What I know about Santini's all urban-legend stuff. There's half a dozen like him that you hear about on the street. You know they're mixed up with something illegal, and you know it reaches into the halls of power."

"Then why doesn't anyone do anything about it?"

"Because you know that if you try you'll get nowhere."

"Because there are people in the department who'll stop you?"

"I'm not going to say any more about this."

"Why not?"

"Because it's pointless. Look. You wanted to find out how dangerous a character you've gotten yourself mixed up with. The answer is, fairly."

"Very comforting."

"But if you play along with him, nothing's going to happen to you. These guys, they protect their people."

"I'm one of his people now?"

"He's got a lot of people."

"What if he asks me to do something illegal?"

"He won't. These guys have other people for that. Here's our food."

I couldn't get anything else out of her. Eventually I got tired of trying.

The blue-and-white fish watched me again as we were on our way out. I stared at him for a couple of seconds. He stared right back. Then, with a flip of his tail, he swam behind his castle.

The hostess was watching too. "Nice fish," I said.

She nodded. "Very intelligent," she said. "That fish knows many things."

"Does he know who killed Dennis Lennox?" I didn't stick around for an answer.

Dennis's time of death was, best guess, nine-thirty on the night of Tuesday, November 25. Exactly one week later, my doorbell rang.

nineteen

"Who is it?" I yelled.

"Mike."

I let him in. He went right for the couch. I caught a whiff as he went by. "How you doing?" I said.

"You know. Okay, I guess."

"That's good."

"So it's been a week."

"I guess it has."

"So it's time."

"Mike, I—"

"What're you going to do first?"

I gave it a second. "I don't have what you'd call a plan."

"Yeah, well, you and me, we're not the kind of guys who plan things out a lot, are we?"

"No," I said. "We're not."

"I mean, we just go with the flow. Ride the river of life, like the song says."

Not any song I knew. "You've been drinking."

"Drinking, smoking, toking, croaking … what's the rest of the line?"

"Are you supposed to drink when you're on antidepressants?"

"Yeah, well, what the fuck difference does it make?" He picked up the TV remote, pressed a couple of buttons at random, dropped it onto the carpet. "Whoopsie."

"Look. I've been thinking. It's kind of pointless for me to try to find who shot—"

"I really appreciate this, man. 'Cause the cops, you know, they got a lot to do, a lot of dead people to track down. No, wait, it's not the dead people, it's the people who make them dead."

"What I was trying to say is—"

"While you, what else you got to do? So I figure that makes up for the fact that they know what they're doing."

"It—"

"So keep me posted, okay?" And he was up, and he was at the door, and he was out it.

I stood there for a minute, and then reason kicked in, and I ran after him. I needn't have bothered. There was a car out front. The driver, young and long-haired and tie-died, leaned against the fender. A member of Mike's Venice community. "Yo," he said.

Mike turned and saw me. "Don't worry," he said. "I'm not crazy enough to drive around drunk. Got enough dead people in my family already."

The two of them got in. The car pulled away.

The next day was Wednesday. Four days since Gina had gone to stay at her mother's. I'd called a couple of times, got the machine, didn't leave a message. I thought about going over there, declaring I couldn't live without her, begging forgiveness on bended knee.

And yet . . . and yet, I was, in some small way, enjoying living alone. I'd noticed this when Gina was in San Francisco.

Being king of my own realm again, not having to make accommodations to the way the other person liked to live—there was a certain attractiveness to it.

Another thing: I was entertaining thoughts of being with other women. Same thoughts I always had, now tinged with the possibility that at some point in the not-too-distant future I might be able to act on them. I felt guilty for a while; then I didn't. No point to it. I knew as soon as Gina and I had things straightened out, my little masturbatory fantasies would resume their rightful place in that mess I call my mind.

And I was sure we *would* straighten things out. Absolutely positive.

Except for the other half of the time. When I felt doomed to a life of loneliness.

I looked in my closet. What do you wear to lunch with the Mob? There was the suit I had for auditions where I needed to look respectable. And for funerals. Or I could go in a ratty sweatshirt and holey jeans. Go into the bird room and get canary shit under my fingernails. Maybe if I looked terrible Santini would think twice about having me do whatever it was he wanted me to.

I took the middle road. I showered, shaved, and put on the kind of thing I usually wore to an audition when they didn't ask for something specific. Dockers, denim shirt, the kind of Reeboks that look like regular shoes if you don't look close.

I pulled up at the Hotel Chilton, home of Valencio's, at five to twelve. In front of me, Santini was handing the keys to a silver-gray Mercedes to the parking attendant. He saw me and waited while I gave away my own keys and endured the attendant's sneer over my choice of transportation.

Santini wore a white shirt, gray sport coat, black pants. "How you doing today?" he said.

"Not bad. Yourself?"

"Good. It's a good day. Sun shining, birds singing." Very civilized, the two of us were.

It was dark inside and it had been bright outside and I couldn't see a thing. I followed the host and Santini more by sound than sight. My eyes adjusted after we were seated at a table way in the back. Thick dark wood, old-time light fixtures hanging from low ceilings, red-and-white checked tablecloths. The scent of oregano.

A waiter came by. He was seventy or more, with thin hair and a narrow moustache. The kind where, one slip while you're shaving, it's cut in half. He said hello to Mr. Santini, nodded to me, poured olive oil into our bread dishes, asked what we wanted to drink.

"A glass of the Chianti," Santini said.

"Do you have iced tea?" I said.

"Joe," Santini said.

"Hmm?"

"Have the Chianti."

"I'll have the Chianti," I told the waiter, who nodded approvingly, performed a perfect about-face, and made his exit.

Santini picked up the menu. I did the same. "Veal's always good here," he said.

I didn't say anything. Just studied the menu.

"You're not a vegetarian, are you?" he said.

"No."

"But you don't eat veal."

"Or lamb."

"That baby animal thing."

"Yes."

"Gotcha. Know what else is good? The chicken marsala. Let's have that. Marco."

The waiter appeared at my right shoulder. He put two big glasses of red wine on the table. "Yes, Mr. Santini?"

"Two of the chicken marsala."

"Good choice, sir."

He disappeared. Santini picked up a chunk of bread, dipped it in oil, took a bite. He chewed, swallowed, said, "Vito's mother makes the bread here. You remember Vito, right?"

"At your place."

"Yeah. Have some."

We made small talk. The weather, sports, "that freak Michael Jackson." Salads came, big ones with garbanzos and olives. I tried to be sneaky about avoiding the olives, but Santini saw what was going on, called Marco over, had him bring me one without them. "Life's too short to pick stuff out of your food," Santini said.

More nothing talk until the entrees arrived. Santini took a bite, then another. His face was blissful. "It's the spices," he said. "Without the spices, you got nothing. You don't have to be scared of me, you know."

"I'm not scared of you."

"Oh?"

"Okay, I'm scared of you."

"Why?"

"Because I've heard some of your history."

"You scared of your father?"

"Of course not."

"Same history. Mine just lasted a little longer, on account of he got caught."

"Forgive me, but I'm not convinced."

"Who you been talking to?"

"Friend of mine on the police force."

"A cop."

"That's what they're known as, yes."

"Try your food."

I cut off a piece, put it in my mouth. It was good, all right. Without the spices, you got nothing.

"Your father killed a guy. I never did that."

"I'm not sure my father really killed that guy."

"Not hard to understand."

"And if you never actually pulled the trigger…"

He was shaking his head. "You think I got a bunch of triggermen?"

"Maybe not a bunch. Just one or two."

"Maybe I did. A long time ago. Now, things are different. Look…"

He leaned forward, with his elbows on the table and his fingers interlaced. "I tell you things, they stay between us."

"I tell my wife everything." In theory, at least.

"You trust her?"

"Of course I trust her."

"Okay, then. I tell you things, they stay between us and your wife."

"Sure."

"Not your cop friend."

"Of course not."

"Not your father."

"Not a problem."

"Good." He sat back, attacked his food again. The chicken had come with a small pile of pasta on the plate. He expertly used his fork and spoon to whirl some up and put it in his mouth without losing a drop of sauce. "Eat up," he said. "We eat first, talk after. That's how it works."

"That's not how it works on *The Sopranos*. They're always shoving food in their mouths while they're talking about who to whack."

"Must be an East Coast thing. Here, we eat first, talk business after."

We sat at the table, John Santini with his espresso, me with my cup of tea. I'd eaten too much and kept shifting in my seat the relieve the pressure.

He reached into his jacket pocket, unstoppered a pharmacy vial. "Hold out your hand." When I did he shook a pill into it. "Take that. Great stuff."

"What is it?"

"What, you think I'm trying to poison you? If I was going to poison you, why would I spend good money on your lunch?"

"Good point." I took the pill, washed it down with a sip of tea, one of water.

"So," he said. "You're wondering how come we're sitting here."

"Yes."

"I need you to find someone."

"Who?"

"Alma's daughter. Name's Valerie. You remember Alma, right?"

"Your assistant. The one who looks like Mike's wife."

"Uh-huh. Been with me thirty-two years."

"What happened to her daughter?"

"Moved out of her place, didn't tell anyone."

"Her place where?"

"Studio City. Apartment building off Laurel Canyon."

"How old?"

"Twenty-eight."

"Actress?"

"How'd you know?"

"Wild guess."

"See? You're the right guy for this."

I shifted my weight, realized the pressure in my gut had already lessened. "Great stuff, those pills."

"I'll get you some."

I downed my tea, dumped more water over the bag. "Why me?"

"You're good at finding people."

"Based on a sample of one?"

"Two. That rock and roll guy."

"Want to know a secret?"

"Won't be a secret anymore."

"I didn't really find him."

"Doesn't matter. I got a feeling about you."

"Even if I were good at it, aren't there people who'd be better?"

"Like who?"

"Like some hired killer. They always find who they're looking for. Just make it clear to them beforehand, stop short of the gun part."

"You're a funny guy."

"Or a private detective."

"Tried one. Got nowhere. I need someone who knows the business."

"The business."

"The acting business."

"I'm pretty much on the fringes."

"That's not what my research says. The Altair Theater. All that."

Many years ago. Before I got involved with commercials. "This is the same research that told you about Toby Bonner?"

"Had to get something for my money from the detective." He reached inside his jacket, came out with a plain white business-size envelope. "This is something to kind of help you along." He handed it to me.

I turned it over. It was sealed. I flexed it. Felt around the edges of the contents. "A photo?" I said.

"Yeah."

"You have a photo?"

"Course I have a photo. Don't open it yet. Wait until you need a little motivation."

"This from that detective of yours?"

His smile was impossible to read. "Doesn't matter," he said. "Now get to work, Joey-boy."

twenty

I found a pay phone and called Alma Rodriguez. She said she was too busy to see me until the next morning.

When I got home I put the envelope on my dresser. Then I opened a drawer and slid it under my socks. I didn't need to see the photograph inside. Its very existence was enough motivation.

I checked the message machine. Two calls. Both from Mike Lennox, wanting to know what I'd discovered.

Not a thing, Mike. I've been too busy on another case. It's a little more important now. You see, there's this envelope with a photo in it. No, I haven't seen it. But I can only imagine it's Ronnie and me doing something we shouldn't have.

But, with the rest of the day to kill, I might as well do something to make it look like I was doing what I'd told him I would. There had to be someone whose brain I could pick.

It took a while, but inspiration struck. I got out the phone book and found Channel 6. I played Voice Mail for a minute or two until I got hold of a live person in the newsroom. I asked for Claudia Acuna. A young male voice asked who was calling. I said my name. The voice turned excited when he heard it. But he was sorry to report she wasn't there. He could try to get her on her cell phone, though, and have her call.

It wasn't three minutes before the phone rang and she was on the line. "The famous Joe Portugal," she said.

"That's me."

"What can I do for you?"

"It's what I can do for you that's important."

"Which is what?"

"I can help you with the Lennox business."

A long pause. "Sure, why not. Come by the station tomorrow at two. I'll show you some things." She gave me an address on Gower in Hollywood. "See you tomorrow." She hung up.

I killed the rest of the afternoon and early evening staring at the TV, with only occasional trips to visit the envelope in my sock drawer to break up the monotony. It stayed sealed. Around eight I took a couple of Dramamine. I wasn't worried about motion sickness. I wasn't going anywhere. But they made dandy sleeping pills.

There was a tiny lot by the Santini Imports loading dock. One spot was marked for visitors. I claimed it and got out of the truck. Vito was running a forklift, unloading a truck full of cartons. Whatever was in them was MADE IN CHINA. He saw me and grunted. Santini must have given him the word that I was okay. I returned the grunt, climbed the stairs to the loading dock, let him let me in the interior door. "She's up on Three," he said.

I found myself in the same corridor I'd been in the other day. I went up the stairs, took them all the way to the top. There were boxes everywhere. Boxes in piles, boxes on pallets, boxes on top of boxes. At the far end a freight elevator ground to a halt, and a skinny guy in the de rigueur shapeless pants pulled off a hand truck overloaded with still more boxes.

I spotted Alma when she walked over to talk to the guy from the elevator. She wore a thin white garment like a lab coat. She pointed to another hand truck, this one piled with the kind of cardboard cartons you keep papers and records in. The guy went after it. Alma stopped him just before he got back on the elevator with it, made a couple of marks on the clipboard she was carrying, let the guy go. The elevator clattered back to life and was gone.

I watched all this, trying to decide if, were I all the way across Staples Center, I could have mistaken her for Donna Lennox. Never having seen Donna in the flesh, I couldn't be sure. And what was the point? Mike clearly had made the error. Whether it seemed reasonable to me didn't matter.

Alma saw me, motioned me over, led me to one of the corners, to an office of sorts. There were glass walls, seven or eight feet high, broken by a doorless entryway. She un-buttoned her lab coat and sat behind an old metal desk that nearly filled the partitioned area. Her chair came from the same litter as the one downstairs in Santini's office. I had my choice of a folding metal one and a battered wooden barstool. I went for metal.

There were dozens of pieces of paper taped to the glass walls, and a half dozen nails in the plaster one, all but one with clipboards dangling. Some of the papers were curled and yellowed. Some of the tape was antique, shiny on one side with gum that had turned a glorious golden brown on the other.

Alma told me to hang on, flicked on a desk lamp, checked the clipboard she'd been carrying. She flipped over the top page and ran her finger down the one behind. Then she hung it on the vacant nail, turned off the lamp, looked at me. "Before anything else, I want to tell you that this isn't my idea."

"Okay."

"Just 'okay'?"

"What else am I supposed to say? I'm not even sure what it is that isn't your idea. Looking for your daughter? Having me do it?"

"The first. You getting involved, what do I care? I don't know you from Adam."

"Okay."

"Don't say that again, all right?"

"Okay."

She looked at me, cracked a smile. "Funny guy."

"I try."

"I've spent half the morning looking for a box of records that disappeared. Got me a little irritable."

"Find it?"

"Yeah. Buried under about a hundred cartons of stuffed animals."

"What kind?"

"Lions and tigers, mostly."

"No bears?"

The phone on the desk rang. She picked it up, said, "Yeah," listened. Whoever was on the other end was loud. I couldn't make out what they were saying, but I got the rhythm. Someone was unhappy. "Tell him to shove it," Alma said. She put her hand over the mouthpiece. "Goddamned Armenians." Back into the phone: "He'll have his bobble-heads this afternoon. I promise. Yeah. Same to you." She put her finger down to break the connection, hit three numbers. "Vito. Get the bobbleheads out, okay? Know what, better deliver them yourself. Make sure you get a certified check."

She hung up, pulled down another clipboard, turned on the lamp again, checked the paper over. I watched her eyes. She wasn't really looking at it. She was stalling. Deciding.

She hung it back up, doused the lamp, said, "Her name's Valerie."

"That much I know."

"What else do you know?"

"That she's an actress, and that she moved out of her apartment in Studio City and didn't tell anyone."

"And?"

"That's it."

Again she went after a clipboard, like she was going to do the deciding act again. This time it never made it off its nail. She brought her hand back, lay it and the other one on the desk, palms down, like it was going to levitate and she was trying to keep it from doing so.

I said, "Why don't you want anyone looking for her?"

"What good would it do?"

"You'd know where she is. What she's up to."

"You think I care?"

"I don't know. Do you?"

"Not a whole lot."

"Are you estranged?"

"Big word."

"But you know what it means."

She nodded. "Yeah. We are."

"How come?"

"Some things she did. Some things Mario and I did."

"What kind of things?"

"She'll take care of herself. She always has."

I got up, picked one of the clipboards off the wall. Looked it over. Some kind of form. It had been xeroxed crookedly, so the last column was cut off toward the bottom of the page. The first third or so was filled in. Dates, numbers, names of customers. A Post-it note was stuck on, with a red arrow pointing at an amount, with three exclamation points after the arrow.

"What are you doing?" Alma said.

"Deciding." I hung the clipboard back up. The Post-it came off and fluttered to the floor. I started after it.

"Leave it," she said. "Bastards are never going to pay anyway. What were you deciding?"

"If I want to pursue this thing. See, what's weird to me is, if you and your husband are so blasé about finding Valerie, why does Santini give a shit?"

"You'll have to ask him."

"I think you know."

"You calling me a liar?"

"I could wrap it up in a pretty package, but basically, yeah, I am."

She was silent. Her eyes went to one of the clipboards.

"Please," I said. "We've exhausted that routine."

A couple more seconds of quiet. Then, "Sit down. You're making me nervous."

I sat.

"I find out you tell anyone this, I swear to God, I'll come after you and knock the shit out of you."

"Duly noted."

"Valerie's his daughter," she said.

twenty-one

"I thought so," I said. "So you and he ..."

"No. Nothing like that. Not on my side, anyway. There was a girl working here."

"A girl."

"Don't give me any of your politically correct bullshit. She was barely seventeen."

"Santini got her pregnant."

"Yes."

"Did his wife know?"

"No. Far as she knew, Patty had a boyfriend that knocked her up and ran off."

"So, jumping ahead here, Patty gave birth to a baby girl, who you and Mario raised as your own."

"Yes."

"Because you couldn't have kids of your own."

"Wrong, Mr. Smart Guy. We have two other children."

"You estranged from them too?"

I expected, at the least, a dirty look. Instead I got a sad smile. "Look, here's the thing. John cares about Valerie, even if I don't. No reason for me, no matter what's up with her and me, to keep anyone from finding her."

How to phrase this? "How familiar are you with his other business ventures?"

"You mean, do I know he's, what do they call it, an organized-crime figure? Of course I do. Though if it wasn't for me, he wouldn't be half as organized. Wait. That might give you the wrong idea. This place is strictly on the up-and-up."

"You're sure of that."

"I do the books. I'm sure."

"He tried to give me the impression he's kept his hands clean lately."

She nodded. "This is pretty much it now. That other stuff, it's all in the past. Just like your father."

"He told you about that?"

"There's not a whole lot that goes on with him that I don't know about. Tell me something. Your father. He probably says he's following the straight and narrow."

"Not just says. He does."

"You're sure of that."

Was I? He was still in contact with some of his old cronies. Like Sonny Patronella, who'd followed me around that time. And Heinie Silverberg, at least until he kicked the bucket. If that one last score beckoned, would he be able to . . .

"Yes," I said. "I'm sure."

"Yeah, well, I'm sure too." She stood. The interview was over.

I got to Channel 6 just before two. The source of the young male voice I'd spoken to on the phone was pleased as punch to see me. He was thin, dressed all in black, and strikingly handsome, with jet black hair and innocent blue eyes. He told me Claudia'd gotten stuck in a meeting, but would be free in a few minutes. Would I like some coffee? Tea? Mineral water? I said I was fine, and sat down to read about heart disease in a weeks-old *U.S. News and World Report*.

But he wouldn't leave me alone. Was I *sure* I didn't want a refreshment? To shut him up I asked for some water. Then he went down the list of waters. I said anything's fine, he came back with an Evian, opened the bottle, poured, hovered.

I looked up. "Is there something else?"

"Well…"

"Go ahead."

Suddenly he was crouching beside me. "Mr. Portugal, I… I saw that you're a very successful actor in commercials, and I've recently—"

I stuck out my hand. "Give it here. I'll let my agent see it. No promises."

He practically popped with glee. "Thank you. Thank you, thank you, thank you." He dashed over to the desk, where he'd stashed his photo and resume for easy access, and placed them reverently in my hand. "Mr. Portugal, I just know I can—"

"Kid."

"Yes?"

"Mr. Portugal is my father."

"Yes, sir."

"Joe."

"Yes, Joe."

He fluttered back to his seat as a door opened. "Sorry about that," Claudia Acuna said.

She was a lot better looking when she wasn't in TV reporter guise. More natural, with just some eyeliner and lipstick. She was wearing flats, snug jeans, a white blouse. Were I single, I would have been instantly attracted to her. Hell, cut the *were I single*. There was something about her that reminded me of Gina. Acuna was taller, more buxom, some years younger. But there was that spark in her eyes, the one that said she didn't suffer fools gladly, and that if you got on her good side you could count on her, and that she could give you a hell of a time in the sack.

We went back through the door and down a stark hall. "I see you met Keith."

Who burst through the door behind us. "Your water … Joe."

"Thanks."

An obsequious smile, and he was gone.

I looked at the picture. *Keith Colbert*, it said underneath. A competent shot, though it didn't fully capture those great eyes. "Good-looking kid. Maybe he has a chance."

"Maybe."

I caught her scent. I'd known a woman once who wore that scent. I associated it with a misbegotten summer.

We entered a high-ceilinged room where a dozen sloppy desks and half that number of frazzled people were scattered around. She led me to one, pointed to the wastebasket at its side. "You can throw that in there."

"Why would I do that?"

"I thought you might have taken it to be polite."

"No. I told the kid I'd show his picture to my agent, and that's what I'll do." She had a bit of a smile on. "What?"

"Nothing."

"Was that a test?"

"What makes you think that?"

"My keen investigative abilities."

She watched me for a beat or two, broadened the smile. "Yes. It was. And I'm sorry. I just wanted to see—"

"How honest I was?"

"I don't know what I was thinking. It was a lame idea. I apologize." She sat down, produced a keyring, unlocked her desk. Opened a file drawer, removed several manila folders full of papers, shut the drawer, turned the key, disappeared the keyring.

She stood. Looked at me. "So? Is the apology accepted?"

"Sure."

"Good. Let's go somewhere more private. My boss is on vacation. We'll use her office."

More stepping down the hall. She moved in front of me to open the office door. I could see the outline of her underthings through the back of her blouse. Something a man never tires of. Yeah, if I were single again...

Stop it, putz. You're not single, you're not going to be, and you're a jerk for even thinking about it. Did you forget that envelope in your sock drawer already?

The office had a desk, a couple of chairs, a small sofa. On the wall, awards and photos. There was a dracaena in the corner, limp and pale. Claudia saw me looking at it. "Right," she said. "The plant man."

"Tell your boss it needs more light."

"I'll do that." She sat on the sofa, a black vinyl thing that creaked when she settled herself. I joined her. It wasn't really a sofa. More of a loveseat.

She opened the first folder, paged through a couple of papers, pulled one out, handed it to me. It was a photocopy of an ad for an X-rated tape called *The High Hard One*. The picture of the box showed a couple of babes wearing baseball caps and unbuttoned jerseys that said *Yan* on one side of their magnificent cleavages and *kers* on the other. The dark-haired one had two baseballs in her hand. The blond held a bat suggestively. One of them was Penelope Pope and the other was Letitia Lawrence, and their unseen co-star was Johnson Johnson. Across the bottom was the punchline to an old joke. *He kissed her between the strikes ... she kissed him between the balls.* There was some sales info alongside and under the photo, the price, distributor, that kind of thing.

"Lovely," I said.

"Either of the women look familiar?"

I brought the page closer. Then tried farther away. I was going to need reading glasses soon. But further examination showed me nothing. "No."

"It's Trixie Trenton."

I inspected the blond more closely. Tapped her picture on the page. "No way."

"Not her. The brunet."

Again I looked. I squinted. Then Claudia pulled out a tearsheet from the *Times*, something from the last week's coverage. There was a photo of Trixie. Suddenly I saw it. The eyes. They were the same eyes. "So it wasn't just *soft*-core."

"No."

"Is she Penelope or Letitia?"

"Penelope."

"How old is this?"

"It came out in '97."

"She must have been pretty young."

"Nineteen."

"Are there others?"

"A few."

I handed the pages back. "So she was a porn star. So what?"

"So nothing. I said I was going to show you some things. I didn't say they were going to add up to anything."

"True enough. Why haven't you used this on the air yet?"

"Why embarrass the girl?"

"Come on. You people love to embarrass people."

"'You people.'"

"Local news people."

"Believe it or not, we do have consciences. At least I do. No one else here knows about this. At least not yet."

"Where'd you get it?"

"Sources."

"You have anything else on her?"

"Nothing much. Exercises a lot. Has a shih tzu."

"I knew that."

"She's into that human-potential crap."

"Right, she was at that Ambiance place right before Dennis got killed. Anything else?"

"No."

"Who's next?"

"Do you want to see what I have on you?" She was looking at me in a way that, in my single days, would have had me calculating how to ask her out.

I turned away. "Not unless there's something I don't know about."

"How about your friend Ronnie MacKenzie?"

I had to think about it. What if Claudia had uncovered something less than flattering? What if Ronnie turned out to have an X-rated background too?

And what if she did? "What have you got?"

"Not a whole lot," she said. "Not much of anything, as a matter of fact. She grew up in Arkansas, which I'm sure you knew. Her father died when she was two—"

"Run over by a semi."

"A semi? How awful. What I have just says a truck."

"Makes pretty much the same spot on the pavement. So nothing else before she got to L.A?"

"No," she said.

"And after?"

"Moved into her cousin Thelma's house on Madison Avenue in Culver City."

"Thelma?"

"Yes."

"She goes by Theta."

"My name was Thelma, I'd go by something else too."

"Anything more?"

She checked her notes. "Works out at the Spectrum Club … well-liked on the set … dating a producer on *Protect and Serve*."

"Eric something."

"Stahl."

"Go on," I said.

"She's pretty much, what you see is what you get. Who would you like next?"

"Might as well finish off the cute young things."

"Samantha Szydlo. Let's see." She shuffled papers, brought out a few. "Born December 4, 1974, St. Louis. Grew up there. Went to college at Cooper Union."

"Where's that?"

"New York. Small school, art, architecture, engineering. Graduated in '96, moved to Chicago, then to L.A. in '98. Had a few group exhibitions. Active in Heal the Bay. Has a small trust fund. That's pretty much it."

"Nothing very—"

"Except for the restraining order," she said.

twenty-two

It took me a second. "When was that?"

"In '98, in Chicago, a little before she moved out here. There was a man she was seeing. He broke it off. She began harassing him."

"How?"

"Phone calls, mostly, mixed in with some stalking. Plus going through his garbage. He was another artist. His website got hacked. The police thought she had something to do with it, but never proved anything."

"Anything violent?"

She scanned the page. "No. Why?"

I looked at her. I flashed on the other woman who'd worn the same perfume. I couldn't remember her name. But I could remember one hot summer night...

Better you should remember the envelope.

I stood, stepped away, leaned against the desk. "I had lunch with her, the day Dennis died. She wanted to get together and come up with a way to get back at Dennis."

"Interesting."

"Some of the ideas were pretty drastic."

"Violent drastic?"

"Yes. But I thought it was just talk."

"She's been in therapy practically since she moved to L.A."

"Is it working?"

"That I don't know."

"I suppose the police know all about this."

"They must," she said.

"So they would have talked to her about it."

"Yes."

"Grilled her, if they thought they had to."

"Most likely."

"So probably this is nothing."

"Probably. Anyway, her alibi looks good. The roommate."

"Carrie."

"Yes."

"Mike's girlfriend. That's Dennis's father."

"Yes. The two of them were home watching TV until she left for Dennis's house. The police got tapes of what they said they were watching and quizzed Samantha. She seems to have watched what she said she did."

"Or Carrie watched it and filled her in. Or taped it for her."

"Seems a little far-fetched," she said.

"I suppose. Even if she was there, it doesn't say she wasn't behind it. She could have hired somebody."

"Took out a contract on Dennis? Seems even more far-fetched than Carrie covering for her."

"More far-fetched than her hiring someone to hack the other guy's website?"

"Good point." She switched to another file. "That's about it on her. On to Sean McKay. He's—" Her cell phone went off. She answered it. After a few seconds she said, "Now?" Then, "Okay." She clicked off. "Late-breaking news."

"High-speed chase?"

"Better. Jumper on the Stack." The downtown freeway interchange. Four levels of road all atop one another. "We'll finish later," she said. "I'll show you out."

"Can I use the phone?"

"Sure."

I found the number in my wallet. Samantha Szydlo's cell phone. She'd given it to me at Mao's, "just in case." I caught her somewhere called Gallery Gaga. She told me she'd be there a while. I told her I was on my way.

Claudia'd listened in. "You work fast," she said.

"When I feel like it," I said.

Gallery Gaga was at the end of Washington Boulevard, the last building on the south side before the ocean. As I walked the two blocks from my parking place, the sun disappeared behind a huge mass of gray clouds scudding in from the west. I found the gallery and entered. A tall thin woman with blond hair to her waist asked if she could help me. I said I was looking for Samantha, and her face lit up. She told me how lucky they were to have her and said Samantha was in the back room and I should go back there.

Paintings leaned all along the foot of the wall. The ones on the left were abstracts, filled with big patches of red and green and purple. The kind of thing that, if you hung them upside down, no one but the artist would know anything was wrong. Those on the right were more representational, the stark brown and black figures in each surrounded by auras of pale color and speckles of something that glinted in the fluorescent lighting.

I stopped to check out the pieces along the back wall. I hoped they and not those on the sides were Samantha's. Then if she asked me what I thought of her work I wouldn't have to lie. The people were identifiable as people, the vehicles as vehicles, the buildings as buildings. I recognized a couple of the locations. One was the building downtown with the giant basketball players painted on, only it was from some past day when baseball was in season. You only saw the lower halves of the athletes, and standing down at the bottom of the building were four small figures engaged in some activity that kept them clustered around a spot where the wall met the ground.

Another had a woman standing next to a lamppost. In the background on the right was the El Rey Theatre. The woman was dressed in a tight red T-shirt and cutoff jeans. Her hair was short and as red as the shirt. Up the post, barely making it inside the top of the painting, was a sign that said *Miracle Mile District*.

I got the feeling the woman in cutoffs was the only person on Wilshire Boulevard for miles around. That the four figures at the foot of the building populated a downtown that, save for them, was as empty as the one in an after-the-nuclear-holocaust movie.

"You like them?" Samantha asked. She'd come out of the back room.

"A lot."

"You know art?"

"Not at all. But you know what they say. I know what I like."

"They do say that."

"And you probably hear it ten times a day from know-nothings like me."

A smile. "No more than five."

"But I really do like them. You get a feeling of, I don't

know, aloneness. Like you dropped these people into deserted cities."

"Kind of what I try for."

"They remind me—I mean, they don't look like it or anything, but the feeling I get—you know that painting *Nighthawks*?"

"Of course. Edward Hopper."

"Right. Him. That's the feeling I get."

"He's an influence."

"Who else is an influence?"

"Would you know the names if I said them?"

"Probably not."

"Then I won't say them."

I moved closer to the one with the four figures. "What are these guys up to?"

"Pitching pennies."

"Hard to tell by looking at it."

"I suppose so. But I knew while I was painting it, and that's what matters. Anyway . . . turns out I have less to do here than I thought I did. So we can go somewhere else to talk."

"No."

"You want to stay here? That's fine—"

I shook my head. "Not, no, I want to stay here. I meant no, you didn't overestimate what you had to do. You wanted me to come here to see your art."

"Why would I want to do that?"

"To see my reaction."

"That would be awfully devious."

"Did I pass?"

She laughed, shook her head. "You barely know me, and you have me all figured out. Yeah, that was the plan. And yeah, you passed."

"Good."

"But I've spent all day here, and I'd just as soon go somewhere else."

"Fine."

We made for the door. Samantha stared at the sky. "Where'd all this gray come from?"

"Just rolled in."

Right on cue, rain pittered down on the sidewalk. Then it turned harder. I said, "Maybe we ought to change our plan."

"We could, but... Ellen? Would you happen to have an umbrella around?"

"There's a couple in back," the blond said. "People leave them, you know? Hang on." She went in the back room and returned with two of them. "Plain black or gray with ducks. Your choice."

"Joe?" Samantha said.

"Let's go with the ducks," I said. "Because it's—"

"Nice weather for ducks. I get it."

She opened the umbrella as we stepped outside. The hard rain had advanced to a downpour. People were running for shelter. I moved under the umbrella. "Where are we going?"

"Back to my place."

"That's a bit of a walk."

"Dumbass. Where's your truck?"

I told her.

"My car's on the way. So you'll drop me there and get the truck and meet me at my place. You remember where it is?"

"Uh-huh."

We started walking. It was a small umbrella. I was getting wet. "You can come in closer, you know," she said. "Touching me isn't going to sully your marriage."

twenty-three

I didn't take her suggestion. The one about coming in closer. Instead, I stepped back, involuntarily, out from under the umbrella.

"Jesus," Samantha said. "You sure are jumpy."

I mumbled something.

"You'd think I propositioned you or something. I mean, no offense, you're okay-looking, but you're a little old for me. Now get your ass back under the umbrella."

I did as I was told. She gave me a look, then a couple more before I dropped her at her Thing.

Her house was minutes away. Carrie's Civic was in the driveway and there was only room behind it for Samantha's wheels. Samantha, waiting by the front door, yelled that Carrie was gone and she didn't have a key to the Civic. Which meant once again I had to go more than a block away to find parking. I squeezed into a spot, turned off the engine, sat there wondering what to do. Wait until she gave me tea and crumpets and say, "Hey, Samantha, I heard you were a stalker." Maybe Carrie would come back. I could watch the horrified look grow on her face as she learned she been living with a psychotic.

The rain had slackened, but it was still coming down hard,

and a little river ran along the curb near Samantha's house. It carried leaves and styrofoam packing noodles and a Snickers wrapper down to the sea. The wind was blowing the chimes into a frenzy. I went through the gate and up the walk and up to the door. It opened before me. She'd already changed from the jeans and sweatshirt she'd been wearing into a tank top and a pair of running shorts. Nothing on her feet. "Come on in." I left the umbrella outside and entered. She pointed me toward the sofa. "Something to drink?"

"Whatever you're having."

"I'm not having anything."

"I'll have that."

She eased down onto the rug that covered the center of the hardwood floor. She leaned back against an easy chair, looked at me, forced a smile.

"Where's Carrie?" I said.

"I'm not good enough?"

"Its just, her car's here, she's not …"

She was looking up at the ceiling. "She went shopping with her mother. Do you have any idea why spiders build their webs up there where there's nothing to eat?"

A question I'd asked myself many times before. "Instinct, I guess."

"A lousy instinct. Hang on a minute, this is driving me crazy." She went into the kitchen, came out carrying a glass. She dragged a chair over to the corner, got up on it, stretched to reach the spider. Her shorts rode up, exposing a lovely expanse of firm young buttock. "Come on, get in, you stupid thing," she said. Then, "Gotcha." She climbed down, dumped the spider outside the front door, under the roof overhang. Then she resumed her position on the floor.

How many times had I done the same thing with spiders

who lodged themselves in a corner? Only now, with my alternate reality kick, a new angle crept in. Every time you saved a spider, how many insects did you doom who otherwise never would have encountered it? And—

And she was saying something. "I'm sorry," I said. "What was that again?"

"I said, I know what you're thinking."

"I doubt it."

"You're thinking, here's a woman who saves spiders that get themselves stuck in the house. Can I really suspect her of murder?"

"What makes you think I do?"

A shrug. "A feeling I get."

"If I suspected you of something as bad as murder, wouldn't I also suspect you of saving a spider just to make yourself seem like someone with an overwhelming reverence for life?"

"Do you?"

"No. I think you really were concerned for the spider."

"Why do you think I killed Dennis?"

"I don't think that. But I'm not convinced you didn't."

"Because?"

"Because I found out what happened in Chicago."

She kept a straight face. "Who told you?"

"Someone you don't know."

She sprang up, paced the room, kept throwing half-assed glares my way.

"It's a good thing," I said, "that you're the spurnee who's not an actress."

"What do you mean?"

"You're trying to convince me you're angry that I know about Chicago. And not doing much of a job of it. So sit down and stop trying to fool me."

She was still pacing, but next time she passed in front of the easy chair she stopped and dropped down into it. "Every time someone finds out, I think I should feel violated." She was still acting. But her work was much better now. Underplaying. That's the key.

"Does Carrie know?"

"Yes," she said. "Of course I told her. Before she moved in. I didn't want her to find out for herself and think I was hiding it from her." She climbed down so she was leaning back against the chair again. "I don't go around telling everyone about it, but I don't hide it either. Look, I was a fucked-up kid. Too many drugs and too much art will do that to you. Didn't you do stupid things when you were young?"

"Not ones that resulted in restraining orders."

"I didn't kill Dennis."

"Then who did?"

"Any one of dozens of people. Women he's fucked over, you've probably got a dozen suspects there alone."

"Yet you got involved with him anyway."

"I didn't know his reputation when I started seeing him." She got up again. "You still having what I'm having?"

"Sure."

She went in the kitchen, came back with a couple of beer bottles. Handed me one, returned to the chair. Took a long pull. I looked at mine. Not beer. Dead Guy Ale.

"Saw it at Trader Joe's," she said. "Seemed appropriate. Where was I? On our second date he mentioned a chick named Leslie Shanis. In the context of a story about something that happened on the set of one of his shows, the one with the rocket scientist."

"*Blast Off.*"

"Yeah. That one. She really was tangential to the story, but he took the time to say something like, 'She was someone I went out with, but it was only once or twice.' I thought that was weird at the time, like he was making a point of letting me know about her, but the conversation went on and she didn't come up again. So I forgot it. I mean, I had other things I was thinking about."

"Like?"

"Like how much I wanted to fuck him."

"Oh. That."

"Shocked?"

"No."

"You are."

"Just a little. Somehow I think of people being less likely to jump in the sack with each other these days. What with HIV and all that."

"He had a health certificate."

"And he just, what, flashed it and said, don't worry about me, I'm clean?"

"A little more gracefully than that."

"And did you have a certificate to show him back?"

She smiled. "Of course not. But I'm pretty careful, and I've been checked. Not that he asked. Maybe he slept with so many women because he *wanted* to catch something. Maybe he had a death wish. Anyway … he was good-looking and charming and funny and there was chemistry. And my thought was, even if this goes nowhere, I'm going to get some good nookie out of it. I forgot about this Leslie person. Until I ran into her."

"Go on."

"It was two weeks later, and Dennis was taking me to a movie premiere. We ran into a guy he knew, an actor, and the actor's date was this Leslie. Dennis did introductions, and again he mentioned that he went out with Leslie, and I thought that was kind of off, because it made all the rest of us uncomfortable. And he didn't have to do it. He could have just introduced us all and we would have shook hands and that would have been the end of it. But he went out of his way to do it the way he did. Then later I ran into her in the ladies' room."

"What a coincidence."

"It wasn't. She saw me go in there and followed me. And she gave me her card and said I should call her. She put her hand on my forearm, like this—" Samantha demonstrated on herself. "And she said, 'It's for your own good.' Well, my first reaction was, whacko." She smiled. "I mean, I know something about girls getting spurned and going weird. But something in her eyes stuck with me. They were all about concern. So I called her. We got together for a drink. At a nice public place, just in case."

She downed some of her Dead Guy Ale, reminding me mine was untouched. I tried it. I liked it. I took another slug.

"She wasn't a whack job," Samantha said. "Not at all. She told me Dennis had led her on, told her she was the only one, how he hadn't met anyone like her for a long time, blah, blah, blah, you probably know the routine—"

"I've been on the receiving end a few times."

"And all the while he was seeing someone else behind her back."

"You believed her?"

"Enough to ask Dennis."

"And he said…"

"That yes, he was seeing someone else when he was dating

her, but he'd never given her the impression it was exclusive. The way he said it seemed too polished, I guess. But when you're overcome by the general wonderfulness of the person, you let things like that slide. Since you know about Trixie, you know what an idiot letting it slide made me."

"I wouldn't use that term."

"Maybe you will after I tell you something else."

"What's that?"

"There was more to what Leslie told me. She knew of two other women he'd done similar things to. One of them, practically the exact same thing he did to her. The other he publicly humiliated. Took her to a dinner party, she spilled soup on her dress, he started telling her she was a whore and had no class and sent her home in tears."

"In front of the whole dinner party?"

"Yes."

"He got away with an awful lot."

"He was so charming."

"Charm can only go so far."

"And powerful."

"Still. Sounds like he got away with an awful lot."

"But he didn't," she said.

"What do you mean?"

"Somebody killed him, didn't they?"

We exhausted all things Dennis and moved on to other topics. Her opening, for instance. It was a week away, and I was invited. We went off on a discussion of her art career. She had several patrons who she could count on to buy something anytime she did an exhibition or participated in one of the street art fairs. The two most reliable ones were older collectors, one male and one female, both hopeful of getting into her pants. With her art and her trust fund, she avoided a day job.

Carrie came home partway through, carrying several Nordstrom bags. She changed, then made a pot of some new blend they'd gotten in at DL and brought it out with a plateful of shortbread cookies. The tea sat pleasantly atop the Dead Guy Ale in my stomach.

I enjoyed the way they complemented each other, acerbic Samantha and sweet Carrie. I left them chatting away, having finished the cookies and tea and moved on to a bag of Chips Ahoy and more ale. The rain had tailed off to the occasional shower, leaving the air smelling of ozone.

I was a couple of houses down the block when I heard light quick footsteps behind me. It was Samantha. She was still in her scanty clothes, still barefoot. When she stopped she wrapped her arms around herself for warmth.

"What's up?" I said.

"I just wanted to know if you still thought I did it."

"I never thought you did it."

"But you thought I could have."

"Yeah, I did. I don't think that very much anymore."

"But still, a little."

"A little," I said. "A very little. I can't discount anyone entirely. You shouldn't take it personally."

"I don't," she said. "And just for the record, I'm not totally convinced you didn't do it. On behalf of Ronnie." She stepped up, gave me a quick hug, released me, departed. I watched her run down the sidewalk. She stopped at her gate, looked back at me. "Don't tell Carrie about the hug, okay?" She ran up the walk and the door slammed and I was alone on the sidewalk.

Half a block from the car the sky opened up again. I'd left

the umbrella on the porch. I didn't bother running. It wasn't as if I'd get any less soaked if I did.

When I got home, there was a Volvo in the driveway. Someone was sitting in one of the wicker chairs on the porch.

Gina.

twenty-four

She was wearing a big shaggy sweater pulled tight against the chill from the rain. "I'm back," she said.

"So I see." I stepped up and sat in the other chair. "Going to stay awhile?"

"I think so."

I shuffled my chair over next to hers. Flashed on what I had hidden away in my sock drawer. Took her hand. "Are we all right?"

She shook her head. "Not all right. But better."

"I'm glad."

She took her hand back, ran it through her hair, turned to me. "Not *all* better."

"You know I'm sorry."

She shook her head. "Don't say that anymore, okay? Of course I know you're sorry. But—this sounds like fucking Joyce Brothers—a marriage is supposed to be built on trust, and if I can't trust you to tell me everything like you told me everything when we were just friends—then maybe we shouldn't be married."

"You don't mean that."

"I don't know what I mean. What I do know is that, after spending a few days away from you, I've realized a lot of stuff is eating at me, and I'd better get it all out if this is going to have a chance of working." Again she dragged her hand through her hair. "Remember, before we started having sex, we didn't want to do it because we thought it would screw up what we had?"

I nodded.

"And it didn't. Everything was the same, except we were sleeping together. We were still Gina and Joe, best friends, who shared everything. Then we got married. Why did we do that?"

"Ostensibly because you were moving in and you didn't want your mother to think we were living in sin."

"The right answer is, it was the next logical step. And that describes our relationship. The whole thing's very logical. There's no passion."

"You're saying—"

"I don't mean physically. Emotionally."

The rain took its cue and came down harder. There was a stream running past the driveway, like the one in front of Samantha's and Carrie's house. When I was little and it rained like that, I would build dams out of twigs and rocks right there, wearing soggy sneakers and my yellow slicker with the hood.

Gina said, "I thought it would be different somehow."

"How?"

"Hell, I don't know. More … spiritual, I guess."

"You're the least spiritual person I know."

"Look, I'm reaching here. I'm trying to put into words stuff I can't even get a handle on in my head."

"We're way beyond Ronnie here, aren't we?"

She nodded. "At some point we should find out what happened. But if you can't even remember, how can I be mad about it?"

I thought of Santini's photo. Decided it could wait.

"No," Gina said. "This is about our whole lives together." Now it was her turn to take my hand. "While I was at my mother's, I kind of boiled what I think our problems are down to two things. One was what I just said, about our whole relationship being kind of la-dee-dah, we're together and we get a kick out of each other and the sex is good, but it's lacking *something*. But I think maybe we can get around that, because it may be that I'm only feeling that way because of the other thing."

"Which is?"

"I don't want you to go all stupid about it, okay?"

"Kind of hard to guarantee not to go stupid if I don't—"

"I'm starting not to like you."

I wanted to find a boat and sail down the Madison Avenue River. Pick up Culver Boulevard Creek and follow it all the way to the wetlands. Live in a tidepool.

"I still love you," she said. "I love you as much as I ever did. But something that was easy to ignore when we had our own places kind of snapped into focus when I moved in, and it's making me not like being with you."

"Going to tell me what it is?"

"You just go along."

"You're saying I'm too agreeable?"

She shook her head, fast, hard, like the way I took her comment was so wrong it needed to be flung away. "With life. You just go along with life. You just wait for stuff to happen to you. There's nothing you really want to do. To accomplish. You go with the flow, and that's fine to an extent, but not when it's all you do and I have to live with you."

I opened my mouth to offer a rebuttal. And shut it again. How could I argue? She was absolutely right.

"I know how it was that you never got around to telling me what happened with Ronnie. You kept waiting for an opportunity. Then you found a reason to disqualify every one that came along. You never just said, I'm going to get this done. And after a while it became less important. If Ronnie hadn't opened her mouth, you never would have told me, would you?"

"Probably not."

"And that's what your life is about. You wait for stuff to happen. You don't have anything that's important enough for you to put any effort into. When I had my own place, it didn't matter. We could hang out, and then I'd go home or you would, and I'd do my thing and you'd do yours and the next time I saw you we'd do something together. But now, I go off to see clients, and you're lying around the house, and when I come home there you still are, and I know you haven't done anything worthwhile in between, but just hung out and waited for stuff to happen to you."

"I'm not any different than I ever was."

"Did I say you were?" She looked me in the eye, touched my cheek, my chin. "While I was over at my mother's, I decided I couldn't put up with it anymore."

My eyes welled up.

"But it would have been really chickenshit of me just to let us fall apart, and not tell you what was going on. So here I am. Shit, Portugal, don't start crying on me."

I blinked the tears away. "So now what?"

"So now I'm going to tell you something I should have told you a long time ago. Actually, I think I did once, but I should have been more assertive about it."

"Go ahead. Tell me."

"There's only one thing I know of that gets you stirring.

One thing you ever get proactive about. One situation where you seem to have any goal in your life."

I hadn't the slightest idea what she was talking about. Certainly nothing to do with acting. I didn't care a whit about it, save maybe for the income. My plants? I'd lost interest. Music? I'd had a burst of inspiration, but it faded more swiftly than I could have imagined.

I could see disappointment brewing in her eyes. I started to say something, anything, just to break the silence, and the answer came.

"Solving murders," I said.

Her eyes lit back up. "Murders, disappearances, all that stuff. When you were looking for Mike's wife, I had a little hope. There was some life in you. But as soon as you found out it wasn't her, you became the same old lump."

"I'm a little old to become a policeman."

She shook her head. "I don't want to hear any objections. No excuses. This is something that gets your blood going, and for some obscure reason you're good at it. You need to figure out a way to make it part of your life."

I thought about it.

I kept thinking about it.

We sat there for without a word for half an hour, until a Wagner riff erupted from her purse. She pulled out her cell phone, checked the screen, turned it off. "Well?"

"Do they have schools for this kind of thing?"

It was the biggest, most genuine smile I'd seen on her in a long time. "Maybe you can look in the Yellow Pages. Or find that guy that came over after we figured out who Aricela was, the one who tracks down lost kids."

"Jack Liffey, he said his name was."

"Yeah, him. See how he got started. I'm cold. You cold?"

"No."

"I'm freezing my ass off. Come inside."

"Think I'll stay out here a while."

She stood, found her key, bent to kiss me. She went inside and I sat there, thinking some more.

Then I went in and told her about the photo.

twenty-five

The phone woke me. Gina was nestled in my arms. We hadn't made love. Neither of us was ready.

I craned my neck to see the clock. Quarter to twelve. Gina stretched, reached behind her, picked up the phone. She listened, frowned, handed it over.

"Joey-boy," John Santini said. "Got to see you right now."

"It's the middle of the night."

"Not where I come from."

There was clearly no point to further protest. "Where?"

"Fabrini's. You know it?"

"On Sepulveda."

"That's the place. Five minutes from your house. You'll be in, out, back in bed with that cute little wife of yours in no time."

"I'll be there."

I relayed Santini's end of the conversation. "If you're going," Gina said, "that cute little wife of yours is coming with you."

"No, you're not."

"Why not?"

Good question. If it was because of danger, why was *I* even going? "You need your sleep."

"That is so lame." She pulled some clothes on. "You're worried about me getting hurt. Babe, if you're going to be a crimestopper, this kind of stuff is going to happen all the time. Might as well get used to it. Where's that picture Santini gave you?"

"My sock drawer. Why—"

"Going to give it back to him."

"You don't want to see it?"

"Much as I'd like to see Ronnie naked, no, I don't think either of us needs to see the picture."

"I love you."

"Me too," she said. "You know where I put my keys?"

Fabrini's was pretty much like any bar I never went to. Neon beer signs in the windows, a crooked happy-hour announcement. Inside it was red vinyl and battered wood and old-beer smell. There was a pool table where an oldster with a furry caterpillar of a moustache was beating himself at eight-ball. Two TVs, ESPN talking heads and a soccer game. The jukebox was playing "Something Stupid," and Frank still sounded a lot better than Nancy.

John Santini sat alone at a table at the back. He stood when he saw us. He had a bottle of wine and three glasses set. One of the glasses was full, and as we walked back he poured wine into the other two. I introduced him to Gina. She offered a hand. I wondered if he'd kiss it, but he shook it like a nice boy.

We sat. Gina opened her purse, passed the envelope with the photo over to Santini.

"What's this?" he said.

"We don't need it," she said.

He looked down at it, back at us. "Suit yourself."

I gestured at the three glasses. "You were watching my house."

"Please. Why would you say such a thing?"

"How else would you know I was bringing somebody?"

A minute shrug. "Had a feeling."

"Mr. Santini," Gina said.

"John."

"John. Three words. What the fuck?"

He stared at her, smiled, burst into laughter. "'What the fuck?' I love that. What a woman you got here, Joey-boy."

"Answer her question, why don't you?"

He looked at me, stopped laughing, kept the smile on. "Fair enough. You can stop looking for Alma's daughter."

"They found her?"

"She was never missing to begin with."

My turn. "What the fuck?"

"Alma knows exactly where Valerie is. They get along just fine together. We made all that other stuff up, including the part about Valerie being my kid, which was kind of fun to invent, though I had a hell of a time convincing Alma to go along with it. It was a test, Joey-boy."

"Explain, please, and for God's sake don't call me 'Joey-boy.'"

"Had to see if your word was good."

"Why wouldn't it be?"

"Always got to see. You never know otherwise. I call in a favor, the guy doesn't come through, who knows what could happen."

"So I came through once. Doesn't mean I would again. When—I'm assuming—you ask me to do something for real."

"You would."

"Mr. Santini," Gina said.

"I told you, it's John."

"You're a bastard, John."

He looked her over, turned to me. "She's a good one. Ordinarily, I wouldn't even have a woman in on a business conversation. I'm old-fashioned that way. But I'm trying to change. Got to change with the times, you know?"

"John," Gina said.

"Yes, doll?"

"When I said 'What the fuck?' before, I wasn't talking about tonight. I was talking about the whole thing."

"What whole thing is that?"

"You getting Joe mixed up in your shady business."

"Joe," he said. "I thought we had this conversation. I'm totally legit these days."

"You're about as legit," Gina said, "as I am blond."

"Little lady—"

"Don't call me 'little lady.' Don't call Joe 'Joey-boy' and don't call me 'little lady.' Or 'doll' for that matter. Call me—"

"Gina," Santini said, and someone else was sitting there. Not some jovial import-export business owner. Instead there was a man I'd never seen before. A man with eyes that had seen things I would never see and never wanted to. A man who knew not only where the bodies were buried, but how deep and what the soil composition was. A man who could eat the likes of Gina and me and all the bad people we'd run into over the last few years for breakfast and still have room for a waffle or two.

"Yes?" a very small girl in Gina's body said.

"Enough with the tough girl act. It's all very impressive, but you know and I know it means nothing."

She stared at him. Under the table, her hand clutched mine, her fingernails dug into its back.

"That's better," he said. "Look, the two of you. I'm not gonna get either of you involved in anything dangerous or anything against the law. But you're honest and you're tough and sometimes I can use people like that. And the way things have worked in this city for a long time is that when I need people, I have them."

I was certain Gina's nails were drawing blood.

"So cut the shit," Santini said, "and think about your place, and everything will be just fine. You got that?"

We both nodded.

"Say it. Say, 'I got it, John.'"

"I got it, John."

"I got it, John." I wasn't sure which of us said it first.

As quickly as he'd come, the scary man went away, replaced by my old buddy John Santini. "This is the part I like. Business is over. Have your wine."

We had our wine. Quickly, and without tasting it.

"One more thing," Santini said.

Gina and I exchanged looks. "Isn't there always?" I said.

He picked up the envelope, ripped off the end, shook the photo out. He pushed it in front of us.

There was a woman in it, all right. She was dark-haired, but that was where the resemblance to Ronnie stopped. She had a weak chin and long hair that wasn't right for the shape of her face. She was looking right at the camera. She was alone.

"Alma's daughter," Santini said.

I stared down at it.

"You thought it was something else," he said.

"Yeah," I said.

"Something you don't want people to see."

"Yeah."

"Figures," he said.

"Why?" Gina said.

He turned to her. Regarded her with a smile.

"Everybody has something like that, doll," he said. "Everybody does."

twenty-six

We talked about it when we got home. We talked about it each time we woke up, clinging to each other, in the middle of the night. We talked about it around six when we both realized there was no way either of us would get any more sleep.

I got out of bed and threw on some sweats and sat on the front porch wishing that just this one morning the sun would rise in the west so I could watch it. Gina came out at seven with mugs of tea. A breakfast blend, she said, from my box from the tea store. Eventually we talked about Santini some more. Didn't come up with anything new. Then Gina looked at me and asked if I was having any doubts about my new career path. That I'd probably be meeting more fearsome people like John Santini and having more scary sit-downs at more seedy spots.

I said if that was the way things were going to be, so be it. We'd deal.

She smiled. She laughed. Me too.

Then we went inside and screwed like there was no tomorrow.

Gina left for an appointment at eleven-thirty. I picked up the phone, put it down, went out to the truck. I wanted the element of surprise. If my quarry wasn't home, I'd figure out another plan.

Twenty minutes later I was pushing the doorbell at my father's place. A few seconds later the door opened. Mary Elizabeth was standing there. She was wearing a robe. There was only one reason I could think of that Mary Elizabeth would be wearing a robe at my father's house.

When you first learn about sex, the thought of your parents having it appalls you. It's something you don't want to consider. You wish you'd been dropped by the stork. Then you get older, and it's not so bad. You're an adult, they're adults, it's what adults do. Then you get to be middle-aged, and your parents get to be senior citizens, and once again the image of them sweatily thrashing about in bed is one you'd rather be without.

My mother died in 1968, and, though I couldn't believe my father'd been celibate since then, this was the first time I'd come across evidence to the contrary. I wanted to turn and flee. Especially when my father came out of his bedroom, asking who was at the door, wearing only boxers and black socks. I hadn't seen him without his shirt in a very long time. The term *silverback gorilla* came to mind.

"Joseph," Mary Elizabeth said. "Why don't you come in?" She'd picked up the *Joseph* business from my father, doubling the world's supply of people who called me that.

"I'm sorry," I said. "It seems you're busy."

Her cheeks reddened, she looked behind her at my father, then back at me. "A few minutes ago we were busy. Now we're not. Come in."

I looked at my father across the living room. He was smiling. No, he was *smirking*. He was smirking like the rooster who'd just serviced every hen in the henhouse.

I walked in. Mary Elizabeth closed the door behind me.
"Dad," I said. "Go put some clothes on."

"My place. I can go naked if I want."

The Moby Grape song popped into my head. *Would you
let me ... walk down the street ... naked if I want to.* "Fine. Go
around naked. See if I care."

"You're embarrassed. Hey, Mary Elizabeth, he's embarrassed. My son is embarrassed about natural body functions."

"Harold," she said, "you're embarrassing me too. Go put
something on. Joseph, you want some tea?"

"Okay."

She put the kettle on and headed for the bedroom, grabbing my father's arm on the way by. In a couple of minutes
they both came out, fully dressed. By that time the water had
boiled, and I had a pot brewing.

We talked about this, that, and the other thing for half an
hour, until Mary Elizabeth had to leave for her volunteer job
reading to the blind. When she was gone my father sat down
at the dining room table with that shit-eating grin on again.
"There's life in the old boy yet," he said.

"No one said there wasn't."

"Though, these days, once and I'm done for the night."

"Can we not have this conversation?"

"Why not?"

"Because the conversation between father and son about
sex was supposed to happen when I was twelve or thirteen.
Not now."

"We never talked about this before?"

"Not that I remember."

"But you learned."

"Kids do."

"And you did okay."

"I did fine."

"Good."

Silence.

"It's getting pretty serious with Mary Elizabeth," I said. "Isn't it?"

"You think because I'm doing it with her, it has to be—"

"Not that. Because of the amount of time you're spending with her."

He thought about it. "Serious, shmerious. I'm having a good time, she's having a good time. You don't mind?"

"Why should I mind?"

"You don't think I'm being unfaithful to your mother?"

"Of course not. I'm sure that, wherever she is, she's very happy for you."

"Where do you think she is?"

"Heaven, I guess."

"You believe in heaven?"

"I'm not sure. I like to think there's something after this."

"You believe in God, Joseph?"

"Does it matter?"

"To me, it matters."

"I'm an agnostic, Dad. I don't believe for sure there's a God, and I don't believe for sure there's not one."

He nodded, slowly, considering. "Good enough, I guess. So. Why did you come to see me today?"

"Do I need a reason?"

"Every time you come over I ask why, and every time you say, do you need a reason, and every time there is one."

"Okay. There's a reason."

"Not to talk about God and Mary Elizabeth, is what I'm guessing."

"I want to know about you and John Santini."

"Who?"

"John Santini. Don't play dumb. I know you know him."

"Is he still around?"

"You know he's around. I told you at Thanksgiving how he helped me find the woman my friend Mike thought was his wife."

"Oh, *that* John Santini." His lower lip was pooched out. Thinking, or angry.

"I hate when you play dumb."

"Then I won't. Yes, I remember you telling me you met him. I haven't seen him since I got out of jail."

"Have you talked to him?"

"No."

"But you did know him before."

"You know I did."

"You worked together."

"Yes."

"How much?"

"That's enough." The lip was way out now. And he wasn't thinking. That left one thing. "Don't ever treat me like one of your suspects in your detective games."

They're not games anymore, Dad. This is my true calling. Aren't you proud?

"I'm just asking a few questions. What's the harm in—"

"You want to know about me and John Santini? I'll tell you. I worked for him. Me, and Sonny, and all the other guys. We all worked for John Santini."

He sat back in his chair. His arms were crossed. His lip had resumed its normal position.

"Are you happy?" he said.

"Not particularly. That night—"

"That night, the night when the fellow got killed, we were on a job for him."

"Was Santini there?"

"I don't remember."

"Fuck that, Dad. You have to remember."

He picked up his long-empty teacup, looked into it, put it back down. "He wasn't there. He never went out on jobs." He stood suddenly, began to gather the cups and saucers. "Got to get started on dinner. I told Leonard and Catherine I'd make blintzes."

"It's not even noon."

"Blintzes take a long time."

With all the dishware precariously balanced in his hands, he sped off for the kitchen. I jumped up and followed him. "Finish the conversation. There's something about Santini you're not telling me."

He spun around. A cup went flying and crashed to the floor. "If there's something I'm not telling you, there's a reason. And if I have a reason, it's a good reason. And if I have a good reason, I don't want you pestering me for an answer I'm not going to give you. Do you understand?"

"I suppose."

"Not, you suppose. Do you understand?"

"I understand."

"Good." He looked at the shattered remains on the kitchen floor. "Catherine will kill me. Those are her favorites." He put the rest on the sink, opened the cabinet underneath, found a brush and dustpan. I took them from him. He began to protest, thought better of it. As I began sweeping up the cup, he started out of the room.

"Dad?"

He whirled. "Now what?"

"We can find a replacement. She'll never know it's missing."

"Where will you find a replacement? Those are from when she got married."

"On eBay."

"You can get things like that there?"

"You can get anything on eBay. Or so Gina tells me."

He nodded, started out of the room. Then he turned in my direction again. "It's for your own good," he said.

"It's okay, Dad," I said. "Everybody needs some secrets."

Later that afternoon. Back out on my front porch. I had a pad and a pencil and a bag of almonds. I wrote down things I knew about Dennis Lennox's murder. I drew arrows between ones that seemed to be connected. I kept changing my mind and erasing the arrows. After four or five the eraser broke off my pencil. I'd learned my first lesson in detection. Always have a Pink Pearl on hand.

I'd been out there an hour when Ronnie emerged from her house. She cut across her lawn and mine and without a word took the other chair. I held out the bag of almonds.

She shook her head. "I'm sorry," she said.

"What for?"

"For getting mad at you. No, for *staying* mad at you."

I helped myself to a nut. "No big."

"I think getting mad when I heard what had happened made sense. But ever since, I've known something that should have made me get over it. And I wasn't ready to."

"What did you know?"

"Dennis came on to every pretty girl on the show, did you know that? Cast, crew, girls with the caterers."

"I'm not surprised."

"I figured he'd get around to me sooner or later, but I never thought—"

"That when you turned him down he'd do something really heinous to get back at you? You did turn him down, didn't you?"

"Of course I did. He's not … he wasn't my type."

"What's your type?"

"Less full of himself."

"Like Eric."

A shy smile. "Gina told you?"

"Yeah." *Not to mention a reporter who's been digging into your life.*

Our mail carrier Rose came up the walk. She said hello, handed over the day's load of crap, retreated. I looked the stuff over. Somewhere I'd gotten on a list as Joseph L. Portugal, and Joseph L. got mail nearly every day. This time it was frequent flyer miles if I'd just sign up for some credit card. Kind of wasted on a guy who'd never been on an airplane in his life. There was also a J. Jill catalogue. Since Gina moved in we'd been getting three or four a month.

"Let me see the J. Jill," Ronnie said. I handed it over. She thumbed through. "He was a bad person, wasn't he?"

"You don't know the half of it. He had something to do with what happened to you and me that morning."

"I know about that. The night he died, when he called me, he said he was sorry about that, and he needed to straighten everything out."

"That's when I found out too. His call to me."

"This is cute," Ronnie said. She dog-eared a page, closed the catalogue. "You're used to it, aren't you? People killing other people."

"I don't think anyone ever gets used to it. But, yeah, it's not as big a deal as it was the first one or two times." *Or three, or four, or …*

"Eric says the world is better off without him."

"Pretty ungrateful, considering the guy gave him what's no doubt a ridiculously high-paying job."

She frowned. Maybe I'd cut too deep. "Eric sometimes

sees things a different way from you and me. Kind of from the outside of things. He says that though he liked Dennis personally, overall it's no loss that he's gone."

"Maybe he killed him."

The frown was gone. "He said the same thing about you."

"Yeah? What else did he say about me?"

"Nothing."

"Liar."

"I really shouldn't say."

"If you don't, I'll imagine the worst."

"He says you were the one who gave me whatever it was that knocked me out and gave me amnesia. Because you wanted to go to bed with me."

"And then, because I was so happy with how well it worked, I took some too."

"He said you made that part up. That you … did it with me, and then acted like you didn't know what happened either."

"But no one did it with you."

"Theta *told*?"

"I wormed it out of her. Look. Dennis drugged us, undressed us, dumped us in bed together. End of story."

"Because I wouldn't sleep with him."

"I think so. But he wasn't satisfied with that, so he fired you and let me take the blame."

She opened the J. Jill catalogue again, found the page she'd marked, un-dog-eared it. "I don't really need this. Tell Gina I'm sorry I messed up her catalogue." A big sigh. "It's terrible, isn't it, not being able to remember part of your life. One minute I was standing there with Eric, and the next—"

"Whoa, back up. Eric was there? Then what did you need me for?"

"He wasn't supposed to be. He went to Chicago for some family business. But he caught an earlier plane than he was supposed to and came right to the party. Though I guess I never got to introduce him to you, or if I did it was during the part I don't remember."

Maybe admitting I wanted to be a detective had awakened something. A sensor went off in my head, and I didn't think it would have gone off if I'd heard this story a week or two earlier. There was something not quite right about Eric Stahl's suddenly appearance at Dennis party. "What *do* you remember? I mean, what was the last thing?"

"Let me see. Okay, Eric showed up, and we walked around some, and then he went off to talk to Dennis. And then I saw you out by the pool—"

"I was by the pool? I must have really been loaded."

"I think you'd smoked a lot of pot. You said your throat hurt from it. I gave you the rest of my Coke." She smiled, shook her head. "You know what? That's the last thing I remember. Next thing I knew, there I was opening my eyes and seeing you there."

"Why'd you run away?"

"I just panicked. I mean, seeing you there, and having that big piece of my memory missing... and being naked... all I wanted to do was get out of there."

"Makes sense."

"Joe?"

"Hmm?"

"You hadn't told Gina about what happened, had you? The night I came over."

"Nope."

"I spilled the beans."

"They needed to be spilled."

"Everything okay with you two?"

"It is now. We had a bit of a rough patch."

"I saw her car was back this morning. So things are better?"

"Yes. Thanks for asking."

"It was all my fault."

"No, it was my fault, for trying to hide something from her. Don't worry about it. It's all over. Everything's fine."

She looked at her watch. "I'd better get going. I'm having coffee with David E. Kelley. He's got a pilot for next year."

"So you're not going back to *The Galahad Sisters*?"

"I don't know. I don't know what I'm going to do. And you know what? I feel okay about that. Whatever happens, happens."

She cut back across the lawns and reentered her house. I gathered my nuts and my detective kit and went inside to decide what to do about Eric Stahl.

twenty-seven

Seeing Ronnie, remembering what I'd done for her and where it had led us, reminded me of Keith Colbert, the kid whose picture and resume I'd taken at the TV station. I dug it out, called Elaine, told her I'd promised him an interview, gave her his info. She said she'd get him in. Then I asked if she knew anything about Eric Stahl. She'd knew the name, knew he worked on *Protect and Serve*, but that was it. If I wanted, she could make some calls.

I told her not yet and got off the phone. Soon as I hung up, it rang. "Hello."

"It's me." Claudia Acuna.

Me was reserved for Gina. But I let Claudia get away with it. "Hi."

"Let's get together," she said.

"Fine. Burton Chace Park."

"Perfect."

"You know where it is?"

"If I didn't, would I have said 'perfect'?"

"You're a smartass, Acuna, you know that?"

"Of course I do," she said. "That's what you like about me."

•

Burton Chace Park is right on the water in Marina del Rey. There's lots of grass, plenty of benches, sun and sea and boats. All the seagulls you need. The occasional pelican.

I put money in the meter and walked toward the water, past the building housing the community room. Through the sliding glass doors I saw a group of seniors sitting around a long table, engaged in a crafts project involving pine cones. An energetic young woman flitted about, offering encouragement. Ten, twelve years in the future, that could be me sitting in there. Gina too. We'd have a pair of pine cone projects to hang in our bedroom. Assuming it got built by then.

The young woman bent over the table. One of the men copped a feel. She shot erect, her face shocked. Then it melted into a smile. She looked at the man and waggled a finger at him and moved on to the next oldster.

I walked around the building and found a bench with a good view of the boats going by. The sky was clear, with just a few high white clouds. But way off in the west a new load of darkness hovered over the water.

Claudia showed up ten minutes after I did. She had on a windbreaker and jeans and white canvas tennis shoes. Her hair was back in a ponytail. She was carrying a thin briefcase and a brown Peet's bag.

She spotted me, sat, looked out at the boats. "Pretty out here," she said. "I don't get out here enough."

"Me neither."

She smiled like she remembered it was the thing to do. Then she unzipped her jacket halfway. The white top underneath was cut low. I had to drag my eyes away.

She sat, picked up the brown bag, opened it. "I stopped on the way," she said. "Thought we could use some refreshments." She withdrew one, then another to-go cup, each with an insulating collar. "Pride of the Port, they call it." She handed one over.

I sniffed it through the drinking slot in the cap. "How'd you know I was a tea drinker?"

"Wild guess."

She put the other cup on the bench, produced a couple of blueberry scones. She gave me one, reached into the bag once more, distributed napkins. We ate and drank in silence, enjoying the cool air, the warm sun, the sounds of children at play. A seagull landed on the sidewalk and, ever so casually, came closer, soliciting a treat. I tossed it a bit of scone. The bird snapped it up and flew off. Another took its place and got its own snack. Then a pigeon showed up. It got a fragment too. I said, "That's it, guys." I guess the birds understood, because they didn't come back.

When we finished our scones Claudia gathered up the napkins and bags, took them to a trash can, sat back down. "I quit my job," she said.

I wanted to kiss her. Not enough to do anything about it. But enough to scare me. Gina and I were back on the right track. I was supposed to be a one-trick pony again.

I found a way to scoot a few inches farther from her. "That was sudden," I said.

"Not so." She smiled, and it was a different smile than I'd ever seen on her before. Relaxed. Contented. Genuine. "I've been thinking about it for a long time."

"How long?"

She watched a boatload of fishermen go by. "Eighteen years," she said. "The usual story. Idealistic young journalism student works for peanuts on an alternative paper. She's lured by the glamour of television news. She gets further and further from anything worthwhile." She turned to me. "I was all, I'm over forty, it's tough for female reporters over forty, I have to do whatever it takes to keep my job."

She pulled the zipper on her jacket back up a couple of inches. The sun was low, and to the west the dark clouds were closing in. "How do you feel about epiphanies?"

"Since I'm guessing you had one, I think they're just fine."

"I finally saw that, no matter how good I was, how much I tried to stand above the crowd, when you got to the bottom of it I was just another bimbo doing on-the-scene reports."

"Walking and pointing and putting on the concerned look."

"Yes. And I realized that there was a reason women my age shouldn't be doing that anymore."

"That reason being?"

"That they can be doing better things with their life. Oh, it sounds so, so …"

"Airy-fairy?"

"Yes. Airy-fairy. This magical realization that, gee folks, what I've been doing most of my whole adult life just isn't cutting it anymore."

It must have been going around. The only difference was, what I'd been doing my entire adult life was nothing. "So you went in to your boss and quit."

"Pretty much. Except my boss is out of town, so I went to her boss."

"And the reaction was?"

"'Maybe you should take a few days off.'"

"Maybe he was really concerned."

"This is my life crisis. Don't go shooting holes in it."

It was eerily similar to a conversation I'd had with Gina a while back, in the middle of my own midlife crisis. Or maybe it was hers. One of us had told the other to stop shooting holes. It only bothered me a little that I couldn't remember who was the shooter and who the shootee. "I'll be quiet."

"He tried halfheartedly to talk me out of it and said he'd be sorry to see me go and told me to put it in writing and go see human resources. He won't be sorry to see me go. He'll replace me with someone younger. Maybe fill one of his minority quotas too."

"Right. There's always a couple of black reporters, a Latino or two, and one Asian who looks just like Terry Takamura. But isn't Acuna a Hispanic name?"

"I'm only a quarter. Not enough to fill the quota."

"Got it."

"Anyway, that's my story. So I'm unemployed. And, so far, I like it." She stood, walked halfway to the water, whirled around with her arms spread. "Unemployment. Isn't it wonderful?"

"Stop that. You look like Mary Tyler Moore."

She spun once more, caught her breath, returned to her seat. "Now, let me give you the rest of this material and I can be done with it." She opened the briefcase, took out a manila folder, handed it over.

I said, "You stole this from the station?"

"Why, no, Mr. Portugal, sir. That would be illegal. Not to mention morally reprehensible."

"Not to mention."

"I made copies before I quit and stashed them in my car."

"The morality of which is unquestioned."

"Exactly," she said.

"Why?"

She flushed. "Thought you might...appreciate it. Let's see. We'd pretty much finished up on you and all the women, so that leaves Sean McKay."

"So what did you dig up on Seanie?"

"He produced three class-Z movies. Two of them went straight to video."

"He said Dennis stole his script."

"Right." She dug around in the folder, pulled out a few sheets clipped together, handed it over. The first was a cover page for something called *Rushing to Nowhere*. It was A SCREENPLAY BY SEAN DAVID MCKAY. There was contact and copyright info and what may have been—it was hard to tell through who knew how many generations of photocopying—a coffee stain.

WE OPEN ON A DARK ALLEY, said the script, proceeding to tell us what happened in said alley. There were two characters, JENKINS the cop and WHISKEY BOY, a stool pigeon. There was a conversation about some criminal enterprise about to go down. WHISKEY BOY told JENKINS he was dead meat if somebody named Rubber Man found out what he was doing. Then there was a flashlight beam and A VOICE said, "Got you, you fuckin' stoolie," and that was the end of what I had.

I looked up. "This sounds like every other cops-and-robbers movie I've ever seen."

"It sound a *lot* like one Dennis had in development."

"Dennis was doing movies too?"

"New worlds to conquer."

I glanced at the script again. "So he did steal this from Sean?"

"It's pretty damned similar. The two guys in the alley are shot down, Jenkins's sister goes on a quest to find out who did it, she hooks up with a ninja master, they—"

"Not a ninja master."

"And not just any ninja master. A time-traveling ninja

master. They go back, undo the shooting, screw up the world. One of those things, you go back to the dinosaur age, step on a butterfly, that one thing creates ripples in time, you come back and find the Nazis won World War Two."

"But she only goes back, what, a few months?"

"A year and a half. So what happens is that she appears in the alley and ninjas the bad guy into submission. And there's a cat in the alley, which originally ran off in one direction, but it runs off in another. And the cat has an encounter with a dog which it didn't have before, which changes the dog's plans and ... well, suffice it to say that the president ends up dead and the government is taken over by right-wing fanatics."

"Just like real life."

A smile, and she caught my eyes. We sat that way, face to face, maybe moving imperceptibly closer, maybe not, for several seconds longer than we should have. Her scent passed through me, working its magic.

Finally—because I had to do something—I looked down at the file. "Didn't Sean register his script with the Writers Guild?" I turned to her again. The moment had passed. Thank God.

"He did. The script Dennis is using changes the ninja to a white witch, and changes the dog-cat-president thing, and changes the right-wing takeover to a religious fanatic one. There are enough changes that you couldn't be certain he based the whole thing on McKay's version."

"But he did," I said.

"How do you know?"

"Because everyone he called up there that night was someone he'd screwed over."

I popped the top off my tea. There was half an inch of

liquid in there, with leaf dust swirling around the bottom. I dumped it on the grass behind the bench, took the cups to the trash can, stood by the railing, watching the charcoal clouds soaring quickly to shore. The sun was barely over the horizon now. It was appreciably colder than when I'd gotten there. Most of the people had disappeared.

I returned to the bench but remained on my feet. "That guy Eric Stahl that Ronnie's dating?"

"What about him?"

"You know anything else about him?"

"Not that I remember. Why? You think he's involved in this?"

"I think he's involved in something."

"I'm not doing any more research."

"No one's asking you to. Look, thanks for all the info. It's a big help."

"You're welcome. If you have any questions, call me next week, when I get back from New York."

"What's in New York?"

"There's a man there ... we've been having a long-distance thing for a couple of years. I think it's time to see if it's going to lead anywhere."

"Yeah, well, good luck with that."

She was standing now too, facing me, too close for polite conversation. Somehow the jacket had gotten unzipped again, held together by only an inch of YKK's best way down at the bottom. "You sound like you don't mean it."

I forced my eyes not to drop. "I mean it."

"You're feeling it too."

"Feeling what?"

"An attraction."

I looked away. Back at her, and now her face was even closer. "Yes, and it's making me really unhappy."

"Why?"

"Because I love my wife."

"I love the man in New York too. Doesn't mean we can't be attracted to each other. We're not going to do anything about it, are we?"

Again, her perfume filled my head. *She wants you to. Just one kiss. One little kiss. What harm could that do?*

I took her hands, but as I did I took a quarter step back. "No," I said. "We're not. Maybe in some other universe we would, but not in this one. Go to New York, get married, have a couple of… well, go to New York and get married. Have a long happy life, and leave the crimefighting to me."

Was she disappointed? I like to think so.

She let go my hands, zipped the windbreaker, adjusted the strap of her purse. "Joe Portugal, master crimestopper."

"At your service," I said.

The minute I got home: "I had lust in my heart for Claudia Acuna."

"Meaning?" Gina said.

"She kind of came on to me and I kind of got turned on."

"Did you do anything about it?"

"Of course not."

"Then that's that. Babe?"

"Uh-huh?"

"You don't have to report to me every time you flirt with somebody."

"I think it was more than flirting."

"Scale of one to ten. One is checking her out when she

isn't looking, ten is a night of torrid sex with toys, whipped cream, and jungle sounds."

"Three, I guess. Somewhere between two and a half and three and a half."

"Not reportable. Four is reportable. Five if you're drunk or high. You know, I think she's kind of sexy too. Reminds me of me, if I was six inches taller and had big boobs. Maybe you and she and I should—"

"Don't even say it."

I made a call. It didn't take long to get through to who I wanted. Elaine knows a lot of people.

twenty-eight

Eric Stahl couldn't possibly see me until the following Wednesday. At least, that's what his assistant told me. I accepted the slot and wondered whether he was avoiding me. Decided it didn't matter.

The rain came again that evening. It continued overnight and into the morning, and kept up with hardly a break all weekend. It broke on Monday, but the sky stayed gray and the weather chilly. Showers drifted down every couple of hours. The folks at Channel 6 broke out their slickers and did on-the-spot reports and publicly wondered if the heavens would every be blue again.

It would have been a good time to stay indoors and cocoon by the fireplace. Too bad we didn't have one. We would someday, in the bedroom, if the addition ever got finished. And if there was a *we*. The chances seemed better now. But it wasn't something I would ever again take for granted.

I phoned around and used Gina's computer to surf the Net and quickly came to the conclusion that I hadn't the slightest idea what I was doing. By the time Monday, then Tuesday rolled around, the biggest progress I'd made was to stop by Office Depot and stock up on Pink Pearls.

Gina'd lollygagged on a proposal and spent most of the weekend working on it. She was gone all day Monday presenting it and, because she thought it hadn't gone well, all day shopping Tuesday.

The Dennis Lennox saga still dominated the local news. Channel 6 had replaced Claudia as lead on the story with someone named Linda Madera. She was short and cute and very young, and she filled the Filipina quota. She put together a series on Hollywood murders. Starting with Thelma Todd, then Sal Mineo and Bob Crane. O.J., of course, though that always seemed to me more a sports murder than a Hollywood one. Robert Blake and Phil Spector.

Mike called every day, and twice on Sunday, to ask about my progress. I said I had a few things to follow up on. This seemed to satisfy him. On Monday he told me Lu was out of the hospital and staying at his place in Venice. She had a full-time nurse and was making an excellent recovery.

He also said the police had been around several times, questioning him about his whereabouts at the time of his son's murder. Two detectives, both young and eager, both TV-star pretty. One was a man and the other a woman, and Mike had dubbed them Starsky and Bitch. When he said that I bit my tongue. He didn't need any of my politically correct bullshit just then.

Each time the police came for a visit he told them he'd been home alone, watching TV. Were there any witnesses, they wanted to know. There weren't. He didn't know why the sudden interest on the cops' part, but attributed it to frustration at the lack of leads. He didn't hold it against them. Just doing their jobs.

I sat in bed Tuesday night with the newspaper, poring over coverage of the Lennox case. Gina was in the living room, watching an old Cary Grant movie. I put the paper down and went out there. I lay down on the sofa with my head in her lap and watched Cary do his debonair thing. A commercial came on, the one with the guy throwing the football at the tire at the end of a rope. It was the first time I'd paid attention to what they were saying. It was for some Viagra-like drug, and the football going through the tire was symbolic of, well, you know.

"Subtle," Gina said.

"Like a truck."

"You think you'll ever do commercials again?"

I looked up at her. "Sure. Once this dies down."

"Do you care?"

"Not particularly."

"So you're going to live off me."

"At least until my private dicking gets going. Would that be a problem?"

The merest hesitation. "Not particularly," she said.

I began to have second thoughts about my new career choice. I didn't doubt that Gina was right. That it was high time I got some direction in my life. I just wasn't sure this was the *right* direction. Because I wasn't coming up with much of anything about Dennis Lennox's murder.

But…one day in the mid-nineties I got a fortune cookie. I held onto the fortune, tucking it between my bedroom mirror and its frame. I'd look at it every few months, consider tossing it in the wastebasket, give it another reprieve.

Quietly and carefully contemplating or planning an action is part of that action.

The process would take as long as it took. In the end there would be a result. Or there wouldn't. No crimefighter got his man a hundred percent of the time. But the bottom line was that I got a kick out of chasing people around the city and seeing what kinds of lies they could come up with. And of distilling the fairy tales they invented and watching the truth drip out the bottom of the still.

If I put some evildoer away, so much the better.

Early Wednesday morning Gina found out her presentation hadn't gone as badly as she thought. She left for Malibu to meet with her new client. I made a mug of Yunnan from my kit and sat on the porch, watching the latest iteration of the lousy weather. It had been a difficult winter, and it wasn't even winter yet. There'd been a hailstorm a couple of months back. It moved in, stalled over Watts, and dumped a foot and a half of hail in an hour. The next day the airwaves were filled with images of kids throwing hailballs, building hailmen, making hail angels. It was the kind of story local news stations covered best.

But on Wednesday it wasn't hail, and within five minutes it wasn't rain either. Ten more, and there was blue sky in the west. I went inside, put on something decent, and went off to badger Eric Stahl.

twenty-nine

Lennox Productions had its offices on the Fox lot. I drove in the Pico entrance and up to the guard gate. "Joe Portugal, to see Eric Stahl."

The guard inspected me. He moved on to my truck. It clearly wasn't the sort of vehicle Eric Stahl's visitors usually drove. His expression said he'd be awfully surprised if my name was on his list. He picked up his clipboard, leafed through a couple of sheets. "You're not on here." Now his look was one of boredom. He'd done this a thousand times. Booted people who tried to finesse their way onto the lot.

"I just spoke to him," I said. "Probably didn't have a chance to call down yet. Call his office."

"Ought to be on the list." He stared at me, like I was expected to admit my guilt and bolt. I stared back. Finally he picked up the phone and made the call. "Guy here says he's got an appointment to see Mr. Stahl. Name's—yeah, that's him. Okay. Right away." He hung up, regarded me with suspicion, wrote out a pass, gave me directions. As I drove off I glanced at the rearview. He was still watching me. I stuck my arm out the window and waved. When he turned away I gave him the finger. That ought to show him.

Eric Stahl's office was in an older brick building, its trim freshly painted, neat and tidy in the emerging sunlight. I walked up some stairs and down a hall and into the office. Stahl's assistant looked up. She was short and stout, with spiky black hair. She smiled at me like I was somebody important. "Mr. Portugal. Mr. Stahl's on the phone. He'll just be a minute. Can I get you anything?"

"I'm fine."

"Have a seat. It'll just be a minute."

It was a lot more than a minute. I sat in a cushy chair in front of a cushy table and leafed through that day's *Variety*. There was buzz about the upcoming Oscar nods. Some big exec I'd never heard of was getting married. His wife-to-be was a non-pro.

After the first ten minutes and the first four apologies from the assistant, I started to wonder if Eric Stahl was really on the phone. Maybe it was all a power thing. He was showing me who was boss by keeping me waiting.

Finally, after close to twenty minutes, he emerged from his office. He had short blond hair and a goatee the size of a postage stamp.

"Joe. I can't tell you how sorry I am." He shook his head. "Agents. Ought to take them all out and shoot them."

"My cousin's an agent," I said.

"Well, not all of them. Come on in. Did you want anything to drink?"

"I didn't, and I still don't."

I followed him into the inner sanctum. The desk was impressive. Polished wood, nice detail. There was a small sofa and a couple of chairs, leather, black, uncomfortable-looking. A huge window overlooked the lot. Not far off, a couple of space aliens walked down a turn-of-the-century street.

The office was loaded with pictures of kids, two boys, on the wall in baseball outfits, on a coffee table at the beach, on the desk in one of those Sears-finest shots. He saw me looking, picked up the Sears one, brought it over to where I'd planted myself on the sofa. "This is the most recent," he said. "Brian's ten and Ricky is eight."

"You can't be more than—"

"Twenty-six. They're my stepkids. Their mom was quite a bit older than me. She died four years ago."

Did Ronnie know about the kids? My guess was there was a lot about Eric Stahl she didn't know. "Sorry," I said.

"Thanks, but ... thanks." He put down the photo and clapped his hands together, signaling a change of subject. "But you didn't come here to talk about my kids. You want to talk about Dennis."

"Yes."

"You realize, of course, that I've gone over everything half a dozen times with the police." He looked me over, and evidently decided it was okay to be seen with me in public. "This might take a while. Let's get lunch." He didn't wait for my reaction, stepping into the anteroom and saying, "Becky, get us a table at Silversmith." He stuck his head back in. "Come on, let's go. Suddenly I'm starved."

"I—"

"Don't worry. I'm paying."

I followed him out and down and to the minivan in his private parking place. I removed the baseball glove on my seat and dropped it among the McDonald's wrappers at my feet and we were off.

Silversmith was on Beverly Drive, south of Wilshire. Reservations for dinner were supposed to be scarce as hens' teeth and lunch was even tougher. But when we walked in, after leaving the van with a parking attendant who looked like Johnny Depp, we were immediately escorted to a table.

Ramon Silversmith had been a short-order cook at the Norm's on La Cienega. Then he won twelve million dollars in the lottery. He took it in a lump sum and partnered up with a long-time restaurant manager named Robin Boston and hauled out all his parents' Argentine recipes. They took over a space that had housed half a dozen restaurants in as many years and turned it into an overnight success. Industry types flocked there. Scenesters made it their destination. S. Irene Virbila crowned it with one of her scarce three-star reviews in the *Times*.

I knew all this because Robin Boston was an old girlfriend of Gina's. After they broke up they stayed friends, and when Robin partnered up with Ramon Silversmith she hired Gina to do the interiors. We got to go to the opening-night party, hated it, left after stuffing ourselves with hors d'oeuvres. I never expected to be back.

But there I was, and in the company of, if the staff's behavior was any indication, their favorite customer. By the time we'd been there five minutes we'd been visited by two waiters, three busboys, the sommelier, the water sommelier, and Ramon Silversmith himself, who greeted Eric with kisses on both cheeks and me with a hearty handshake. He hung onto my hand, trying to figure out where he knew me from. I told him. He said, Ah, what Gina did for this place, I should give her a cut, then sniffed the air, grimaced, dashed back into his kitchen.

Bread, water, tapenade appeared on the table. A young woman with collagen lips materialized. Eric introduced me. She fluttered her eyelashes at me.

Eric watched her walk away. "Dennis would have loved that," he said. "Quite the ass on her, huh?"

Anyone else, I would have said something like, "I thought her nipple was going to poke me in the eye."

But I said nothing.

He broke off a piece of flatbread, dipped it in the tapenade, tossed it down the hatch. "Did you see the parking attendant?"

"Yeah," I said. "Looked like Johnny Depp."

"It was Johnny Depp. Doing research for a role."

"Really."

"I've been trying to get him to do a guest shot on *Protect and Serve*. He says he's not interested, but that's all part of the game."

Who did this guy think he was fooling? Johnny Depp's *21 Jump Street* gig notwithstanding, him being on a cop show was as likely as me being featured on *Meet the Press*.

Our waiter appeared. I let Eric order for both of us. He picked what he wanted and asked the waiter what he thought he should bring for me. The waiter said he knew just the thing and went away. I'd either been dissed or treated like a king.

I took in the throng. "I heard this place was hard to get into."

He smiled. "One of the perks."

"Must be a lot of them."

"If somebody wants them."

"You don't?"

"Ones like this, yes. Not a lot of the others."

"Like the girls and the drugs."

"Where are you going with this?"

"Just making conversation."

The wine came. Eric and the sommelier went through the showing, pouring, sipping, approving routine. I tried it. Red wine is red wine.

"With Dennis gone," I said, "you must have more to do at work."

"Not really. He wasn't that involved with day-to-day operations. He was more the visionary." There was no irony in his voice.

"How did the two of you get along?"

He frowned. "Just fine."

"Because Ronnie said you said the world might be better off without him."

He waited a beat. It was deliberate. "I didn't mean it that way."

"How did you mean it?"

I never found out, because someone else came over to pay his respects. A character actor who always played the put-upon neighbor or minor functionary. I'd seen him in dozens of things, didn't know his name, forgot it again the second he retreated.

After a couple of bites of salad I said, "Most of the people I've met who knew Dennis, he did something lousy to. Take Ronnie, for example. Do you know why he fired her?"

"She told me."

"That was totally cold-blooded. Not just firing her because she wouldn't sleep with him, but dragging me, a person he barely knew, into it. And then before that. With the roofies. Did you know about that?"

His blinked a couple of times more than he should have. "He was trying to change."

"Please."

"No, seriously. Regardless of what you might think about

Dennis, he did have a conscience. He did sometimes feel bad about the way he treated people. He fired me twice, did you know that?"

"No."

"And each time he bought me an expensive gift to make up for it."

"Real thoughtful of him."

"I know, I know. But lately … well, actually, just in the couple of days before he died … something was different."

"How so?"

"He'd stumbled on something … I don't know what it was."

"I don't get it."

"Me either. We just talked about it on the phone once, for half a minute. He said it was going to change his life."

"Forgive me if I'm not convinced."

"Understandable. I'm sorry. That's all I know." The waiter came and took away our salad plates. "Look," Eric said. "Dennis is dead. What's the point in talking trash about him?"

"The point in talking trash is that his father asked me to help figure out who killed him. And when someone's an asshole and he gets shot, one natural conclusion is that he got shot *because* he's an asshole."

"You know, it's not very graceful, letting someone take you to lunch and subjecting him to the third degree."

I almost broke it open right then. But I was determined to play it cool, keep him on the line as long as possible, extract every bit of information I could. "Hey, lunch was your idea. I had every intention of subjecting you to the third degree right there in your office."

Our entrees came. His was steak. Mine was slices of beef

and some root vegetable in a sauce. It was good. Not three-stars good. S. Irene Virbila, I was sure, had awarded the place for its in-factor, maybe for Gina's design, definitely for the way it made S. Irene feel like she was somebody important.

We behaved ourselves through the main course. We talked about his stepkids, and my remodel, and Iraq. He ate the next-to-last bite of the green stuff that was his side dish, put down his fork, said, "You want to talk about Ronnie." No question mark.

"You know me so well." I pushed a bread crumb around with my fingertip. "I understand you suggested to her that I might have murdered Dennis."

He'd mastered the all-will-be-taken-care-of smile. "Not seriously. Just exploring possibilities. And I understand you said the same thing about me."

"You told her I was the one who drugged her."

"Where'd you hear that?"

"From her."

He leaned forward. "All right. So I said it. So what. It's a natural conclusion, how gorgeous she is."

"You're right," I said. "A woman that gorgeous, a guy would do a lot to get her in the sack."

His eyes fluttered, darted away, came back. His cheeks turned a shade paler. "What's that supposed to mean?"

"It means that you were frustrated as hell that you couldn't talk her into bed with you."

"This is none of your—"

"And I guess while you were out of town you decided to do something about it. So you charmed her by showing up at the party. It was a nice move. Very romantic. Stop looking for the waiter and look at me, you piece of shit."

He turned and saw my face. The air went out of him.

"But the romance routine wasn't enough for you. You put something in her drink. I've been going under the assumption it was a date-rape drug. Am I right?"

"That's the most ridiculous accusation I've ever heard."

"Really? Of all the accusations you've heard in your entire worthless life, it's absolutely the most ridiculous?"

"It's libel."

"I think you mean slander. Libel's written, and so far I have written anything about it. So far."

"You'll never prove anything. It's way too late for that."

"Maybe I'm wearing a wire. That's what they'd do on *Protect and Serve*, right? They get the bad guy in a situation where he'd have no reason to think he was being recorded and—" I patted my chest, about where I thought the microphone ought to be. "—and everything's all cleaned up neat and tidy by the end of the fourth act."

"Stop it. Stop it right there." His eyes were glazed. His breathing was shallow. "This meal is over," he said.

"You haven't finished your greens."

He stood, pulled out his wallet, tossed a hundred and a fifty on the table. He brushed off all attempts at communication as he made his way outside. A couple of minutes later Johnny Depp brought the van around.

I finished my meal. Did a quick calculation. I could have dessert and still leave the waiter a healthy tip.

The pear tart was definitely three-star. The tea was excellent too.

thirty

There's a popular misconception that nobody walks in L.A. There was even a song back in the eighties with lyrics that said so. But lots of people walk in L.A. It's usually good walking weather, except for the dozen days in the winter when it rains and the half-dozen in September and October when it's too hot. If you pretend your neighborhood is a small town you can get by for days without a vehicle.

So it wasn't a big deal for me to make my way on foot back to the Fox lot. It wasn't more than a couple of miles. A half hour stroll. I took Olympic most of the way, cut down Avenue of the Stars past the office tower where they shot *Die Hard*, finished the trip on Pico. I paid my respects to my friend the guard, walked to the truck. I drove out and west on Pico, looking for a pay phone. The first one I spotted was outside a Kentucky Fried Chicken. It was broken. The next was in the lot at a 7-Eleven. It didn't work either, and ate my coins to boot.

Sometimes you resist something so much that opposing it becomes a point of pride. Even when all the evidence points to capitulation, you continue struggling against it, convinced that to give in provides evidence of some inner weakness, some flaw in character that, once recognized, will result in awful consequences.

Sometimes you just say to hell with it.

I thought of all the times I'd wanted to check in with Gina but couldn't because I couldn't get to a phone; all the abuse I'd endured from Elaine because she couldn't get in touch with me about an audition; all the 7-Eleven lots I'd stood in, cursing Alexander Graham Bell for starting the whole thing.

And Gina had demolished my objection about the cost. A couple of days ago she'd presented me with a brochure for a prepaid plan that would only cost us seven or eight bucks a month. And with my new vocation, I could write even that small sum off.

I vaguely remembered an AT&T store somewhere along Pico. I found it in a building shared with a piano showroom and a party store. I went in and half an hour later walked out with my brand new Nokia and a fuzzy idea of how to use it.

My first call was supposed to be to Gina. I reached a tire store. An auspicious entry into the world of digital communications.

I managed to dial Mike's number. He picked up. I told him what I wanted. He said he was gassed that I was coming over.

I hadn't been to his place before. Everything we'd done had been east of my house and it always made sense for him to pick me up or drop his car at my place while I drove. Not to mention the parking situation, which was even worse in Mike's neck of the woods than in Carrie's and Samantha's half a mile away.

But I got lucky. As I drove up Pacific I glanced down one of the narrow side streets and spotted someone pulling out. I hung a *Dukes of Hazzard* right and snapped up the spot.

Two minutes later I was at Mike's. It was one of those two-story places overlooking the boardwalk. The bottom floor was Feed Your Head and the top his apartment. I'd finally figured out that he moved into the apartment after Donna went missing, and that he rented out the house they'd lived in together.

It was always noisy there on the boardwalk, what with the skaters and tourists and homeless people beating drums. It wasn't where I would have chosen to recover from blunt force trauma to the head. Were I Lu, I would have gone back to Dennis's place. But maybe she couldn't go back, just like Gina never went back to her condo in West Hollywood after someone met a violent end there.

I climbed the staircase leading up to Mike's front door. A tattered and faded Christmas wreath hung there. Knowing Mike, probably left over from last year. I rang the bell and the nurse answered. She was a Filipina, very short and perky and younger than I would have thought. She said Mike was downstairs in the shop. I asked how Lu was and got told she was feeling a little bit better every day.

I went back down and around to the shop. The Yardbirds were blasting from inside. The front window was filled with hash pipes and water pipes and a bunch of gadgets I didn't recognize. Technology had caught up with the dope-smoking industry. There was also a fancy golden hookah, hand-painted in reds and blues and yellows. *On Special*, said the sign. *Makes a Great Xmas Gift.*

Inside. More paraphernalia. Twenty or so kinds of rolling papers. Scales and tiny pruning shears and plastic bags guaranteed to repel ultraviolet light. Posters with peace signs or long-dead rock stars. Black lights from six inches on up.

Three of the five people inside were drinking Snapples

around a wooden table. There was a spindly old guy with a gray ponytail, a middle-aged heavyset man wearing a FREE HUEY T-shirt, and a teenage girl in a bikini top and overalls. They were discussing how we were going to get rid of W. The girl's position was that Howard Dean was going to be the salvation of the Democratic Party. The heavy guy said he was unelectable. The senior citizen said it didn't make any difference, politicians were all the same.

A woman my age was buying rolling papers. She couldn't decide between two kinds. She was on her cell phone with someone named Dewey, insisting he make a choice. Mike stood behind the counter, wearing a tolerant smile. He was nodding in time, more or less, with the Yardbirds.

Mike spotted me and waved me over. "Tell Belinda here which papers to get." To the woman: "Joe here's an expert."

Belinda said, "Hold on," and took the phone from her ear.

"What are my choices?" I said.

"The JOB Tribal or the Bob Marley King Size Pure Hemp."

"I'd go with Bob."

"But the JOBs are chlorine-free," she said.

"Bob would never steer you wrong."

She nodded, told Dewey she'd made her choice, finished the transaction. She was about to walk out when Mike said, "Oh, hell," and threw the JOBs in the bag too. "Try 'em for yourself. The best way."

The woman thanked him and made her exit. "An expert?" I said.

"Whatever. Made her happy. Come on upstairs. Summer."

The teenager looked over.

"Man the store for a while. I'm going upstairs."

Summer made a face. "Don't you mean 'staff the store'?"

"Whatever."

Mike led me through the back room and out the back door. I said, "Isn't she a little young to be working in a head shop?"

"She doesn't work here. Just covering for a while. Lots of people do that sometimes."

The door deposited us at the base of the stairs. We went up and into the apartment. The inside was cluttered but functional. A sliding glass door led out to a balcony directly over the boardwalk. The living room was dominated by a giant TV. There was a food show on with the sound way down low. They were showing us how Hershey's Kisses were made.

Mike went in the back, returned, told me Lu was tied up with the nurse and sat me down at the dining room table. A Chinese checkers board was set up on it. There'd been one at Dennis's house too. One of the ties that bound father and son.

A couple of marbles had rolled onto the floor. I picked them up and dropped them into random slots on the game board.

"Been playing some with the nurse," he said. "She's good."

"Who's paying for her?"

"Dennis." He was rolling a couple of marbles around in his hand. Made me think of Captain Queeg.

"How you doing?" I said.

"Okay. You want some tea?"

"You should take a vacation."

"Where would I go?"

"Las Vegas. Mount Rushmore. Liverpool. Hell, I don't know."

"Maybe China, huh?"

"If you want."

"Starsky and Bitch were back this morning."

"What'd they have to say?"

"They asked if I'd remembered anyone who could pin-point my whereabouts."

"What'd you tell them?"

"Same thing I told them all the other times. That there wasn't anybody."

"Any reason you can think of that they suspect you?"

"Nope. I guess 'cause everyone else didn't pan out."

I picked up a red marble and a white one, put them back in each other's spot. I glanced at the entrance to the hall that led, I assumed, back to where the bedrooms were.

"Joe?"

"Yeah?"

"It's okay to sit around not saying anything."

"Really?"

"Really."

So the two of us remained silent. I scooted my chair around to look at the TV. After a while they moved on to Peppermint Patties.

"Love those things," Mike said.

"Really."

"Haven't had one in a while," he said. "Last one I had was the night they killed Denny. I remember, 'cause I offered to share it with Carrie, and she said she didn't like 'em. Can you imagine that? Not liking Peppermint Patties."

thirty-one

"Carrie was here that night?" I said. "You told me not five minutes ago you were by yourself."

"Huh? Oh. Right. You know what? It couldn't have been that night. I was alone that night, till I got the—"

"Bullshit."

"Damn it. I promised I wouldn't tell anyone."

"You promised who? Her?"

"Yeah, her, of course her."

"Why? So she could provide an alibi for Samantha?"

"Well, yeah, I suppose."

"You suppose."

"Yeah."

"So it was more important she provide an alibi for Samantha than one for you."

"She needed one right off. I didn't need one till later, when the cops decided to get up my ass. By that time it was too late to change her story."

"Did you guys watch TV that night?"

"Yeah. Couple hours worth, I think. Hey, man. What's with the third degree?"

"What's with it is, why would Samantha find it necessary to set up a fake alibi? Did Carrie say anything?"

"No. I mean, I didn't really think about it. Didn't make a whole lot of difference to me, and if you remember I wasn't exactly in the best shape those couple of days to spend a lot of time on it."

"You sure you didn't tell the police this?"

"I'm sure. Stop asking all these questions."

"It's just that I find it a little odd that you managed to keep it quiet from the cops but managed to let it slip to me."

"Maybe I let it slip on purpose."

"Why would that be?"

A shrug. "Friends shouldn't keep secrets from each other."

"You keeping any other secrets from me?"

He was. The miserable attempt at an innocent expression on his face told me that. But before I could press him—

"All done." It was the nurse. Mike introduced us, and I immediately forgot her name. She went into the kitchen.

"So," I said, "getting back to—"

"Drop it, okay? Carrie was here, she wasn't with Samantha, that's all I know. You want to see Lu or not?"

I was certain there was more he wasn't telling me. But I'd gotten to where I could read him pretty well, and knew he was ready to stonewall. At the moment, finding out what Lu had to say was more important. "Lead the way."

He took me to her room. She was on the pale side and she was thinner than when I'd seen her before. She was in a hospital bed, with the head section adjusted up. It must have been hell getting the thing up those stairs.

She had a TV of her own, and the same channel was on. They were still making Peppermint Patties. They went in one side of a machine naked and came out the other covered in chocolate.

"I want one," Lu said.

"Not on your diet," Mike said.

"Who cares about my diet?"

"You're the worst patient I've ever had."

"I am the only patient you ever had. Now go away. I want to talk to Joe."

"In a second. Your pillows are all screwy."

He went over and adjusted them. Not that they needed it. When he was done they looked just like they did before. She clutched his hand and patted it.

He left the room, and I pulled over a straight-back chair. "How's your head?" I said.

"Not bleeding anymore."

"Does it hurt?"

She shrugged. Her nightgown slipped down, exposing a shoulder. She looked down, frowned, hiked it back up. "Stupid bed. What did you ask?"

"If your head hurt."

"Once in a while. We Chinese have a saying. Do not look down upon your position, for tomorrow you may sleep on the carpet."

"You just made that up."

"I did?"

"I'm pretty sure Confucius never came up with that one."

"Him. What does he know? So. What you want?"

"I need a question answered."

"What question?"

"Right before he died, Dennis told a man who works for him that he'd discovered something which was going to change his life."

"That is not a question."

"I was thinking that, being there in the house, you might have known what it was."

"Still not a question." If the housekeeper thing didn't work out, she could get a job subbing for Alex Trebek.

"Do you know anything about that?"

"Yes."

"What is it that you know?"

"Let me think." She closed her eyes. They were still closed when she said, "Ah."

"What is it?"

"The club."

"You mean like a nightclub?"

Her eyes opened. "No, not that. Some club he went to. I don't remember. I need a nap."

"Just try, please."

"Tomorrow. Come back tomorrow. You are very nice. You are almost as nice as Mike." Her lids snapped shut.

Only to pop open again. "Beyonce," she mumbled.

"Beyonce?" I said. "Is that what you said? Do you mean Beyoncé? Beyoncé the singer?"

Again her eyes closed. She did something with her head. It could have been a nod. I decided it was a nod.

"Lu? Is that who you meant? Was Dennis seeing her too? Did he meet her at some club?"

But she was asleep. I watched her until I was sure. Then I got up and stood over the bed. The pillows were still in perfect array. I adjusted them anyway.

I asked Mike if he knew of any connection between Dennis and Beyoncé. He didn't know who she was. Not surprising, since his knowledge of popular music stopped at about 1978. I told him about Destiny's Child. That didn't help. Then I said, you know, the chick in the last Austin Powers movie. That did the trick. Yes, he knew who she was. No, he didn't think Dennis had ever had anything to do with her.

Before I left I asked him if there was anything he'd "forgotten" to tell me. He said there wasn't. I knew he was lying, and he knew I knew. I didn't push it. When the time was right, he'd spill. I'd see to that.

I'd never been to Lawndale, but a few years back one of my murders brought me to Hawthorne. Lawndale was right next door, and it was from the same mold. The houses were well-kept, most of them, with the same Honda Civics and tricycles and pots of geraniums. And here too, you got the feeling that, once you turned off the main street, you'd passed through an invisible curtain that had dropped you a decade or two in the past. It was comforting. Also disturbing.

I was in Lawndale to visit Sean McKay, who lived there with his father. I parked across the street from the address in the file Claudia Acuna had given me, behind a Termites R Us truck. The house right across from Sean's and his father's was being tented. Before we started the remodel we'd done the same. Gina and the canaries and I spent a couple of days at Elaine's. The birds enjoyed the excursion.

The McKay house was white stucco. The trim was part light green, part dark. The dark part was being applied over the light by a man who had to be Sean's father. He had the same build and pretty much the same face. He wore a white painter's suit and hat. When he saw me he put down his brush and took off his hat and wiped his forehead with his forearm. He introduced himself as Tom McKay and said Sean had run down to Vons for bread and milk. I skipped the strikebreaking discussion.

"You can wait inside or out back," Tom McKay said. "Or you can stay out here and keep an old man company."

"You're not an old man, Mr. McKay."

"Old enough. You're that fellow from the TV, aren't you? The one with the bugs."

"That's me."

"That was there the night that Lennox fellow got killed."

"Me again."

He'd picked up his brush again and had started back in on a half-finished window frame. "And now you think Sean might have shot the man."

"I don't think that, sir. I just want to—"

"It's all right. I don't think he could hurt a fly, but he's enjoying the attention, and that's all right with me. Hand me that rag, would you?"

I gave him the orange mechanic's cloth. He used it to wipe some spillage from outside a paint can.

"Go ahead and ask me what you want to ask me," he said.

"Which would be?"

"Was Sean really here watching TV with me that night, up until he got the phone call from that Lennox fellow?"

He was concentrating hard on the spot he was painting. It must have been a tough spot. He went over it again and again.

"Was he?" I said.

"I'll tell you the same thing I told the police."

"Which is?"

"He sure was."

"And would that be the truth?"

"It sure would." He looked out into the street. "Here comes Sean."

He turned to his painting gear, and I walked to where Sean was pulling his Jetta into the driveway. Sean saw me, waved, stopped the car, got out. He opened the trunk and pulled out a couple of grocery bags. They were from some-place called Royal Market.

"Thought you were going to Vons."

"And cross the picket line? Not me. It's a little ritual, Dad's and mine. He's not very big on unions. So I tell him I'm going to Vons, and we don't get in a fight, and I bring the stuff home and tell him I remembered I had a coupon for Royal or something. Come on inside."

He opened the door and led me in. The place was neat. The furniture was decent. There was a row of bowling trophies on the mantel.

"Your dad must be quite a bowler," I said.

"Those are mine. From when I was younger. Come in the kitchen."

He put the grocery bags on the floor, started unloading. He'd gotten quite a bit more than bread and milk. Oranges, Milanos, Glad Bags.

"You're surprised I'm a bowler," he said.

"A little."

"Is it because I'm gay?"

"I really hadn't given much thought to your sexuality. It's because I just don't associate people trying to claw their way to the top in the entertainment business with bowling."

"It's very relaxing."

"Knocking over all those pins. Yes, I guess it must be."

"You bowl, Joe?"

"Not very well. By the way, did you kill Dennis?"

"Of course not. I was sitting at home watching TV with Dad, just like I told the police about a thousand times."

"But you had reason to."

"So did you. So did dozens of people, most of them people who weren't even there that night."

All of the groceries were put away. He opened a can of

Pepsi, poured himself a glass, asked me if I wanted any. I shook my head. He drank down half of it, put the glass on the counter.

"This place," I said. "It doesn't fit my picture."

"I'm supposed to be living up in West Hollywood or somewhere like that."

"Somewhere closer to the studios. And to the action."

He smiled, picked up his Pepsi, drained it, rinsed out the glass and put it in the dish drainer. "Staying here with Dad. It centers me, you know?"

"Plus it provides an alibi when you need one."

His smile was preoccupied. "It's handy that way. What did you really want to see me for today?"

"I guess I wanted to get a sense of you. When we weren't running around in dishwashing gloves freaking out over a dead body."

We had a lovely little conversation, there in the kitchen. He told me about growing up in his blue-collar neighborhood, starting to realize he was different from the other boys, hiding it behind teenage bombast. How it was a blessing that he was so good at bowling, because it let him get points for sports from the other boys while doing something he at least liked. How he went to El Camino College and got interested in making movies, and how his father staked him for a couple of years while he got his career going. And how after that he'd lived off a rich old man who, when he died, turned out not to be as rich as everybody thought. That was when Sean moved back home.

"So?" he said when he'd brought me up to date. "What sense do you get?"

"That you're basically an okay guy, but you're hiding something."

"Like?"

"I don't know. I don't think it's that you killed Dennis. But I'm not a hundred percent sure."

I heard footsteps. Tom McKay walked in. He'd lost the painter outfit and had on cutoffs and a white T-shirt. "Gonna shower up," he said. He looked at the empty grocery bags still on the floor, smiled, turned to me. "Staying for dinner?"

"Love to, but I've got plans."

He knew I didn't, but since he'd only made the offer to be polite, it didn't much matter. "Good enough. Nice to meet you." And he was gone. A minute later, so was I.

thirty-two

I called Mike. He wasn't there, but the nurse said Lu was asleep and she wasn't going to wake her to ask about any rap music star. I didn't think Beyoncé did any rapping, but the nurse was younger than me and maybe knew things I didn't.

I dug out the phone number I'd gotten a million years ago at Voom. Dialed it, got a teenager, asked for Sarah. "Maaa! It's for you!" The phone clunked onto something hard, and a few seconds later got picked up. I identified myself, said I was in the neighborhood, Sarah expressed delight. I got an address.

Fifteen minutes after that I was pulling to the curb in front of a good-looking house on a Torrance cul-de-sac. I rang the doorbell and was greeted by a teenager with a stud in her nose and blond pigtails. Sarah appeared behind her and invited me in. "Joni, this is Joe Portugal," she said. "He was in a band with your father when I was just a little older than you. Joe, this is my youngest, Joni."

Joni gave me ten seconds of her precious youth and fled the room. "She'll be out of here soon," Sarah said. "Then it'll be that empty nest thing for Tone and me. Come, have something to drink."

Soon we were sitting in the living room, her with a cup of coffee, me with a mug of Red Rose. I looked around, noticing how solidly middle-class everything was. Bookcases with an assortment of mystery novels and self-help books, and one shelf filled with an antique World Book. Nice furniture, comfortable, worn. A Hendrix poster, the same one a couple of players in the Toby Bonner affair had had, but this one nicely framed and hung next to a reproduction of those Van Gogh irises at the Getty. There were photos of their three daughters—the others were Judy and Janis—and of the grandkids I'd avoided at Voom. I looked them over, made the appropriate comments, related my own childless state.

We talked about old times, touching on that night up at Pyramid Lake. I told her how good it had made me feel when she pulled me into the huddle with Tony and her. We did the discussion I was having uncomfortably often, the one about where did the time go and how could it be that it was forty years since the Beatles showed up and was it or wasn't it about time Jagger stopped strutting about onstage like a demented rooster.

Joni stopped by, guitar case in hand, on her way out. She was headed for practice. Her band was called the Felonious Monks, and they did acid-folk-punk. Sarah told her to make sure she got something to eat. Joni rolled her eyes and escaped.

Tony came home from his job at the Mobil refinery, and things grew more nostalgic. They invited me to dinner. I called Gina and told her what was up and accepted the invite. While the food was cooking Tony pulled out a couple of acoustics, and we revisited some of the old repertoire. After we ate we reminisced some more, with the soundtrack to the sixties on the stereo. Tony fell asleep on the couch, woke up, took his leave. When Sarah and I sat down again I remembered what it was I'd come for.

"I wanted to talk to you about Mike," I said.

"I thought so."

"Oh?"

"Just a feeling. A vibe."

"Heavy."

She smiled, took a candy from a dish on the lamp table, unwrapped it, sucked on it. "Like I need to be eating this."

What do you say to that?

"It's okay," she said. "I stopped worrying about my weight long ago." She dropped the wrapper on the coffee table. "How long have you known Mike?"

"Month, month and a half."

"I've known him twenty-five years. Almost since he took over at Feed Your Head. Went in one day for a birthday present for Tony. The four of us, we saw a lot of each other for a while."

"What was she like?"

"She was a good woman. We weren't that close, actually. Never did anything just the two of us, but Mike and Tony and me really got along and she came along for the ride. She and Mike were really tight." She eyed me. "By the time she disappeared, we'd stopped hanging out so much. You know how that goes. Saw each other a few times a year." Her teeth cracked down on the candy. "You probably think he's a big goof."

"Kind of."

"He always was. But there was another side of him back then, a practical one. He may have run a head shop, but he ran it well."

"He's not still running it well?"

"He's got people running it well. He's pretty much hands off. He just comes in and hangs out with the people you and Tony and I would have ended up as, if we hadn't gotten straight lives."

The music had run out. She got up, took out Jefferson Airplane, put on Dylan. "Rainy Day Women" came over the speakers, and I nodded my head in time. Sarah dimmed the lights, lit a couple of candles, sat back down. She took off her shoes and curled her feet under her. "Just like the old days," she said.

"It'll never be like the old days. Even the old days weren't like the old days."

"You're saying we remember it better than it was."

"Everyone does. Our parents did. The thirties, the forties, it was all great. Conveniently forgetting the Depression and the war and all that."

"You've become quite the philosopher."

"I've become quite the cynic, is what I've become."

A key in the front door. It opened and Joni came in. Sarah asked if she'd had fun and Joni said she had, and that they had a new song that was really cool. Generations came and generations went, but *cool* stuck around.

Joni said she was going to bed. She and Sarah hugged. It was clear that they loved each other. Liked each other too.

In one of those alternate universes, Sarah and I got off on a discussion of kids, my childlessness, the possibility of adopting, all that crap. We never talked about the late Dennis Lennox.

In the one we were actually in, I said, "You knew Dennis when he was growing up, right?"

Her eyes met mine. "Uh-huh."

"When did he start being such a shit?"

"He wasn't so bad."

"Sarah. This is Joe you're talking to. Velour Overground Joe. Pyramid Lake Joe. I spent a rotten evening up at his house with a bunch of people he'd screwed over, while the cops scraped him off the rug."

"Okay. I can tell you exactly when it was. It was in high school. His junior year. There was a girl. They were in love, in that high school way. They one day she was in love with another boy. Dennis took it hard."

"How hard?"

"Trying-to-kill-himself hard."

"I didn't know."

"Only other person you've met who'd be likely to know is Mike—well, and Tony—and Mike's not likely to bring it up."

"What'd he do?"

"Tried to hang himself in his room. They put him in an institution for a while. Got him therapy. He got better."

"How much better?"

"Enough to go back to school and on to college. Not enough to ever have a normal relationship with a woman again."

"He wanted to hurt them before they hurt him."

She nodded.

"And that never stopped," I said.

"Right."

"And he found out he liked it."

"That's the feeling I get."

"So much that he started acting that way with everyone."

"Yes," she said. "There were only two people who weren't fair game for getting run over."

"Mike and Donna."

"They never stopped trying to straighten him out. It was very frustrating for both of them. But when Donna disappeared, Mike did stop trying. He just let Dennis do his thing."

"You know a lot about this," I said. "Considering you and they weren't that close anymore."

"We had an interest, Tony and I."

"What kind?"

"Our oldest. Judy. They went out for a while. Six, seven years ago."

"I'm sorry."

"By that time, we knew what he was like. We warned her. She wouldn't have any of it. She thought she was the one who could make him straighten up and fly right."

"What did he—no, forget that. I don't need details."

"She was lucky. She met a guy not long after." She turned to the pictures of her grandkids. "There's the result."

I left Sarah and Tony's near midnight with promises that the four of us would get together soon. That would go one of three ways. It might happen, and we'd all really hit it off and become good buddies. Or it would never happen; there might be a call or two, but somehow we'd never find the right date and after a while the calls would stop.

The most likely scenario was that we would uncover a night that matched all our schedules, and one couple would come to the other's house, or we'd meet on neutral ground, and the evening would be pleasant enough. There might even be one more. But after that I'd never see Sarah and Tony again.

Gina barely noticed when I got into bed, and I fell asleep quickly. We both woke up a little after three. There was a helicopter overhead and a searchlight flashing in and out of our window. I felt my way into the living room and peered out into the street. A man was running by, wearing only a sweatshirt and one flip-flop. He stopped in front of the Clement house, looked up at the helicopter, turned and ran back the way he came. A few seconds later a cop car went by, siren blaring, lights flashing. This major threat to society must have been captured shortly thereafter. The loud noises went away. The lights that had popped on up and down the block blinked out.

We went back to bed, but I couldn't sleep. I tossed and turned and drove Gina crazy. I got up and went in the living room and watched more James Bond. When it was over the penis enhancement infomercial came on. I switched channels until I found a show about otters and watched it until I fell asleep. In my dream, I was playing a beat-up acoustic guitar. I'd removed all the frets above the seventh because I never played that far up the neck. Then the frets I'd taken off turned into worms and grew enormous and took over the world. I woke up on the floor between the couch and the coffee table. There was vague daylight beyond the windows.

I hauled myself up, went out and retrieved the newspaper from the lawn. I checked out the obits and Ramirez's latest reactionary editorial cartoon. Then a quick scan of the front page. Then onto the Calendar.

Where, on the first page, there was a big article about Beyoncé Knowles. How she was going to continue recording with Destiny's Child, even though her solo career was going great guns. She seemed like a nice enough young woman. Levelheaded. Probably kind to dogs and children. Multitalented too, judging from that Austin Powers movie.

Only her name bugged me. That accent over the second

e. It seemed pretentious. But I supposed it was necessary. Because her name was *Bay-on-say*, not *Bay-onss*, and—

I called myself names.

It wasn't "Beyoncé" that Lu had mumbled as she was nodding off. It was something else entirely. She'd swallowed the first syllable. And I was the one who'd added the *-ay* sound.

What she was saying—and what she had referred to as a club, something I conveniently forgot—was "Ambiance."

And I knew just who to call to find out more about that.

thirty-three

I searched the file Claudia Acuna had given me, found the number I needed, dialed it. The woman who answered said she'd been awake; her tone said otherwise. I told her what I wanted. She said she'd be happy to see me. She either meant it or was a better actress than I'd suspected.

Trixie Trenton's place was in Beachwood Canyon in Hollywood. It was just up the block from the former home of another actress I once knew. I hadn't been up the canyon since, and as I drove past Laura's place I saw her orange cat, which a couple of neighbor boys adopted after she was murdered. He was sunning himself on the hood of a car. He lifted his head and watched as I drove by.

Trixie lived upstairs in one of the dozens of dingbat-style apartment buildings that lined the street. There was a bookcase with five or six books. The rest of the shelves were loaded with cheerleading trophies, cast-and-crew photos, porcelain animals, a bowl with two goldfish. And a shrine. It included a foot-tall stone statue of some Asian deity with several extra arms, a couple of candles, a bowl of what looked like cornmeal. Plus a wooden frog and a plastic duck. The candles were lit and made the place smell like vanilla. The whole thing reminded me of Donna

Lennox's memorial at DL Tea, though this one was a fair bit tackier.

Exercise equipment dominated the living room. A stairclimber and a Bowflex were the main pieces of apparatus. The Bowflex looked a lot more like a medieval torture machine than it did on late-night commercials.

Trixie was barefoot, wearing a loose T-shirt and running shorts and an Angels cap with a ponytail pulled through the opening in back. She came across a whole lot better than in the urban slut outfit she'd worn at Dennis's.

Snoogums, though, looked the same. He flew in from the bedroom, sniffed my shoes and cuffs, sneered, hid behind the stair-climber.

I sat on the sofa, accepted a cup of chamomile tea, commented on all the exercise gear.

"I'm kind of a fanatic," she said. "Always have been, ever since I was a kid."

"Why here? Why not go to the gym? This stuff takes up a lot of space."

"This is so much easier. And here I don't have to worry about guys staring at my boobs and coming on to me."

"Don't they have all-women gyms?"

"Then I'd have girls staring at my boobs and coming on to me. Who do you think goes to all-women gyms?"

"Never thought about it. Did Dennis ever come over here?"

She picked up her mug, blew on her chamomile. "He never saw the place. His driver did once."

"He sent a driver?"

"And I, stupid little idiot that I am, thought that was oh so romantic."

"You must have known about him when you went out with him the first time."

"I'd heard stories. You hear stories about a lot of men. Sometimes you know they must be true, and you think, who cares, I'll have a good time, I'm not looking for Mr. Wonderful. I didn't think I'd fall for him."

"How long did you go out?"

"Just a few weeks. Maybe a month"

"Where did Cozumel fall in there?"

"You know about that?"

"Samantha told me."

"Samantha. That girl and I ought to get together." She'd curled herself up on her end of the sofa with her feet under her, just like Sarah the night before. "It was about a week in. That was where he wove his spell on me."

Wove his spell. This didn't sound like the ditz I'd seen up at Dennis's place. And her voice hadn't a trace of the grating quality I'd heard before. "Was this before or after you took him to Ambiance?"

"Before."

I turned to the shrine. "How long have you been involved?"

"Two years."

"Has it helped?"

"It got me out of those Playboy Channel things I was doing."

"What about the hardcore stuff?"

She frowned. "Let's make a deal. Why don't you tell me everything you know about me, and stop dishing it out one little piece at a time."

"That's everything."

"You're sure?"

"I'm sure."

"Okay, then. Yes. It got me out of hardcore, softcore, the website, everything."

"There was a website?"

"Oh, yes. Sign up for nine ninety-five a month, get to jack off to pictures of Penelope Pope playing with herself."

"And you say Ambiance got you to stop."

"Yes."

"How?"

She looked away, patted the arm of the sofa. "Snoogums." He came running and jumped into her lap. She turned to me. "You don't know anything about Ambiance, do you?"

"I know that it's another one of those pop-psych movements that sprout in L.A. every couple of years, that attracts people like you who are looking for something to belong to, and that makes a ton of money for whoever's behind it."

"In other words, you don't know anything."

"Why don't you tell me?"

"Because it'd go in one ear and out the other."

"I thought people in these things were always proselytizing, trying to get everyone they know to join."

"We're not like that. We're like vampires. You have to invite us to tell you."

I thought of the commercial shoot where I ran into Roberta Salkind. Trixie was right. Roberta had never suggested I check the place out, though at the time I thought that was because I escaped before she had a chance to.

"Okay, fine. Tell me. I invite you to tell me."

She glanced at her shrine, looked back at me. "It's run by a man named Ike Sunemori. He's taken the best of Eastern religions and the best of human-potential movements and molded them into something that really helps people."

"Which Eastern religions?"

"Hinduism, Buddhism, mostly. There's a little Taoism."

"No Confucianism?"

"Don't be a jerk, okay?"

"What about the human-potential stuff?"

"Regardless of what you might think, those things aren't completely a bunch of baloney. Lifespring, Scientology, all the others I checked out, sure, the people that ran them were in it for the money and the power. But I did get something useful out of each. Ike has just put all those useful pieces together."

I knew someone else who'd been into that stuff. Someone who lived just down the block. "Did you happen to know a woman named Laura Astaire?"

Her face went slack. "Yes. She lived—"

"I know."

"She was kind of a big sister to me. You knew her?"

"I was the one who found out who killed her."

"Oh." She tried to say more. Nothing came out. Then tears were dribbling down her cheeks.

"I'm sorry," I said. "I didn't mean to make you cry."

She waved her fingers. *Don't worry, it's nothing.* I scooted over to comfort her, but Snoogums growled when I got too close, and I resumed my position.

Trixie tossed the dog down, got up, ran into the bathroom. When she came out her eyes were red but dry and she was more or less composed. She patted her lap and Snoogums returned. "Now where was I?"

She was going to go back to her Ambiance orientation talk, and I didn't want to hear it. It was the same thing they all did. We've taken a little of this, a little of that, and we've come up with something that will turn your life around in *X* months flat for a mere *Y* dollars. Payable by cash, check, or credit card.

I was more interested in Dennis's involvement. "Why'd you take Dennis up there?"

"I told him about it, of course. He invited me to tell him more. So I brought him to a gathering."

"What happened?"

"He acted like he was really into it."

"Acted like?"

"I thought he really was. At the time, anyway. He seemed so interested. Asked a lot of questions. Spent time with Ike one-on-one. You know where this is headed, don't you?"

"I think so."

"A lot of girls like me. Come to L.A. to become famous, lose their way, find life in the big city's too tough for them. They need something to center them."

Everyone did. For Sean McKay, it was moving back in with his father. A far better choice than the Charlatan-of-the-Month Club. "A treasure trove for someone like Dennis."

"But you know what? Ike saw right through him. He took me aside and told me. I watched Dennis the rest of the day. Once I knew, it was so obvious that he was scouting out the girls. You could almost see him making a list in his head."

"Yet you were still hurt when he dumped you."

A helpless gesture. "I tried to tell myself he was a bastard. Then he'd look at me with those green eyes and—"

"You didn't hire one of your fellow Ambiance people to whack him or anything?"

A giggle. "Actually, by the time he was killed, I was pretty much over him. A couple of days, that was all it took."

I picked up my chamomile tea. It was cold. I drank it down anyway. I wasn't sure why I'd come, what I expected to find out. The only thing I'd really discovered was that maybe, just maybe, Ike Sunemori and his crew weren't quite the money-grubbing pirates I'd assumed. "So did Ike tell Dennis not to bother coming back?"

"Because Dennis was only acting interested for the women?"

"Yes."

"No."

"So he was willing to take his money anyway."

"He thought he could change Dennis."

"Just like that. Guy's been an absolute prick since high school and just like that he's going to change."

"Ike has a lot of confidence. And he really wants to help people."

"I see."

"And he wouldn't see it as his place to tell anyone not to join Ambiance."

"So did Denny Dear go back up?"

"I've heard he did, that Sunday night between when he dumped me and when he got himself killed."

We kept talking. When the conversation began to repeat itself I got up to go. Trixie stood too, walked into the kitchen, came back with a brochure for Ambiance.

"Here," she said, handing it over.

I took a quick look. Young people with troubled expressions. "Proselytizing?"

She shook her head. "I'm guessing you're heading up there next. There's a map on the back."

I turned it over. Ambiance was in Altadena, at the foot of the San Gabriels. Half an hour, thirty-five minutes, if traffic was light.

I let her escort me to the door. When she opened it, I said, "Speaking to you today, and meeting you up at Dennis's, it's like two different people."

"How so?"

"You're clever, articulate, charming. The person up at Denny's was a typical blond bimbo."

"That's for my public."

"Cut it out."

"It works. It's gotten me work."

"Porn work."

"No, other work since then. A couple of sitcoms. And I was on *Angel*. Though you couldn't really tell it was me."

"Were you a vampire?"

She shook her head. "I'm not exactly sure what I was. But I was purple."

"You've met my friend Ronnie MacKenzie."

"That night."

"She used to do the same thing. I got her to stop it. Now she's a regular in prime time."

A broad smile. She looked over to where Snoogums had fallen asleep on the sofa. His doggie snores stopped, he yawned, he turned his big brown eyes to her. She looked back at me. "Maybe," she said, "I'm not ready for prime time."

thirty-four

Hollywood Freeway north, Ventura east, off at Lake. The long gradual climb to the foothills. Pasadena turned to Altadena. I pulled to the curb, checked the Thomas Guide. Five minutes later I was there.

Ambiance.

Huge old trees, pines and oaks, dotted the grounds. A couple of dozen people in ones and twos, reading and talking. A group of seven or eight, sitting cross-legged, watching raptly as a woman scribbled on a flip-chart mounted on an easel. They all had golden nametags pinned to their chests.

It had been a Catholic high school at one time, the brochure Trixie'd given me said. There were several brick buildings, a basketball court, a grassy playing field with a three-story, more modern building where an end zone should have been. Nine or ten signs told me it was the orientation center. I ignored them and headed for the one remaining structure. This one was a big old house. The front lawn was split by a walkway. Each half hosted a thick-trunked palm tree, the kind a whole kindergarten class could hide behind. Last time I'd been up close with one of those had been over a year before, in the Valley, at a house I visited with one of my fellow Platypuses. That one was a gun dealer's. Maybe I was moving up in the world. Maybe not.

I rang the bell. There were footsteps. The door opened and a young woman stood there. She was tall and dark-eyed, wearing a simple, pale yellow dress that reached her ankles. Her nametag identified her as Vikki Rodman. She looked slightly familiar. Probably an actress I'd seen at an audition. They flocked to these places. "May I help you?" she said.

"Guy I know's been coming here, and it sounds like something I could use. So I'm here to check it out."

A lovely and, as far as I could tell, sincere smile. "You want the orientation center. That's in the building on the playing field."

I frowned and shook my head. "I want to meet the head man."

"Sir, Mr. Sunemori is a very busy man. You'll have an opportunity to meet him—"

"Forget it then. See, I thought you guys could help me. But I see I'm just gonna get the same old runaround I got at Scientology. They wouldn't let me see that Hubbard guy either. Waste of my time." I turned and stormed back down the walkway.

She came running after me. "Sir, I'm sorry. I didn't know you were so in need. Of course you may see Mr. Sunemori. Please." She took my arm, turned me around, led me inside. Mission-style furniture, lots of stained wood, exposed beams on the ceiling. Thick rugs on a terra cotta tile floor. Above the fireplace was a painting of an aged wispy-haired Asian man seated at a window, gazing out at a verdant landscape.

"Mr. Sunemori is on a call to Nepal," she said. "So it will be a few minutes."

"I can stand that."

"Have a seat, please. Would you like some tea while you wait?"

"Yeah, okay." I fell into a leather chair. As soon as she was gone I jumped up and checked out the nearest bookcase. Aristotle, Sartre, Dale Carnegie, Billy Graham. The Torah, the Koran, the Book of Mormon. The books were spotless, the rich old shelves without a mote of dust.

There was a shrine on a nearby table, similar to the one at Trixie's, much bigger. The multi-armed goddess was bronze, the cornmeal bowl silver, the frog and duck both wooden and exquisitely carved.

A quick check of the rest of the bookcases gave up more philosophy and religion, some psychology, and two shelves worth of L. Ron Hubbards in matching gilt and leather bindings. Probably Sunemori's role model.

A set of French doors led to a big back yard. I tried one, found it unlocked, let myself out. The yard was filled with cacti and the like. A couple of gigantic prickly pears. A year or two before I would have been able to tell you the species. Now it was lost among the other detritus filling my head. There were several big cereus, still bearing the previous summer's fruits. Four or five mature agaves. Lots of smaller plants too, in the ground and in pots scattered everywhere, on the concrete and on benches and hanging. There was a rose garden too, a dozen or so plants, some still in bloom.

The showpiece was the biggest saguaro I'd ever seen. As tall as the house, with a couple of arms giving it the characteristic shape you see in every Western, whether or not it takes place in Arizona.

I heard someone behind me and turned. Ike Sunemori. I recognized him from the brochure. He was wearing a robe of the same color as Vikki's dress and an infuriating self-congratulatory smile. He carried a delicate tray with a metal teapot like those at Donna Lennox's store and two tiny earthenware cups.

"It's been here for eighty years," he said.

"Blooming?"

"Of course. You know saguaros?"

"Yes. As it happens, I have a cactus collection."

"Ah. One of those. Come. Over here."

He walked to a heavy wood table with appropriately massive chairs. When we were seated he poured tea. Something green. I picked up my cup and sniffed.

"A simple sencha," he said.

I drank a little. It was too much like vegetable broth for my taste. He sipped his own. I wanted him to speak next. I wanted to have him start his little game on me. Start enticing me in.

He waited until we'd each finished one cup and he'd poured us refills. "So. Tell me what you need."

"Like I told the young lady, I have a friend who—"

He was waving me off. "Please. Mr. Portugal. There's no need for the facade."

"What are you—" I shut my mouth. He knew my name. I wasn't likely to fool him about anything else. "How?"

"I've kept close tabs on Dennis Lennox's murder. I know all the players. I know you like to imagine yourself a detective. Do you like the tea?"

"I prefer black."

His nodded. His expression implied those who preferred black tea were savages. But noble savages.

I said, "Why the interest in Dennis's death?"

"As you know, he was here shortly before he died. There are those who would take any opportunity to tear down what I've built here. Bad publicity would provide them fodder."

"As I know?"

"Why else would you be here? I suppose you spoke to Miss Trenton. A nice girl."

"For a porn star."

He shook his head. "That comment wasn't worthy of you."

"How do you know what's worthy of me and what isn't?"

"That comment wasn't worthy of anyone."

I didn't say anything. When I thought about it, the son of a bitch was right.

He said, "You want to know about Dennis's visit."

"Yes. Trixie told me that he used it to scope out women."

"His first visit."

"He came back?"

"I invited him back."

"Willing to take his money."

"Mr. Portugal, we have two choices. We can argue the merits of what I'm doing here, and waste a lot of your time and mine, or I can simply tell you what happened. Which will it be?"

I didn't dislike this guy as much as I expected to. He did have a certain charm. And I appreciated his cut-the-crap attitude. "The second," I said.

"Good. So. What did Trixie tell you?"

I filled him in.

"That's a fair picture," he said. "I saw right away what he was up to. It's not the first time some Casanova has viewed Ambiance as a fertile hunting ground. So I took him aside and said it simply wouldn't be tolerated."

"To which he said?"

"He denied it, of course. They always do. I let that pass. He said he'd like to return."

"And he did."

"It was on a Sunday night, about a week later...two days before he died."

"That explains something."

"Oh?"

"He got rid of both Trixie and Samantha—you know who she is?" He nodded. "He dumped them both the Saturday before he died. Clearing the way. So what happened Sunday night?"

"Sunday is one of the days when people are most in need of what Ambiance provides. It prepares them for the long work week. Sundays are very crowded. We have our main session in the auditorium, which I myself lead, and other sessions going on in other rooms, other buildings."

"Excuse me, and I'm not arguing merits here, but I really don't understand what goes on at these sessions."

A beneficent smile. "You're welcome to experience one."

"Some other time."

"Of course. Suffice it to say, there is some meditation, some chanting, some sharing, some exercises."

"No biofeedback?" I grimaced. "Sorry."

Still smiling, he shook his head. "Dennis chose to sit in on our main session. I suppose he felt that provided the most women for him to pursue." He poured himself more tea. "Sometimes someone appears whom I develop a particular interest in. Dennis was one such."

"This had nothing to do with him being disgustingly well-off."

"You can't stop yourself, can you?"

"I guess not. Go on, please."

"Sometimes I develop a feeling about a person. I watched Dennis during the session. We keep the lights dim, but not so dim that I couldn't keep an eye on him. And something happened to him. It was toward the end. We were meditating. I felt the energy shift."

He waited for my snide comment. I disappointed him. If I was willing to consider alternate realities, what was a little energy shift?

"It happens occasionally. I can't take credit for it, and I don't know what it is. But I knew, when I left the stage, that Dennis was about to make a big change in his life."

"Did you speak to him afterward?"

"He sought me out. He said that during the meditation he went somewhere and when he came back he was different. I know how mystic that sounds and I don't pretend to know what it means, but I know it happens. People have breakthroughs in different ways. Some in therapy, some in near-death experiences. Some, I believe, here."

"What did he say?"

"The details don't matter. Just know that I spent two hours with him, and when he left here that night he was a changed man."

"Mr. Sunemori. I've learned a lot about Dennis Lennox over the last month. He was a total ass. He had no regard for anyone other than himself, with the possible exceptions of his father and his housekeeper. It wouldn't be below him to give you a total snow job to give himself access to all the women up here."

"Understood. But that's not what happened. I have a doctorate in psychology and one in theology. I may not always be able to see through a single lie, but I can tell if someone is spending two hours giving me a snow job. This was not a snow job."

"He changed. Just like that, he changed."

"You don't have to believe me. It might make things easier if you do. Perhaps this will help you see. He mentioned you by name. And what he'd done to you."

"Oh?"

"How he propositioned the young woman you've mentored, and how he decided to punish her for rejecting him by letting her go from his television program, and how he maneuvered you into a position where you would take the blame for her losing her job."

Who knew about that? Me, Gina, Ronnie. Eric Stahl. Probably Theta. Could Sunemori have found out about it from any of us? It didn't seem likely. And if he had, why bother lying to me? Simply to make his operation look better? It didn't wash. "This would explain why—"

"Why he gathered that particular group of people at his house the night he was killed—merely two nights later? Yes. It would. Unfortunately, between the time he called you all and the time he was going to meet you, the killer struck."

I wasn't convinced that Dennis had had a life-changing experience at Ambiance. But was it possible? Sure it was. "Do the police know about this?"

"The police have been here. I told them much the same story. They seemed not to believe it." He stood. "Now, I have duties to attend to. Ms. Rodman will show you out. I hope I have been of help."

"You have. I appreciate it."

He nodded. He bowed. He left. In a few seconds Vikki Rodman reappeared. I still thought I'd seen her somewhere before. I told her so. She said, yes, she was an actress. But she wasn't putting a lot of effort into her career. She was donating her time to Ambiance. It was a much better use of her energy, she said. I told her I was glad she was happy and walked away.

thirty-five

I put on my nice-dad audition outfit and sat in the living room while Gina decided what to wear. She came out wearing a slinky green dress I hadn't seen in years. I got up and came close. She'd put on a new scent. It was like orange blossoms smoldering. We nearly didn't make it out of the house.

But I had a job to do. It was a tough job, but someone had to do it, and from all indications the police weren't very interested. So we extracted ourselves, she touched up her lipstick, and we went out to her Volvo.

We parked a couple of blocks from the gallery and got out of the car. She smoothed her dress. "How do I look?" she said.

"Didn't I make that perfectly clear back there?"

"A girl can't hear it too many times."

"You look like heaven. I'll be the envy of every man there."

"Sly devil," she said, and took my arm.

We went a few steps. I stopped and swung her around to face me. "Are we all right?"

"As all right as we're ever going to be."

"What's that mean?"

"Can't this wait?"

"No."

"You pick the strangest times—"

"Just tell me."

She looked over at the traffic on Washington, back to me. "I've realized something."

"Uh-oh."

"Shut up, idiot. It's not a bad thing. Not unless you want it to be."

"What have you realized?"

"That this thing we have—this relationship, this marriage—is never going to be one of those exploding fireworks kind of things. And don't make a stupid joke about what happens in bed."

"I wasn't—"

"You were." She grabbed my arm, pulled me out of the way of pedestrian traffic. "What we have is a case of an old married couple who got to be totally comfortable with each other long before they became romantically involved. I mean, not counting that fling we had however many years ago."

"Twenty-two."

"You keep track?"

"I just know."

She nodded. "You also know how much I put on a big show of being a cynic about romance. How I didn't want a fancy wedding and all that. How I used to make fun of my cousins when they got all girly about the guys they were seeing. But deep down, some part of me wanted that. I wanted to meet the man—or woman—of my dreams and feel fireworks in my heart and get sweaty palms and all that."

"I don't give you sweaty palms?"

"Not very often. Shut up and let me finish."

"Sorry."

"So after we were married a few months, I started to feel cheated. Here I was, nearly fifty, finally married, and nothing had really changed from the last few years. More than a few. Since we starting hanging out together, and please don't tell me the year. Except a few years ago we started having sex, and then I moved in with you, and we got married, and it was all kind of ho-hum, because you were still good old Joe."

"I had no idea you were unhappy."

"I wasn't unhappy. I was unsettled. So then there I was, with this vague dissatisfaction, and I found out about what happened or didn't happen with Ronnie—and given the circumstances, it doesn't really matter if it did or not—but what did matter was, you hadn't felt secure enough to tell me. And when you've seen a guy almost every day for years and he's told you everything and now you have what's supposed to be the ultimate relationship and he starts hiding stuff... and when this coincides with you coming to grips with the fact that, okay, this is how the knight in shining armor happened to you, girl, get used to it... and when you're realizing that menopause is on the way—"

"What?"

"—you get upset. You maybe say things that are the farthest from the truth you could ever imagine. So I made that dumb comment about wondering if maybe we shouldn't be married. Of course we should be married. What we have is what we were meant to have. Especially now that you're not sitting on your ass letting life go by anymore."

She stood on her toes, kissed me, kept looking into my eyes.

"Your whole manner's different," she said. "I haven't seen you like this since way back—twenty-two years back—when you were running the Altair. I mean, I can't say I'm one hundred percent convinced I want my husband to spend the rest of his life tracking down evildoers, not after how much death we've been exposed to even from your half-assed mucking around, but I'll just have to get used to it, won't I? Now let's get going. All the horse's ovaries are going to be gone."

"Speaking of ovaries... what was that about menopause?"

"It's coming, babe. Now let's go party down."

There was a lot of black outside Gallery Gaga. Black shirts, black pants, black dresses and skirts and scarves. A couple of dozen trendoids stood around with plastic champagne glasses full of sparkly liquid. Plus professorial types with full beards and corduroy jackets, women with sculptured coifs, a couple wearing matching maroon jumpsuits with coordinated berets. The room was too hip for me, and I wasn't even in it yet.

We squeezed our way through and inside. The moment we'd cleared the entrance a photographer said, "Stop right there," and blinded us with his flash. We stood there while the effects wore off. Someone said, "Excuse me, coming through," slipped by me, stopped. "You came."

"I—"

Samantha grabbed my arm and pulled me away from the doorway. I was holding Gina's hand, so she got dragged along. "You're in the way," Samantha said.

"Old and in the way, that's us."

"Funny man. Is he this funny at home? I'm assuming you're his wife. Gina, was it? If you're not her, I'm in trouble. I'm Samantha Szydlo. I'm why you're here, aren't you? Or do you know another artist? Joe said you were in design, maybe you do know another artist."

"Amphetamines?" Gina said.

"Huh? Oh, because I'm talking so fast? No, there's just so much going on. A mile a minute. I'm glad you came. Huh?" A woman in a red and white polka dot miniskirt was whispering in her ear. "Really?" The woman nodded. "I've got to go. One of my so-called patrons wants to buy one of my pieces." She followed Polka Dottie around a pillar toward the back.

"That was Samantha," I said.

"So she said," Gina said.

"I don't think she does drugs anymore."

"Neither do I, but I might need some soon. Let's get something to eat."

We barged our way to a long buffet table. Some scattered vegetables, a few pulpy strawberries, a basket of tortilla chips that someone had spilled a soda on. Also several empty trays. "You were right about the horse's ovaries," I said.

"We'll eat after. I'm going to go get some drinks. You start detecting." She slipped off. I watched her go. So did several other men. With all the young babes, with all the money that had been spent on beauty, she was still the most gorgeous woman in the room. My humble opinion.

"That your wife?"

I turned. It was Carrie. She done something swirly with her hair and wore a dress cut low in front and looked nearly her age.

"Uh-huh," I said.

"She's beautiful."

"Thanks. I think so too. Mike here?"

"Uh-uh. He's home watching TV."

"Doesn't like this kind of thing."

"Nope."

"Speaking of being home watching TV…"

She was nodding. "He told me he let it slip."

"Samantha asked you to cover for her."

"Yes."

"What was she really up to?"

"No idea."

"Aren't you curious?"

"Samantha's a good roommate and a great friend."

"That's a funny answer."

"I let her have her secrets. That's all I meant."

Gina was coming our way. She saw me detecting and detoured. "What about you?" I said. "Any deep dark secrets?"

"You don't like me, do you?"

"Where'd you get that idea?"

"Because you think I'm too young for Mike, and because you think I shouldn't be trying to fill the space in his heart Donna left."

"Second one first. How Mike chooses to fill holes in his heart is up to him. If you guys are happy, what difference does it make to me?"

"What about the other?"

"The age thing? It's just a little weird, that's all. Hey, if I hadn't gotten together with Gina, I might be hanging out with a young babe like you too."

"Then you don't dislike me?"

"I don't dislike you. If I had a daughter, I'd want her to be just like you. Though maybe I'd want her to cover her chest a little better."

She grimaced and placed a hand in a strategic position. "That's why I never wear this dress."

"Wear it for Mike," I said. "He'll like it. I'm going to look around, okay?"

I left her standing there and tracked Gina down. She was staring at one of the abstracts I'd seen the first time I was at the gallery. "What do you think of this?" she said.

"It has a certain insouciance, with aftertones of oak and peach."

"You hate it."

"I don't think it would look good over the fireplace, if that's what you're thinking. Assuming the fireplace ever gets built."

"Who was that?"

"Carrie. Mike's girlfriend."

"What'd you find out?"

"That I'm going to have to pin Samantha down. What'd you get us?"

"Cheap champagne. Here."

I took the flimsy glass, held it up, watched the bubbles. Then I tossed it down.

"*Très gauche*," Gina said. "You're supposed to sip it."

"I needed fortification. I'm going to track her down."

"I'll be around here. I've got a couple of clients who like this kind of crap."

I grabbed another glass of champagne from a passing tray and wandered toward the back. There were six or seven people checking out Samantha's work. One was a short, amazingly fat man wearing a caftan. He saw me. His eyes lit with recognition. "It takes a bug …" he said.

"To catch a bug."

"I *love* those ads."

He was some indeterminate blend of black and white and maybe a couple of other shades. His brown hair was cut short except for one thin braid that grew from the center of his hairline and was pulled back over his shoulder. He had a soul patch and eyeglasses with mother-of-pearl frames. Behind them one eye was green and the other blue.

I introduced myself and he did the same. I didn't catch his name and I didn't care. I said, "You like her work?"

"It's excellent," he said. "Simply excellent."

"Reminds me of Hopper," I said.

"Really? I don't see that at all."

"Samantha told me he's an influence."

"Really?" He inspected the nearest painting, the penny-pitching one. "Yes, yes, I see it now. The use of light and shadow."

"Of course."

"You know her, then?"

"I've made her acquaintance several times."

"I've only met her briefly," he said, smiling. "Through a relative."

"What's so funny?"

"Oh, nothing."

"Come, tell me. We art aficionados shouldn't have any secrets."

"Oh, all right." He came closer. He smelled of chocolate. "See that man over there?"

I followed his eyes. They led to someone tall, dark, and if-I-were-a-woman-I'd-fuck-him handsome. "I see him."

"My nephew Emilio. Not really much for art, but likes openings, if you know what I mean."

"I don't think I do."

"The women, my boy, the women. Just look around. There are dozens of beautiful women here. If I weren't so damned fat I'd be after them myself. The one in the green, for instance. What I wouldn't give for a night in the sack with her."

"That's my wife."

"Oh. *Oh*." A giggle. "No offense intended, I'm sure."

"I'm sure. Come on, this sounds juicy."

"It is, it is. Emilio met Samantha at an opening some weeks ago. They went back to his place and, you know …"

"Did the deed," I said.

"Yes. They did the deed." He came closer, looked around furtively. Now I smelled coconut on top of the chocolate. "She was awfully good in bed, Emilio told me. So he went out with her a few more times. Then he grew tired of her. You know, Emilio has so many women throwing themselves at him. He met someone else. Samantha's turn was over." He came even closer. His face was within inches of mine. Now there was almond in the mix. He was the world's biggest Almond Joy. "The poor girl, she didn't take it very well. She's a fine artist, but upstairs …" He tapped his forehead. "A little cuckoo."

"What makes you say that?"

"This won't go any further, will it?"

"I swear on my mother's grave—" Sorry, Mom. "I'll keep the secret as well as you did."

"Well … the poor girl … she started stalking him."

"She didn't."

"He spotted her twice. He had to call her and tell her to stop."

"And did she?"

"He thought she had—he didn't see her for weeks—and then he caught her one more time. By that time he was tired of the new one too. He met someone at a cocktail party, and they left together. Poor Samantha was at the party too."

"Poor Samantha."

"He could tell she was upset, but, after all, what was he supposed to do? And it had been several weeks."

"So what happened?"

"They went back to his place, and were, uh..."

"Doing the deed," I said.

He smiled. I wanted to smack him one. But after he finished the story. "Yes. They were doing the deed, and Emilio heard a phone go off right outside his bedroom window. So he pulled out and ran over to look. And there she was."

"Samantha."

"Yes," he said. "She was watching the whole thing. Which, if one stops to think about it, has a certain kinky attraction, doesn't it? Where are you going?"

thirty-six

Emilio stood surrounded by a bevy of female admirers. "I need to see you a minute," I said.

"Do I know you?" He had an accent. It was thin, vague, and fake.

"You're about to. Ladies, would you excuse me?"

"Mister, who do—"

I dropped my voice. "LAPD. You want to do this the easy way or the hard way?"

Impersonating a cop always does the trick. "Ladies," he said. "Will you excuse me?"

They sauntered off. I maneuvered into a spot far enough from anyone else for privacy. "Nothing to worry about, Mister… Emilio. Need to ask you a couple of questions for an investigation I'm running."

He was, I thought, beginning to realize I ought to have shown him a badge or something. "Yes?"

"Just two, really. I understand you found Samantha Szydlo spying on your sexual activities a few weeks ago."

"Really, this is none of anybody's—"

"Just routine, sir. First question, what was she wearing?"

All trace of the accent was gone. "How the hell am I supposed to—"

"Think, man. People's lives depend on it."

"Oh, all right." His face scrunched up. "It was that red number she had. Nice and short. It had some kind of shiny stuff on it."

"Excellent. You're doing a fine job. Last question. Do you remember what night this was?"

"Oh, yeah. That one I remember right off. Lot of excitement, that night. First Samantha spying on me, and then a guy I knew got killed."

"A guy you knew?"

"Just a little. Used to run into him at clubs sometimes. We went out with a couple of the same girls."

"Was this Dennis Lennox?"

"Yeah, that's him. Hey, you got a badge or something you can show me?"

I looked at him. Then behind me. If he took a swing, I'd be able to step back out of the way. "No, dumbass, I don't have a badge. I don't need no steenkin' badge." I stepped over to where the clutch of women Emilio had been with was watching our encounter. "Little word of advice, ladies. You ever hear of Lidovec?"

One of them perked right up. "I saw an ad the other day. That's for herpes, isn't it?"

"Ewww," said one of the others.

"Right on," I said. And I directed a meaningful look at Emilio, who was standing there like the big dumb dope he was.

It took a couple of seconds. But this time, when the "ewww" came, it came from all of them.

I wasn't able to get a minute alone with Samantha, and eventually Gina and I walked down the block and had a drink and some snacks at an Irish bar. When we came back an hour and a half later most of the crowd was gone. A dozen people were left, mostly clustered near the walls, looking at paintings, trying to make decisions.

Gina went to talk to one of the other artists about the piece she thought her client might like, leaving me alone to corral Samantha. When she saw me her mouth smiled and her eyes didn't. She invited me into the back room, sat on a shiny green vinyl couch. I leaned against a desk.

"I saw you talking to Emilio," she said. "And that slimy uncle of his."

I didn't say anything.

"How much did you find out?"

"Everything."

She fingered the slick surface of the couch. "I sold four pieces tonight."

"Congratulations."

"Things are looking up, career-wise."

"But not personal-wise."

"I thought I was over all that."

"Guess not."

"I just ... I don't know. I didn't even like Emilio. He was just a good fuck."

"He said the same thing about you. At least, his uncle told me he did."

She forced out a laugh. "It was Dennis's fault, you know. I was still feeling crappy because he dumped me. I mean, I hadn't even thought about Emilio since I met Dennis, but then when I saw him again at the party I got all jealous. He left with that woman, and it was like someone else was controlling me. I was so embarrassed when he caught me."

"There's a good side to everything."

"And the good side to this would be?"

"Now you have a real alibi to replace your phony one."

"Oh. That." She rubbed her finger on the vinyl again. "Carrie gave me up?"

"No. Mike did."

She frowned. "I should've known he couldn't keep a secret."

"What did Carrie do, take notes on what she was watching with him and fill you in?"

"More or less. Plus I taped *Frasier*. I really like David Hyde Pierce, can you believe that?"

"So you were at that party, then you were lurking at Emilio's. Then, I suppose, you drove right up to Dennis's. Because I'm guessing when your cell went off outside Emilio's window, that was Dennis, telling you he wanted to make all better."

A hoarse laugh. "Once I ran far enough away from Emilio's to answer the fucking phone, yeah, that's who it was."

"So it sounds to me like your time is covered. Which lets you off the hook."

"Sounds like." We stared at each other. "So what happens now?"

"What should happen?"

"I don't know. You tell everyone I'm a whack job."

"Why would I do that?"

"A lot of people would."

"I'm not a lot of people. And given that the cops seem to have accepted your original story, there's not any point to telling anyone, is there?"

"I guess not."

"You need to get help, though."

"Please. I've had help. I've had so fucking much help." She giggled. It wasn't the laugh of a crazy person.

"Get some more," I said. "Most therapists suck. Find the right one."

"How?"

"I don't know. I don't have any answers for you. I don't even have any answers for myself." I pushed off from the table. "Congratulations, by the way. On your sales."

"Thanks," she said. "I owe you one."

"Yeah," I said. "You do."

The worms were back that night, the giant ones that started out as guitar frets. After they'd taken over the world, they pulled ping-pong balls from a bin, and each ping-pong ball represented a birthday. It was like the draft lottery back during Vietnam, only this time the numbers were the order everyone was going to get eaten by the worms. There was a resistance movement, and Ronnie was in it, and one of the things they did was give people a drink that would make them taste bad to the worms. In my dream, she dipped a Flintstones glass into a swimming pool full of liquid that glowed green like the radium in a watch. She offered the glass to me, but I kept shaking my head, saying what was the point, because by the time the worms realized you tasted bad, they'd already have eaten you. Then someone else told me to drink it. It may have been Mike or Dennis or a dream-state combination of the two. I reached out to take the drink and a siren went off.

But it wasn't a siren, it was the telephone, and it was back in the real world. Still half-believing giant worms were in control, I squinted at the clock. Nine thirty-something. The shower was going and, in it, Gina was singing "Livin' La Vida Loca."

I tracked down the phone. It was Claudia Acuna. Ten minutes later I was on my way to Lawndale.

•

A lot of small cities in Los Angeles County don't have their own police forces and are served by the county Sheriff's Department. Lawndale's one of them. When I got there three Sheriff's patrol cars were parked in front of the McKay house. There were also four vehicles from local television stations, a fire engine, and a truck from Termites R Us.

The house across the street was still swathed in a yellow-and-blue rubbery tent. Cops and technicians and exterminators swarmed around it. Reporters clamored for access. Neighbors looked on avidly.

I spotted Linda Madera, Claudia's replacement, standing by the Channel 6 van. I walked over and asked if she'd seen Claudia around.

"She doesn't work for the station anymore," she said.

"That's not what I asked."

"Then why would she be here? Has she signed with KTLA?"

I turned away and spotted Claudia, a house or two down, talking to a man in a sport jacket and turtleneck. I walked over. She made introductions. His name was Fred Johnson. He was a detective with the LAPD. He had no jurisdiction in Lawndale, but had been sent down to check things out once the victim's name was known.

Johnson was my age or a little less, a light-skinned African-American, rail-thin. His head was shaved. We shook hands and the three of us went a little farther down the block. I had a hunch, turned, and sure enough Linda Madera was watching us. She looked like someone had stolen her Easter eggs.

As soon as we were out of anyone else's earshot, Claudia said, "A neighbor kid saw what happened."

"Which was?"

"The young man's a hero," Johnson said. "A little boy lives over there—" He gestured at the white-picket-fenced house across the street from us, two down from the tented place. "He's three years old. His mother goes to take a phone call, kid gets out, walks right down the street, right for the tent. Son of a bitches screwed up, there's a little spot just big enough for a three-year-old to get in. McKay was in his kitchen across the street, sees the kid, sees the spot, runs across and after him. Never came out again."

"The kid?"

"Never even went in. He'd gone around back or something while McKay was getting to his front door. He's fine."

I took in the trucks, the cops, the bedlam. I turned back to Claudia.

She read my expression perfectly. "I had the same thought. He's feeling guilty about killing Dennis, thinks he can make amends. I don't buy it. I think Detective Johnson is right. He's a hero."

"Be more of a hero," I said, "if he'd actually saved the kid."

That got me a matching pair of glares.

"Sorry," I said. "Just thinking too logically."

"My former colleagues will spin the hero version." Claudia said. "And as far as I'm concerned, let them. Too much bad news lately. We need a hero or two."

I took a couple of steps away, thought a bit, came back. "His father?"

"Sedated," Johnson said. "He took it—"

"Pretty hard. I know the routine."

Johnson eyed me, turned to Claudia, said, "I've got to consult with my colleagues from the Sheriff's Department. If there's nothing else ..."

There wasn't, and he took his leave. I asked Claudia how she found out what was going on.

"Fred called me," she said. "He owed me one."

Of course he did. "Why'd you come? Being retired and all."

"I don't know. I guess I missed it a little. The excitement."

"How'd New York go?"

"It's not going to work out."

"Sorry." I looked into her eyes. Realized whatever fleeting attraction we'd felt before was gone. We'd both been at emotional odds, both dealing with life-changing events, both vulnerable. Hormones took over. In the overall scheme of things, it didn't amount to a hill of beans.

"Look at her," she said.

"Who?"

"Linda. She hasn't a clue."

"The teeming masses won't mind."

"I suppose not. You getting anywhere?"

"I've solved the crime."

"Oh?"

I flicked a hand at Sean McKay's house. "With him dead, I've eliminated all of my suspects. Therefore, no one killed Dennis."

"Wow. You're really good."

"The best."

"Look, I have to go. You be careful, okay?" A perfunctory hug, and she was off to her car. I hung around a little longer. I watched Linda Madera do her standup. All things considered, she wasn't half bad.

Ronnie's car was in the driveway when I got home. I hadn't talked to her since my lunch with Eric. I hadn't decided what to do about him yet. Partly, I was waiting to see if he would do the right thing and tell Ronnie what had happened.

With two days gone by, he'd had time enough for that. I went over and rang the doorbell. We sat on the front porch and made small talk. It was quickly clear that she'd seen Eric since I had, and that he hadn't confessed.

So I did it for him.

thirty-seven

"I don't believe it," Ronnie said. She was angry more than hurt. Still, I could see a piece of armor fall into place.

"Understandable."

"*He* drugged us. Not Dennis."

"He drugged you. Then you drugged me."

"My Coke."

I nodded. "Eric gave you the mickey in it, then you shared it with me when I said my throat hurt. There was enough in there to knock us both silly." Maybe there was. But I was already so badly wrecked that I hadn't even remembered getting the Coke. It may not have taken much to render me senseless.

"Let's call the police," she said.

"My first impulse too."

"So what are we waiting for?"

"We're not going to be able to prove anything, at least not without a long, stupid trial."

"I can deal with that."

I said nothing.

"There's something else," she said. "Isn't there?"

"Yes."

"The kids."

"Uh-huh."

"Don't you think a man who did what he did might not be fit to raise them?"

"The thought did pass through my head."

"And?"

"Have you met them?"

"Yes."

"And?"

"Ten minutes ago, I would have said there was no chance in the world he would ever do anything that would hurt them. Now, I'm not so sure."

"Aren't you?"

She gave it some thought. "Know what? No matter what he did to me, I still can't believe he'd hurt the boys."

"But we would, if we made what we know public."

"So now what?"

"I have another idea."

"Like what?"

"I'll tell you if I decide to do it."

She looked me over, realized I meant it, got up and leaned against the railing. "If Eric drugged me, how come Dennis said on the phone he was going to talk to us about what he did at the party?"

"Dennis did do something to us at the party. I'm guessing he came along before Eric had a chance to spirit you off somewhere, and he saw what was going on. Maybe he threatened to expose Eric. Made him leave. Whatever. Then he undressed us and dumped us in bed together."

"But why that? I mean, he could have done all sorts of things to us. Why make it look like we'd slept together?"

"I've been trying to figure that out too. I've only been able to come up with one thing. I told him I was your father figure."

"I don't get it."

"Earlier that night, I ran into him, and we were talking about you, and I just said it. I was loaded already. Dennis had issues with women. I think he had some unresolved feelings about his mother." I didn't know where that last part came from, but it seemed to help my argument. "So he thought, let's see what happens if she wakes up with—"

"Why did you tell him that? That father figure thing."

"I told you, I was loaded."

"It must have come from somewhere."

"It came from ... hell, Ronnie, I do have paternal feelings about you. You must know that."

"I don't get it."

"Last year, when Aricela was around, Gina suddenly got all these motherly instincts she never had before. Biological clock stuff."

"What's that got to do with you and me?"

"Something she said one day. That she didn't want to deal with diapers and all that, but that it might be nice to have a grown child. I picked that up from her. And then when I started giving you advice—"

"I said I wanted to be your protégé."

"I remember. But somehow it transformed into this sur-rogate daughter thing. Like you were the child I never had."

I looked up at her. She turned away. "My father's dead."

"I know."

"I don't need another one."

"I just thought ... I don't know what I thought."

"You're a good friend. And you'll always be my first one out here in California, and that'll always be special. But that's it."

I looked out at the street and nodded.

"I don't ever want to hear this kind of thing again."

I nodded again.

"It makes me very uncomfortable."

I didn't even manage a nod. Without another word, she went inside.

Gina was plodding through *Cold Mountain*. I read the same paragraph in the *Times* Calendar section over and over. Something to do with an opera at the Disney Hall. It didn't make sense. The Disney was supposed to be for the Philharmonic. Opera was at the Dorothy Chandler.

I gave up and turned out my light. Gina did the same. We lay there. Then we did it some more. We'd eaten a whole pizza between us. A medium, but still. The cheese roadblocked my gut. The salt raced around my head, toting thoughts behind it. One kept coming back. The gist was, maybe if I hadn't visited Sean McKay he'd be alive. If I hadn't gone over there, his actions over the next two days would have been a tiny bit different, and he wouldn't have been in the kitchen just in time to see the little boy by the termite tent, and he'd be alive. Then there was the roundabout version. When I parked the truck a piece of paper got stuck under the tire, and if I hadn't come that piece of paper would have blown into the kid's yard, and instead of wandering away his attention was drawn to it, because there was a picture of a doggie on it, and he stayed in the yard.

Again, with the alternate universes, I heard my father say, the way you hear voices when you're teetering on the edge of sleep. It jarred me wide awake.

I looked over at Gina. Only an ounce of light seeped in through the windows, but it was enough to tell me she was in dreamland. I leaned over to kiss her cheek, feared it would awaken her, slipped out of bed instead.

I padded into the living room, flipped the TV on. The same people who'd been selling penis enhancement were hawking something called the Bosom Builder. The woman who'd told us size did matter in the other ad was recounting her miraculous sprouting from a 34B to a 36C, "almost a D." I clicked her away.

I wound my way through the channels, stopping briefly on a Korean soap opera here and a *Gilligan's Island* rerun there, and eventually found what I was looking for. I settled in on the sofa, lying on my side with my head on a cushion.

I was back where I started. With the Dennis Lennox murder, and with James Bond movies. But this time *Dr. No* was just beginning. I could catch up on the part I didn't see however long ago. Then there'd be Ursula Andress again.

A couple of people got killed in Jamaica. Bond was dispatched to find out what was going on. He went home to pack. He opened the door. He switched on the light. He heard a noise. He flipped the light off again.

A simple gesture. One everyone does a dozen times a day.

I muted the TV. I sat up. I thought it all through, and it continued to make sense. I got up and went to the bathroom, and when I came back it still made sense.

Poor Miss Moneypenny. Never did get in the sack with James, and finally she was too long in the tooth and they traded her in for a newer model. The new actress: Samantha Bond. Quite a coincidence, that last name. Maybe she'd changed it. After all, actors often did just that to advance their careers.

I switched the sound back on and resumed the position. Soon Gina wandered in. She sat on the couch, then nestled spoon-like in front of me. I wrapped my arm around her and she took my hand in her own. We lay there quietly until the commercial.

"You figured something out," she said.

"Yeah," I said. "I did."

"Want to tell me?"

I did.

"Makes sense to me," she said.

"You think?"

"I think." She disengaged our limbs and sat up. "Come back to bed sometime."

The flashing light from the television illuminated her exit. The T-shirt she was sleeping in was shorter than most. It barely covered her behind.

The movie was back on. I knew what was going to happen. I turned off the TV and followed Gina into the bedroom.

thirty-eight

Late Saturday morning I rang the doorbell at Ike Sunemori's house. The young woman who answered wasn't Vikki Rodman. She had a badge, but I didn't bother looking at it. "Mr. Portugal," she said. "Mr. Sunemori's not here."

"Does the whole staff know me on sight?"

"Pretty much."

"Actually, I didn't come to see him. I came to see Vikki. Is she here?"

She was. The other woman led me through the house, opened one of the French doors, closed it when I'd passed through.

Vikki was pruning roses. It was a little early in the season for that, but L.A.'s climate lets you get away with a lot.

She was sucking on the side of her hand when I walked up. She saw me and winced. "I stuck myself."

"I figured."

"I was so proud of myself because I'd been doing this for an hour and hadn't gotten thorned. Then I let my attention wander and gave myself an owie."

"Let me see."

I took her soft young hand in mine, inspected the tiny wound. There was a bit of skin pulled away. The moist layer underneath showed. A bit of blood rimmed the edge of the damaged area, but she'd sucked most of it up already.

I gave her hand back. "You'll be fine," I said. "Put some Neosporin on when you get back inside."

"I will." The way she looked at me made me wonder. Did she know I knew everything? Or did she just know I'd figured something out?

"Tell me," I said. "Did you decide to change your name as soon as you became an actress, or did you try Rodriguez for a while first?"

She smiled, took another taste of the side of her hand, picked up the pruning shears she must have dropped when she poked herself. "I never intended changing it at all. But when I got my SAG card, there was already a Valerie Rodriguez. So I changed it. It didn't seem like such a big deal. Anyway, my agent said I'd get more work if I anglicized my name."

"Why not Valerie Rodman?"

"My agent suggested Vikki. Said it worked for Vikki Carr."

I already knew everything there was to know about her agent. He sat in a tiny office in North Hollywood, living off one leftover star from the fifties, and thrilling dozens of hopefuls who couldn't believe their luck at getting an agent with such a history. He was a relic of the glory days of Hollywood, unable to understand that things were different now. Unable to get his clients any work.

Valerie/Vikki snipped off a cane, looked it over, cut it again a couple of buds down. "My father was furious."

"I'll bet."

"But he got over it."

"They do that. Fathers." The expert speaking. I had such good luck with fatherhood, even the surrogate variety.

Another cane bit the dust. She stuck the pruner in a leather sheath hanging off the waistline of her jeans, began gathering up what she'd removed and putting it in a waste bin.

"You should be wearing gloves," I said.

"Living dangerously, I guess."

"Is that what you were doing when you went out with Dennis Lennox?"

"Do you know if we got married and he took my name, he'd be Dennis Rodman?"

"He's dead. He's not marrying anybody."

"Don't tell me you think I killed him."

"I won't, because I don't. But I think you know who did. Or at least suspect."

She watched me, expressionless. "What you said, a minute ago. About Dennis. He did change, you know. Ike told me."

"How'd you get mixed up with him? Dennis. Not Ike."

"I ran into him at the studio. I was on an audition."

"When?"

"Beginning of October. I passed him in the hall. He didn't recognize me. Just gave me the once-over."

"Why would he recognize you?"

"I've known him a long time. Not well, but enough so he would have recognized me before. But I'd changed. A lot of people kept saying I'd get more work if only this, or if only that, so I changed a few things."

Her seeming familiar to me ... it wasn't from auditions. It was because I'd seen the *before*. In the photograph John Santini had given me.

"What did you change?" I said.

"I had a receding chin. We built that up some. And took a little off my nose. And once I had the work done, I redid the hair, makeup, the works. I look a lot better now."

"You getting more work?"

"No."

"Did you really expect to?"

"It was worth a shot."

"Okay," I said. "So Dennis sees you, doesn't recognize you, moves on—"

"And I call out to him, and he turns around and takes a good look, and, well, you can guess what happened."

"How long did you go out with him?"

"Three weeks, four days."

Which meant they were done before the party where I met Dennis. And Mike. Mustn't forget Mike. "You didn't know his reputation?"

She turned away. "I'd heard. I thought, with me it would be different. All his girls think that, don't they?"

"I haven't met all his girls."

"But you've met a couple. That artist. Samantha, was that her name? And Trixie, of course. He was seeing both of them already when he was seeing me."

"Swearing the whole time it was you, you, nobody but you."

She nodded.

"Did he show you his health certificate?"

Another nod. "And to answer your next question, yes, it seemed a little odd that he had it so handy. But I was infatuated. I ignored things I shouldn't have."

"What happened when he dumped you?"

"He just called and said it wasn't working out. Fact is, I was kind of expecting it. I think I knew he was seeing other women. But Dennis, he had a way... you've probably heard all this."

"What happened after he called you?"

"I fell apart. I've never had a lot of success with men. Remember when I said I got surgery and the rest because people said I'd get more work? That was part of it, but a lot of it was stupid me thinking I'd attract more men if I were—"

"Perfect?"

She tossed off a glare, but it melted fast. "Closer to it, at any rate. And then when I got involved with Dennis, I built up my hopes, and of course the higher I built them the farther they fell when the inevitable happened."

"How far did you fall?"

"Big, big depression. Hiding in my bedroom, crying jags, all that."

I said nothing.

"I pulled out of it after a while. A couple of weeks. And—I know you're not going to believe this—Ambiance was a big part of it. Having my circle of people who cared about me, having Ike dispense his personal blend of psychobabble and religious piffle. I got better. I mean, I knew all along what an ass Dennis was. They just helped me admit it, admit I was better off without him."

She was wrong about one thing. I did believe her. It didn't matter how much drivel Ike pumped out. Bottom line was, having all those people who cared about her ... sure, it helped. I had no argument with that.

Only thing was, if she got better, it shot my theory to hell. Unless ...

"A little bit ago. You mentioned Trixie. You know her?"

"I've spent a little time with her here."

"Were you here the day she brought Dennis?"

"Yes."

"Did you speak to them?"

She pulled out the shears, moved to a fresh rosebush, attacked it with more ferocity than it deserved. "I turned a corner and there they were. You know what the bastard did?"

"He told Trixie you two had been seeing each other."

"Yes. But he—"

Her mouth quivered. She ambushed another cane. But she went after it too low, down where it was old and woody. The blade went partway in and got stuck. She squeezed. She twisted. She cursed. The branch withstood the assault.

I stepped over, took her hand, removed it from the pruner, which stayed embedded in the rose as I stood her straight. She looked in my eyes, then put her head on my shoulder and began to cry. No big, wracking sobs. No wailing. Just a gentle flow of tears. I wasn't sure there was even that until she raised her head and I saw the last few glistening on her cheek. I wiped them away with my finger.

She stepped back, smiled ruefully. "It was just the way he was. I know that, but just then … the way he told her we'd gone out, he made it sound like nothing, like a little fun between a couple of friends. And I knew soon she'd be facing the same thing, and after that more girls would, and it would probably go on forever." She returned to the latest rosebush and calmly, effortlessly, removed the shears from where they were stuck and snipped the cane off a little higher up. "I thought I got depressed the first time. This was worse. A lot worse. Before, it was just a stupid disappointment about a worthless man. This time, it was the combination of realizing, really realizing I meant absolutely nothing to him, and knowing how many more women he was going to hurt, and somehow I built that up into how many other guys were out there just like him, and women too, and then there was a suicide bombing in Israel and that same night we accidentally bombed a hospital in Iraq and it was like the weight of humanity had fallen down on my shoulders."

"I'm—"

"Don't say anything. You don't have to say anything."

She sheathed the shears, gathered the last couple of branches she'd cut, dropped them in the waste bin. "I was reduced to a total vegetable. I thought about... well, you know, ending it all. Next thing I knew I was in the hospital under a suicide watch."

"Were you in there the night Dennis was murdered?"

"Yes."

"When'd you get out?"

"Five or six days after he was killed. Somehow... I know it sounds awful, but hearing he was gone gave me hope that things could be right in the world. And that started me back to being better. That and the pills."

"What kind of pills?"

"They have me on Zoloft."

Just like someone else I knew. "I'm surprised they let you hear about stuff like Dennis in there."

"My mother told me." She eked out a smile. "She also told me that story John had her feed you about me disappearing and being estranged from the family and all that."

"I suppose she told him—Santini—what happened between you and Dennis."

"I wouldn't be surprised."

"Would you be surprised if he took revenge on behalf of his most valued employee and her daughter, and had Dennis whacked?"

Up until then, I hadn't been sure. Sure of who did it, sure

of whether this young woman knew. But I saw the hope as she thought I'd come to the wrong conclusion. I saw her turn the actress on. "I wouldn't be surprised at all."

I motioned for the pruning shears. She handed them over. I bent, took a bit off a cane. "This one would have gone off in the wrong direction," I said. "This'll make the plant bushier." I handed back the shears and she put them away. "It wouldn't be very smart for me to tell anyone about this, would it?"

"Not if you like living."

"That's pretty blunt."

"Just a piece of friendly advice."

I let it sink in. Then told her I was leaving. "Take care of that hand," I said.

"I will."

I turned, took a couple of steps toward the house, stopped and faced her again. "I just thought of something."

She knew I hadn't, but she let me get away with the Columbo routine. "What's that?"

"You said you knew Dennis before you saw him at the studio."

"Right."

"Mind telling me how?"

"My mom and Dennis's father. They've known each other a long time. I've known Dennis since I was a teenager."

I almost let it go at that. But you know me. "Santini didn't kill Dennis, and he didn't have anyone do it either."

Again, it was in her eyes. It's always in their eyes. "Sure he did."

"Forget it. I know what happened."

She licked her lips. "What are you going to do?"

"I'm not sure yet," I said, and walked away.

•

I drove back to L.A. picking away at the chain, the string of connections that explained how *A* eventually attached to *Z*. I was nearly sure before my second visit to Ambiance, and I'd just had it confirmed.

The string passed through Mike Lennox.

It was time to talk to him. And find out just how long I'd been played like a piano.

thirty-nine

I parked four blocks away, on the other side of Main. When I got near Mike's a cop car was blocking the narrow side street and another was at the curb on Pacific, in front of a suspiciously plain Pontiac. A pair of moustached officers stood by the second cop car. The prettiest pair of detectives you'll ever see hovered around the Pontiac. Starsky and Bitch, no doubt.

A Channel 6 news van showed up. The driver parked where mere mortals dare not, right behind the Pontiac. Out came Claudia Acuna. Surprised the hell out of me. A camera-woman followed and the two of them moved toward the beach.

The four law officers conferred. Two cops came out of the first police car and joined the party. A surfer dude came by, mumbled something to the gang of six, and headed for the beach. Starsky and Bitch gave Claudia and her pal a dirty look, then made for the house. They walked up the stairs to the apartment entrance. The uniforms spread out along the street. Claudia spewed commentary into her microphone.

Starsky pressed the doorbell. The door opened. Mike was there, in jeans and shirtless. Claudia and her accomplice moved closer. One of the uniforms came over, told them to step back. Words were exchanged. The cops won the argument.

Conversation at the top of the stairs. Mike and Starsky went inside. I tried to go down the street toward the beach, but one of the cops stopped me. I hustled around the block and approached from the other direction. L.A.'s finest had left that route clear.

Neighbors, seeing the excitement, congregated. Summer, the teenager who'd been left to "man" the shop when Mike and I went upstairs last time around, was standing on a park bench and yelling to someone up the boardwalk. She jumped down and ran toward whoever she'd been shouting at.

Like they'd heard jungle drums, people accumulated. The northbound and southbound flows—already heavy with the usual Saturday throng—merged and stopped. Within minutes at least a hundred people circulated in front of Feed Your Head and at the end of the narrow side street. There was a party atmosphere. Everyone knew something exciting was going on, though most of them didn't have a clue as to what it was.

And what of the cops? They were too busy rousting Mike to deal with crowd control. Only the fake surfer was in evidence, arguing with the guy who'd been Mike's designated driver the night he came over drunk.

Then one of the cops filtered out onto the boardwalk. He did a double take and yelled a name. Another cop came running. His look matched the first one's. They both disappeared again.

I checked the landing. Lu was standing out there, alone, perturbed. She scanned the crowd, turned in the direction all the cop cars were parked in, returned to the beach side. She looked right at me. Recognition dawned. Then somebody stumbled into me, I looked away, and when I checked again she was gone.

Summer came back from up the boardwalk. She had four or five men with her. The kind of men that, when tourists see them on their obligatory visit to Venice, they walk faster. They were burly and unshaven and the sleeves of their denim jackets were gone.

A knot formed around them. Old hippies and teenagers on skates and boomers whose shirts bore political slogans. I couldn't see Summer, but I could hear her, yelling about the pigs and the injustice of it all. Then, as one, they moved toward the foot of the stairs leading up to Mike's place.

On the landing outside his door, the woman he called Bitch appeared concerned. She knocked, the door opened, she went inside. One of the uniforms took up a position a couple of steps up from street level.

Someone started a chant. *Leave Mike a-lone! Leave Mike a-lone!* A lot of the crowd had no idea who Mike was. But everyone enjoys a good protest. The volume swelled. Someone added a low harmony voice.

Summer's Army reached the bottom of the stairs. The cop guarding the way yelled at them to disperse. Someone yelled, "Disperse, my ass!"

Up above, Mike's door opened. He and the two beautiful police came out. Mike had a Hawaiian shirt on and was carrying a jacket. Lu appeared momentarily, confused and concerned, then closed the door behind Mike and the cops.

The detectives conferred. I think the blond wanted to wait things out inside, but Starsky went all macho. They started down.

At the bottom of the stairs, Claudia and her camerawoman pushed their way to the front of the crowd. Claudia stuck her mic in one face, then another. She recorded a couple of timeless comments and directed the mic at the cop on the stairs. Like before, he told her to step back. She began to obey, but not quickly enough for the cop. He put a hand on Claudia's shoulder and shoved. A cry of *Free press! Free press!* mingled with the one about Mike.

Then Mike tripped. He and the two detectives were about halfway down the stairs, and he went tumbling the rest of the way, grabbing unsuccessfully for the railing. He crashed right into the uniform, pushing him into Claudia. She fell into one of Summer's creepy guys. The pretty police looked like someone had shit in their mousse. They pursued Mike down the stairs. The uniform was on the ground, trying to wrench his gun from its holster.

I headed for the center of the action, not knowing what I hoped to accomplish, but certain I needed to be there for Mike or Claudia or both. But dozens of other people had the same idea I did, and I couldn't get any closer. A cross-flow of humanity picked me up and deposited me back on the boardwalk.

Things were less crowded there. But a freak-out virus had attacked the crowd. People took the upheaval ten yards away as an excuse to act out their wildest instincts. A man in a judo outfit had a chokehold on a guy with a Gold's Gym tank top and muscles like The Rock. A glassy crash erupted from the pizza place next door to Feed Your Head. People pushed in and ran out bearing illicit slices.

A teenager on a skateboard skidded to a stop too close to an old man with a walking stick. The old man raised his cane. The kid took a swing at him. A middle-aged woman in running clothes stepped between them and got bopped for her trouble. A man moved in to break up the fracas. He got slugged too. It was the guy wearing the FREE HUEY shirt the day I came to talk to Lu. He fell from view. The old man beat the snot out of the teenager with his cane.

More smashing glass, more storefronts ruined. A woman ran by carrying at least a dozen boxes of sneakers, piled perilously atop one another in her outstretched arms. Another grabbed for the box on the top of the stack. The first bared her teeth and the second backed off.

A pear-shaped man with a scraggly ponytail and overalls kicked off yet another chant. *Fuck the pigs! Fuck the pigs!* When no one joined in, he quit it, sat down on a bench, began reading an antique copy of *The Fountainhead*. A seagull joined him and he pointed out a particularly interesting passage to it.

A little boy stood out in the middle of the boardwalk, crying for his mother. A dachshund chased its tail nearby. Its owner kept trying to grab its leash. Finally she did and the dachshund bit her knee.

Someone poked me in the back. I whirled around. It was a fat woman in *101 Dalmatians* pajamas. "You with the news?" she said. "You should see my collection. Fifteen thousand, four hundred and six dalmatians."

I said, "You must be very proud," spotted a lane opening up in the mob, and made like a fullback. Within seconds I was at the bottom of Mike's stairs. I couldn't see Claudia and I couldn't see Mike. I could see the camerawoman. Her camera was on the ground and some parts weren't attached that ought to have been.

A bottle splintered at my feet. I tripped over something and went sprawling. Someone landed on top of me and bounced off. I caught a glimpse of one of the mustachioed cops. He had his gun out and was hollering at people to cease and desist. No one paid him the slightest attention. I have to give the guy credit. He didn't shoot anyone.

Somebody reached out a hand and helped me up. When I got to my feet I saw it was Carrie. She was yelling at me. I pointed to a mound of writhing people. It seemed as good an answer as any, considering I had no idea what she was saying.

Far away, sirens sounded.

I caught a flash of Mike's Hawaiian shirt. I jumped over and began pulling people off a pile. Someone jerked on me from behind. I spun around. It was a square-faced man with a crewcut. I punched him in the ear and returned to undoing the pileup. Then Carrie was beside me. She was strong, that babyfaced young woman. She tossed aside a muscular black kid and one of Summer's Army like they were mannequins. Together we hauled off one of the fattest men I'd ever seen. He made the the uncle at Samantha's opening look like Tom Thumb. There under him we found Mike and The Detective Sometimes Known As Bitch.

Mike's legs were still pinned under God knew who. Carrie went after him, and I assigned myself the lady cop. I grabbed her under her arms, jerked her free, tossed her over my shoulder, stepped back. Her jacket was ripped, and she bled profusely from a gash over her eye. I carted her around under the stairs and laid her between a couple of garbage bins. I checked her over as best my limited knowledge of first aid would allow. I knelt, slapped her face half a dozen times, asked if she was all right. Finally I got an answer. "Pookie," she said.

"On his way," I said, and looked up. Carrie had Mike free and was helping him limp away. Starsky appeared in their path. He had his gun pointed at the two of them. "Stop right there," he said.

"Like hell I will," Carrie said. She tightened her grip around Mike's waist and tried going around the detective.

"I mean it, lady. Stop or I'll use this thing."

She looked him in the eye. "Then either use it or get out of my way and let me get my man to safety."

The gun wavered. So did Starsky. Then he stuffed the thing under his jacket and got on Mike's other side, and together they escorted him away from the roiling mob.

I stood and surveyed the carnage. Claudia had managed to break free and was, bless her heart, still relaying events into her mic. Given the state of the equipment—and of her camera person, who stood to one side, grimacing, holding one wrist with the other hand—it appeared unlikely that anything was going out over the airwaves.

Things were suddenly quieter. I looked around. Fewer people. More breaking glass from the direction of the board-walk. Then more. And shouts and screams and sirens. Some-body nearby was playing an electric guitar with the distortion turned to max. It was either "White Rabbit" or "Amazing Grace."

Fuck the pigs! was back, kept going by two old hippies and the little kid who'd been looking for his mother. He had a slice of pizza in his hand and all over his shirt.

I knelt back down to attend to the blond detective. "Freeze," said someone behind me.

I froze.

"Real slow now, stand up with your hands on top of your head."

I did.

"Now turn around."

I did. And found myself face-to-face with Starsky. He didn't look like a movie star anymore.

"I pulled her out," I said. "She needs medical attention."

"Sure, buddy. Now step away from her."

"She's bleeding like a—"

"I said step away from her!"

"Fine." I took two steps to my left. "Happy?"

"Shut up. Now lay down on the ground with your hands behind your back."

I might have talked my way out of it. But I blew it. "Listen, Pookie, there's no need to—"

I found myself flat on the sidewalk with my cheek rubbed raw. Something encircled my wrists. I heard a ratcheting sound. One of those plastic cable connectors they used for handcuffs. It tightened beyond comfort. They were going to have to amputate my hands because the tissue would die.

"Hey, buddy," I said. "Two things. Could you maybe loosen this? And will you please stop fucking with me and go tend to your partner there. She's badly hurt." The two requests were contradictory, but if I could get him going on either I'd be ahead of the game.

One of the uniforms appeared. The pretty boy told him to keep an eye on me, and finally went off to check on his partner. I jiggled my hands, pressed the wrists tightly together, managed to reduce the pressure to a bearable level.

"Joe!"

I craned my neck up. Claudia stood there, still clutching her microphone. Her clothing was ripped and her face scratched. One of the sleeves of her jacket was gone. So was one of her shoes.

I opened my mouth to respond, but a new cop grabbed her and hauled her away. They dragged me upright and off to a patrol car and shoved me in the back. They disappointed me. They didn't push my head down like in the movies.

forty

It was nine hours before the last police personnel left the riot scene in Venice. Nine hours during which dozens of residents were questioned, during which hordes of press and television personnel descended upon the neighborhood, during which legions of pundits analyzed the situation to death and pontificated on the sorry state of society.

What emerged from all the investigation and analysis was this:

Twenty-seven storefront windows along the boardwalk were smashed. But looting was minimal, limited only to pizza, ice cream novelties, and one or two Philly steak sandwiches. Plus thirteen pairs of sneakers which were taken from a tented booth near the center of activity, then mysteriously returned the next day, along with a note that said *i got cauhgt up in things*.

The only unbroken window along the string of smashed glass fronted an establishment called Feed Your Head. This shop sold paraphernalia for drug consumption and appreciation. It was owned by Michael Peter Lennox, fifty-two, whose apprehension for the murder of his son was the spark that set off the event. Mr. Lennox was treated by one of the medical personnel arriving at the scene in the wake of the unrest for a broken finger, a sprained ankle, and a fearsome bruise to the left thigh. He was then driven to LAPD's Pacific Division, where he was booked on suspicion of murder in the first degree in the death of his son Dennis.

Field reporter Claudia Acuna and cameraperson Felicia Alvarez of KIKB, Los Angeles Channel 6, were charged with inciting to riot for their role in touching off the fracas. The charges were quietly dropped two days later.

Twenty-four-year-old student and bodybuilder Clay Thayer, sixty-one-year-old community activist Harvey "Hemp" Hemphill, and ninety-three-year-old retiree Francois Dulac were booked on disorderly conduct charges. These charges were dropped almost immediately. A fourth man, Ju Daek Kim, was taken into custody, but mysteriously disappeared from police guardianship. "One second he was there, and the next he wasn't," reported the police officer who made the arrest.

No death was attributed to the riot. Injuries were light, given the magnitude and intensity of the proceedings. Thirty-six-year-old Patricia Frankfurter was treated at the scene for a dog bite to the knee. Five-year-old Vinnie James got to sit in a police cruiser while his mother, twenty-two-year-old envelope stuffer Stacie James, was rushed to the emergency room at Daniel Freeman Marina Hospital for the removal of a "really hurty" piece of debris from her right eye. Nineteen other citizens were treated on-scene for misfortunes ranging from a broken leg down to a severe paper cut. This last occurred when "Hemp" Hemphill aggressively stuffed an antiwar leaflet into the victim's hand.

Detective sergeant Mary Ventura, thirty-three, was also taken to Daniel Freeman. She recovered quickly from a blow to the forehead which opened a long, deep, but not particularly dangerous cut, and which caused a mild concussion. After several hours she remembered being dragged from under a pile of bodies by a man in a green shirt. This eventually resulted in the release from custody of fifty-year-old Joseph Portugal of Culver City. Mr. Portugal returned to his home and received aid and succor from his wife, Gina Vela, forty-eight. He then spent several hours trying unsuccessfully to discover the motivation behind the police's persecution of Michael Peter Lennox and, equally without success, attempting to achieve Mr. Lennox's release from custody.

forty-one

I called around some more Sunday morning and into the afternoon. No one at Channel 6 was willing to put me in touch with Claudia Acuna. I couldn't track down Alberta Burns. I did reach Hector Casillas, a detective I'd butted heads with on a couple of earlier homicides, but he either didn't know anything or wasn't telling.

I also got hold of Samantha, who said Carrie had been going through much the same thing I was, discovering only that Mike had been moved, either downtown or to Chatsworth way out in the Valley, depending on who one spoke to.

There was one more person I could call, and as the day went on the itch to do so grew. Gina thought I was crazy to even consider it. She was probably right. In the end it didn't matter, because he beat me to the punch.

The phone rang at two-thirty. "Hello?"

"Joseph?"

"Dad? Is something wrong?"

"Yes, something is wrong. What is wrong is that my son is a moron."

"You going to give me one of your be-careful talks?"

"No. It doesn't do any good, you're such a schmuck. Now come over here."

"I'm kind of busy—"

"Come. Now."

"Dad? Are you all right?"

"Just come." He hung up on me.

I rang the bell. My father opened it immediately, but instead of letting me in, he came out. He locked the door, checking it twice just like he always did when I was a kid.

I started asking questions. He told me to be quiet. There was something in his tone. I kept my mouth shut.

I walked with him over to Fairfax, down past Beverly, all the way to Farmers Market. I didn't say anything and neither did he. I hadn't walked this far with him since...maybe since ever.

We went into Du-Par's and were seated in a corner booth. We both ordered tea and blueberry pie. Then my father said we had someone else coming, and to bring him the same.

"Who's coming, Dad?" I thought I knew. The man I'd been thinking of calling earlier.

"You'll see," my father said.

"Someone I know?"

"Stop with the questions."

Uncomfortable silence. I looked out the window. A young Orthodox family went by. Father, mother, a boy, three girls. The mother wore the standard long dress and tennis shoes. One of the girls was skipping. Her mother watched her adoringly.

I looked at my father. "Do you miss Mom?"

His bottom lip puffed out. Then his face relaxed. "Every day."

"There doesn't come a day, after thirty-odd years, where you wake up one morning and say, okay, I can move on now?"

"You move on, but you still miss her. Don't you?"

"I was fifteen when she died. Sometimes I just remember her like I remember my teachers."

He frowned. Opened his mouth. Shut it.

I said, "Are you disappointed that I never gave you grandchildren?"

"Of course I am." He watched me. "What did you expect me to say? I see Leonard with his grandchildren, I see Catherine with hers, of course I want some."

"I'm sorry."

"Eh. It's not your fault you didn't meet the right girl until you were older."

The pie and tea arrived. A minute later, so did our tea-time companion. My suspicion had been correct. It was John Santini.

He sat beside me, said, "Probably didn't expect to see me again, eh, kid? You want to slide in so I can get the rest of my ass on this seat?" We arranged ourselves. Santini took a bite of pie. "Good stuff."

"What are you doing here?" I said.

My father smiled. He held out his hand, palm up. "Pay up," he said.

John Santini shook his head. He leaned to his right, extracted his wallet from his pants, removed a twenty from it. He handed it over to my father.

"What?" I said.

"Your old man thought that would be the first thing out of your mouth. Me, I figured you'd put two and two together. Or at least not ask something so—"

"Trite?"

"I was gonna say stupid."

"Now that I've asked my stupid question, why don't you answer it?"

"Pushy son of a bitch, aren't you? Horse, how'd you raise such a pushy bastard? What?"

"You actually called him 'Horse.'"

"Well, yeah, that's his name, Harold the Horse."

"I know that. It's just, actually hearing my father called 'Horse,' it's kind of surreal."

"You know why he's called that?"

"I don't think I want to."

"It doesn't have to do with his prick, if that's what you're worried about."

"Look, I'd love to hear where my father got his nickname, and I'm sure there's lots of other stories I'd like to hear you tell, but right now what I really want to hear is the answer to my question."

"Which was what I'm doing here."

"Right."

He looked around. It was an off hour, and no one was seated near us. Still he dropped his voice. "What I'm doing here is getting you to stop sticking your nose into the Lennox business."

I stared at him. I stared at my father. "Dad? You actually thought you had to bring in muscle to keep me out of harm's way?"

"Joseph, you can be such a schmuck sometimes."

"Agreed, but why—"

"Horse," Santini said.

"Umm?" my father said.

"You have to go to the bathroom."

My father thought about it. He put his hand on his stomach. "I have to go to the bathroom. The two of you will excuse me." He got up and headed for the restroom. Except he didn't get there. I saw him push open the door and go outside.

Santini got up, swung around to the other side of the booth, sat where my father had been. I thought of all those movies where someone has a gun under the table, pointed at the other person's crotch. "So," he said. "You know who did it?"

"Yes."

"Who?"

"Alma," I said.

"Now why would she do that?"

"Dennis screwed over Valerie like he screwed over so many other women. Alma found out."

"You think that's what happened?"

"Yeah. I'm right, aren't I?"

He stared at me, and I thought again of what he might have under the table.

"Yeah," he said. "You're right. I figured you were getting close, once I heard you went up to see Valerie again."

"How'd you find that out?"

"Not everyone that follows you around is as lousy at it as Sonny."

"Who was it?"

"Vito. Just the last day or so. He's pretty sneaky for such a big guy, don't you think? So tell me. How'd you figure it out?"

"When Lu went in and saw Dennis dead, the light was on. When I found his body, it was off. Somebody turned it off, and who else was there but the killer?"

"And you found out how nutty Alma is about turning off lights."

"She turned off the one in your office, the day I met her. Twice, she turned the one on her desk on just long enough to see what she had to, the day you were testing me."

"She wasn't gonna kill him, you know. Sometimes it just happens."

"And Lu? Why'd she have to bash Lu?"

"Would've seen her." A shrug. "She didn't hurt her bad."

Maybe on his scale, what happened to Lu equated to not hurt bad. "She could've died."

"She didn't."

I grabbed my teacup, drank most of it down. "Is Mike taking the fall?"

"Nah. That pretty-boy cop got a bug up his ass. Whole thing over in Venice was a big mistake. He's probably out by now."

"What've you got on him?"

"What's that mean?"

"You did something for him. You called in your favor. You had him set up this whole woman-at-the-hockey-game thing just to get me in to see you. So you could help me find her, supposedly, and then I'd owe you one."

"How do you know I even know the guy?"

"You know the guy."

"Yeah, okay, so I know him. So what?"

"See, when I first met Alma, I was surprised that, even across Staples, Mike would've mistaken her for Donna. More I thought about it, the less likely it seemed. But he never thought he saw her. That whole thing was a setup. What did he owe you for?"

"Had a little trouble with his store and the DEA, ten or twelve years back. I pulled some strings, helped him out."

"And you waited this long to call in your marker?"

"Sometimes it takes that long."

I tried to hold his gaze. "I can't just stand by and let Alma get away with murder."

"Even if I threaten to send some big guys after you?"

"Even if you do. But I think you won't."

"Why not?"

"Out of respect for my father."

"Kid. That's not how things work. Your father, I love him like a brother. Hadn't seen him in forty years, still I love him like a brother. But that don't mean anything."

"I'll take my chances."

"Ever had your kneecap shot?"

"No. Though I've been thinking about it since you swung around to the other side of the table. I never got fitted for concrete overshoes or had burning bamboo shoved under my fingernails either."

He broke out laughing. "You got some stones, I got to hand you that. You know, that bamboo business, that's not us, that's the Chinks."

"Doesn't matter. I still can't—"

He had his hands up in submission. "Yeah, yeah. I get it. I can't scare you. So I got to play the other card in my deck."

I leaned in. "You threatening my wife?"

He put his elbow on the table, laid his forehead in his palm, shook his head. "Jesus. Where do they get these ideas?" He picked his head up. "I don't threaten wives. I don't threaten kids. I don't threaten your fucking canaries, for Christ's sake."

"How do you know about my canaries?"

"Forget the goddamn canaries. I'm trying to conduct a little business here."

"Fine. So what's your other card?" I knew what was coming. But I wanted to hear it from him.

"You owe me one."

I looked in his eyes. I wondered what those eyes had seen. How many times they'd taken in scenes like the one in Dennis Lennox's den. "Yes," I said. "I owe you one."

"I'm calling in my marker."

"So helping me find somebody is worth turning a blind eye to murder?"

"A favor's a favor. You don't have big ones and small ones."

I looked out the window. The Orthodox family was still there. The four kids were holding hands, two by two.

"You're not sure," he said. "I understand. So I'm gonna go to the bathroom."

I didn't know how taking a leak was going to convince me of anything. Not until the place he vacated was taken by my third tea companion of the day.

Alma Rodriguez.

forty-two

I said, "I didn't see him call you."

Her gesture said, We have our ways. She said, "Do you have children?"

"Didn't the Great Santini Information Network give you the answer to that?"

"Sorry. I know you don't have children. If you did, maybe you'd understand better."

"Dennis Lennox screwed over dozens of women. None of the other parents felt it necessary to shoot him in the head."

"You didn't see her. She was close to suicide."

"She told me."

"Isn't the world better off without him?"

"Whose decision is that?"

"He was a terrible man. I did the world a favor by shooting him."

"I don't believe that, and neither do you. And anyway, he was about to change."

"Where'd you get an idea like that?"

I just knew the answer would go over well. "Ike Sunemori. The head guy up at Ambiance."

But she surprised me. She nodded and said, "That's what Dennis told me too. When I showed up at his house. He said he'd had ... what's that word?"

"An epiphany."

"Yeah," she said. "One of those. He'd had an epiphany and was going to make everything right, right there that night, with a bunch of people he'd dumped on lately. He said he'd called Valerie too, but couldn't get hold of her and was going to fix things with her later."

"And you shot him anyway."

"Not 'anyway.' I shot him *because* he said that. I thought he was making it all up, that he thought I was an idiot who'd believe such bullshit, and … what, you think I went up there intending to kill him?"

"The thought had crossed my mind."

"I wasn't going to use the damned gun. I don't know what I was going to do, but actually shooting him wasn't part of it. Then he fed me that epiphany thing, and turned away like I wasn't worth his attention, and next thing I knew I'd blown his face off."

"And Lu? The housekeeper?"

"I heard her coming. I wasn't going to shoot an innocent woman too. So I grabbed the first thing I could and hid behind the door and—"

"And clobbered her. And then you shut the light on the way out."

She shrugged. "My parents drilled it into me."

I tried to catch her eyes, but she wouldn't look at me. "And in the weeks since, have you ever thought he might have been sincere about changing?"

"Maybe."

"Because why else would he have gathered us all up there that night? I mean, I think that Ambiance bullshit your daughter's involved in is mostly a load of crud, but I've got to accept that every once in a while it resonates in someone and can make them have—"

"An epiphany."

"Yeah," I said. "One of those."

I looked out the window again. The Orthodox family was gone. Replaced by a couple of teenage girls. One was smoking, the other chewing gum with her mouth flapping open, and each had a ring in her navel. Someday they'd meet shits like Dennis. Everyone did. Didn't matter if they were male or female, rich or poor. Was the world any better if the shits were eliminated?

That was a question for bigger minds than mine. And a pointless one. Because, regardless of John Santini's past and possible present, I'd made an agreement with him. That someday I'd repay his favor with one of my own. There were no stipulations.

I turned my attention back inside. Santini was sitting opposite me, turned away, looking for the waitress. While I was inspecting the teenyboppers, Alma left and he came back. I didn't say anything, didn't make any sign that I'd noticed. I didn't have anything else to say to her.

Santini got the waitress's attention. "More pie, please. For him too." Indicating my father's piece, "And wrap this one up." He swiveled back to the table. He waited for me to say something.

I obliged. "You can get me to stop looking, but you know and I know the cops are a lot bigger threat to you—to Alma—than I ever was."

"Cops are taken care of."

"Just like that?"

He smiled. "It's complicated. Let's just say, everything's gonna turn out all right."

"You have a fall guy."

"You know what? I start telling you shit like this, you could get in trouble. Would make you an accessory after the fact."

"I'm already one."

"Are you?"

"Yeah."

"Meaning, when we get up from this table, we're gonna be even?"

"Yeah," I said. "We're gonna be even."

He pulled off those thick-framed glasses, squinted through them at the light, put them back on. "You're a good kid," he said. "It's tough finding people who're true to their word. You ever want a job in import-export, you come to me, okay?"

"You know and I know that's not likely to happen."

"You never know. Life deals you some funny hands."

Our seconds of pie arrived. The waitress boxed up my father's piece, cleared the other plates, asked if we wanted more hot water. Neither of us did. When she was gone I spoke. "You're not going to pull him back into a life of crime, are you?"

I regretted the words before they cleared my mouth. I saw his eyes narrow. I knew what he was going to do.

His fists flew up in front of him. "Every time I think I'm out…" Elbows jerked back, fists following. "They *pull* me back in. Jeez, I love doing that."

"That's the worst Pacino I've ever seen. Answer my question."

"Of course not, dumbass. Your pop's been straight for a long time. I'm not gonna fuck that up. We're just gonna socialize now and then. Now eat your pie."

"You're going to pay for this."

His expression darkened. "What the hell's that supposed to mean?"

I pointed at the table. "The pie. And the tea. You're going to pay for it."

The menace dissipated. A smile replaced it. "You're a funny kid. Fun to have around. You really ought to think about import-export."

I attacked my second slice of blueberry pie. No, I wasn't going to, at the ripe old age of fifty, suddenly become an import-export baron. Not yet, anyway. Maybe if the detective thing didn't work out...

I waited until his mouth was full and said, "You set the whole Donna thing up just so I'd owe you a favor."

"Jeez—" Bits of blueberry flew. "Are we back on that?"

"And I paid you back your favor. But when you set it up, you didn't know Alma was going to kill Dennis. So you didn't know I was going to repay you by letting her get away with it. So there was something else you were going to have me do."

"I was wondering when you were gonna get around to figuring that out."

"What was it?"

"I'm not gonna tell you."

"Why not?"

"Doesn't matter now."

"Did it have something to do with my father?"

"Why would you say that?"

"Just a guess. So what was it?"

He shook his head. "Not now."

"He's my father. I have a right to know."

He gave me five seconds of the other Santini. The one Gina and I had met at Fabrini's. "No. You don't."

Sometime, weeks, month, maybe years in the future, I was going to find out what his original plan was. And how it concerned my father. Of that I was sure.

But not right then. Not after seeing The Real Santini again. You think I'm an idiot?

We finished our second pieces of pie. Mine didn't sit well. I rubbed my stomach.

"That reminds me," he said. He dug into his pocket, came out with a vial, held it out to me. "Those stomach pills I promised."

"Is this a favor?"

"Nope. This is a gift."

I took the pills, popped one, shoved the rest in my pocket. He paid the bill, we got up and went outside. As, ever so civilized, we shook hands, I said, "Just one more thing..."

"Who are you, fuckin' Columbo?"

"If you can be Michael Corleone, I can be Colombo."

That got a big smile. "Shoot."

"Was Alma even at Staples that night?"

"Nope."

"Are those seats even yours?"

"Hell, no. I got better things to spend my money on."

"So when I was told they were yours, that was just so much horseshit, wasn't it?"

He caught my eyes. He smiled again. He said, "Been nice seeing you, kid. Keep in touch." He turned and walked away.

So that was it. The murder was solved and the person who did it was getting away with it and I didn't mind. Not much, anyway. People got away with murder every day. Everyone said so, so it had to be true, right?

I walked back to my father's house. I rang the bell and he let me in. Catherine and Leonard, he said, were at Beverly Center seeing the third *Lord of the Rings* movie. Rather, Catherine was seeing it; Leonard, being legally blind, was watching vague moving shapes on a big bright screen.

We sat at the table in the back yard and watched it get dark out. He picked at his leftover blueberry pie. Suddenly he was talking about his childhood. I found out things about him I'd never known. Like which elementary school he went to, and who his first girlfriend was, and how one of his best friends when he was a kid went off to the camp at Manzanar and never came back.

He told me the story of how he met my mother. I knew the basics, but most of it was new. It was a Romeo and Juliet tale of sorts, the Catholic girl and the Jewish boy, each family suspicious of the other until one night they all got drunk together on Chianti and Manischewitz and realized their commonalities were a lot greater than their differences. He told me my Aunt Esther disappeared into a back bedroom with my Uncle Anthony, and came out an hour later insisting all they'd done back there was discuss the Red Menace.

Eventually Catherine and Leonard returned. They came outside and said hello and Catherine asked if I wanted to stay for dinner. I told her I needed to get home to Gina. They went back in, and my father pulled out a half-smoked cigar and lit it. He blew a smoke ring, and we watched it dissipate into the near–dark.

"Everything get settled with John?" he said.

"Yeah."

"Anything we need to talk about?"

"No."

"So I don't have to worry about you for a while?"

"Well ..."

I told him about my new career.

When I was done he said, "I knew this was coming. You'll be careful?"

"I'll be careful."

Another puff. Another smoke ring. Then, "I have some-thing to tell you too." He snuffed the cigar on the underside of the table, made sure it was out, dropped it into his shirt pocket. "Mary Elizabeth and me. We're getting married."

"Dad, that's great."

"You're sure?"

"Of course I'm sure."

"You don't think I'm being unfaithful to your mother?"

"Dad..." I got up, knelt by him, put my arms around him. "I'm sure Mom would be ... is ... very glad that you've found someone."

"You like her?"

"Mary Elizabeth? Of course I do."

"You're not just saying that?"

"Of course I'm not. You know I like her. We get along great."

"There's just one thing."

"What's that?"

"I'm going to have Leonard be my best man."

"That's great."

"If he wants to."

"You haven't asked him yet?"

"I wanted you to be the first to know. You're not mad?"

"About what?"

"About not being the best man. Because you had me be yours."

"It doesn't matter. Not a bit."

"Leonard's old. He doesn't have a lot of years left. I think this would make him very happy. Maybe make up a little for him having to find another roommate."

"You're moving in with Mary Elizabeth?"

He shook his head. "She's selling her place. We're getting

a condo. We're too old to deal with a house and a yard and all that."

"What about your posies?"

"You can grow posies in pots. Place we get, we'll make sure it has a nice patio. With plenty of sun and plenty of room for posies in pots. So you're all right with this?"

"Of course. I'm ecstatic. For both of you."

"Not this, the wedding. This, the best man thing."

"I already said I was."

"You can be the head usher."

"I'd be the flower girl if you wanted me to."

Slowly, he smiled. I could smell the cigar smoke on him, bringing memories of summer twilights throwing a softball back and forth where my greenhouse now stood. Underneath the smoke was the harsh-soap-and-cologne scent of my father, the one I imagined I could smell all those years he was away at San Quentin.

"Yes, Joseph," he said. "I think you would."

I'd come to terms with Alma Rodriguez getting away with murder. But there were other things I didn't feel like letting people get away with. Three things, three people.

I talked it over with Gina. She told me not to bother. That I'd been shaken up enough by the goings-on of the last few weeks, and that there was nothing to be gained by stirring the pot. It was a perfunctory attempt at persuasion. She knew I was going to go ahead and stir.

forty-three

I called Claudia Acuna at Channel 6 and scheduled lunch. We walked to a Thai Dishes near the station. But when we reached it she kept going. I'd slowed to enter, caught up to her, said, "Not hungry?"

"You don't want to have lunch with me. You just want to give me a hard time for going back to work."

"Yeah."

"So go ahead. Yell at me."

"I'm not going to yell. I just don't understand. You seemed so happy."

She turned up a side street. It was lined with tiny homes with metal bars over their windows. We walked halfway to the next intersection before she said anything. "You know that joke about the man who gets a job cleaning up after the elephants at the circus?"

"'What, and leave show business?'"

A smile. "That's the one."

"Once you got what you wanted, it wasn't really what you wanted."

"It was that damned Madera. Seeing her face on the screen where mine used to be. She was *so* bad."

I remembered thinking she wasn't as terrible as I'd thought

she'd be. "And if she'd been the best young reporter you'd ever seen?"

"Wouldn't have made a difference. I'm addicted to the celebrity, as minor as it is."

"What about being happy for the rest of your life?"

"Bottom line? After that first flush of liberation, I was happier being on-screen doing car chases than off-screen watching them."

"I see."

"Don't be mad."

"I'm not mad. It's just...you had the opportunity to get what you wanted out of life, and you retreated to what you had before."

"That's not what I just said."

"What you just said is bullshit. You were too scared to change."

We stopped in front of a house with a big pomegranate tree in the front yard, overhanging the sidewalk. Most of the leaves were gone for the winter. A couple of lonely, fractured fruits remained up in the highest branches. She examined the tree, touched a twig, turned back to me. "You're right, of course."

"I know I am."

"But did you have to rub it in my face?"

I started us back toward the station. "That wasn't my intention."

"What was your intention?"

"Maybe to change your mind back."

"Go ahead and try."

"No. Because it's not going to do any good. Is it?"

"No."

"So, fine. It's your life."

We walked on in silence. We were almost back when I said, "I thought they were glad to be rid of you. How'd you get your job back?"

"I called in a favor."

"I see."

"Do you?"

"Believe me, I do."

"Because that's the way the world works, right?"

"Yeah," I said. "That's the way it works."

Having achieved such satisfaction from my showdown with Claudia Acuna, I moved on to the next.

I met Alberta Burns at the bagel place in Marina del Rey. We ordered and went outside, found a couple of chairs the birds hadn't messed up, took our places. "So," she said. "What do you want now?"

"You and my father. Both think I only want to see you when I need something."

She unwrapped her bagel. "This time's different, isn't it?"

"Yeah."

"How much do you know?"

"I know that John Santini found out about me from you. And that my father's name came up, and that was what got this whole thing with him started."

"You're better at this than I thought."

"I also know that you didn't really look anything up when I asked about those tickets. That—Jesus, you had me pegged—that you and he knew that if I had to find out whose tickets they were I'd go right to you."

"Stood to reason."

Except it wasn't me that thought of going to Burns. "Please tell me Gina wasn't in on this too." My stomach was jumping. I wished I'd brought Santini's pills.

"Now you're getting paranoid."

"She wasn't?"

"She wasn't."

"Why were you talking to Santini?"

"It was about something else entirely. Your name came up in passing."

"Alberta."

"Whoa," she said. You could count the times I'd called her by her first name on the fingers of Mickey Mouse's hand.

"You knew what I was asking."

"Hey, what about those Lakers?"

"Stop it."

She opened her bagel, found nothing unexpected, put the halves back together. "You want to know why I was in a position to be having a conversation with him at all."

"Uh-huh."

"And I can't tell you."

"Please. Cut the secretive shit."

"No, I can't. I'm sorry, Joe, I really can't."

"Can you tell me how long you've known him?"

"Almost ten years."

"And have you been involved with him all that time?"

"Part of what I can't tell you."

"Goddamn it, Burns."

"Maybe someday I can tell you. Maybe a day not too far off. But not now."

"I could go to the press."

"But you won't."

Of course I wouldn't. What would it accomplish? And why would I want to hold her up to the kind of inane public scrutiny my former comrade Claudia Acuna and her tribe would subject her to? "You owed him a favor, didn't you?"

"I owed him a few. I'm still in the red."

"What if I tried to find out the history without your cooperation?"

"Don't."

"Why not?"

"Because I'd have to stop you. And you wouldn't like how I would do that."

"Oooh, I'm scared."

"And he'd have to stop you too."

"And I wouldn't like how he did that?"

"You wouldn't care. You'd be dead."

"Oh." I picked up my bagel. Put it down. "There's one thing I don't—"

"The subject is *closed*."

She bit into her bagel. A dab of cream cheese deposited itself at the corner of her mouth. I touched myself in the same place, and she wiped it away.

"One more question," I said. "I promise, just one more, and we'll be done with this until you decide to bring it up again."

"Would it do me any good to say no?"

"Of course not."

"Then shoot."

"How did he manage to fix me up with Mike? I mean, he comes up with this plan, he drags Mike into it, and then I just happen to be at a party where Mike can latch onto me?"

"Why do you think he picked Mike?"

"I don't get you."

"It's simple. Once John decided to do this, he quizzed me about you. I mentioned your little friend next door. He knew Dennis produced her show, and that Mike was Dennis's father. That's when he picked Mike. Other circumstances, your friend was on a Bochco show or something, it would have been someone else. He's got lots of people in this town. Dozens. Hundreds."

A lot to think about. Santini's tentacles extended throughout Los Angeles. Who knew how many public figures were in his debt? And what he'd done to put them there?

But that wasn't what I found most interesting about this last disclosure. What I found most interesting was that she'd called him by his first name.

"Still buddies?" she said.

"Yeah."

"But you're still mad at me."

"A little."

"Trust me on this," she said. "All will be revealed. All in good time."

"It better be," I said.

A couple of days later, the police closed in on one Robert Leighton "Bobby Lee" Fillmore at his Gardena apartment. Shots were fired. Bobby Lee Fillmore died on the scene. The police announced the solution of the Dennis Lennox case. Bobby Lee's sister Janeen had worked in the commissary at the studio where Dennis had his office. They'd gone out a few times and Dennis had dumped her. Bobby Lee took offense and blew him away. When reporters searched down Janeen Fillmore for her comment, they found she'd returned to her Missouri home. When one went so far as to look for her there, she found a community intent on giving Janeen her privacy.

Bobby Lee Fillmore was a creepy little loser. No one would miss him. Probably not even his sister Janeen. If she even existed.

•

The day after Bobby Lee Fillmore's untimely demise, Gina and I were awakened by a hubbub in our back yard. We stumbled outside and found half a dozen men hard at work on our new master bedroom. When asked about the sudden burst of activity, the guy in charge gave me a queer grin and said something about an opening in the contractor's schedule. If I knew what he meant.

I knew what he meant. What I didn't know is if this added to my favor account with John Santini. Was it a favor if you didn't ask for it?

Spring eventually made its appearance. Our remodel, once it got going, was accomplished in record time. Gina and I greatly enjoyed our new bedroom. It's good knowing people in high places. Or low places. More I see, more I think they're the same places.

One thing we loved about our new bedroom hung over the long-anticipated fireplace. It was a painting of a woman in T-shirt and cutoffs standing by a lamppost near the El Rey Theatre. A sign on the lamppost said *Miracle Mile District*. Samantha dropped it by one Saturday afternoon. She said she had a new therapist. Things were going well. Another six months, she said, and she wouldn't be any crazier than I was.

They announced the schedules for the fall TV season. Though *Protect and Serve* and two of Dennis Lennox's sit-coms continued as before, *The Galahad Sisters* was no more. Stephanie Urbano, the blond sister, was scheduled for a new show about an ornithologist and a beekeeper who meet cute and fall in love. It was called *Birds and Bees*.

And Ronnie? With her name all over the papers, other producers got interested. So she let her firing stick. And moved to a new hour-long police drama called *Badges*. It was based on the exploits of a former LAPD homicide detective named Alberta Burns. Ronnie was cast as the young white detective taken under the wing of the older black one who was Burns's alter ego. Burns's partner Paul Witten was one of the producers. I had a small part in the pilot. Very small. "Over there, officer."

Eric Stahl continued at *Protect and Serve*. One morning in January a very large man materialized in his office and told him that if he ever went near Ronnie again, or if he ever even thought about using anything other than his natural charm to get a woman in bed with him, his two boys would be short both a mother and a father.

I owed John Santini one again, and I wasn't too surprised to find that it didn't bother me very much. Part Two of *The Life of Joe* was beginning, and I had a feeling that John—as I found myself thinking of him—was going to be of as much use to me as I was to him.

I'd never gotten around to dealing with the last person who'd let me down. I talked to him on the phone a few times, but sometimes you need to see a person's face, and as the days grew longer and warmer I never got to do that. As with so many things, the more time went by, the less important it became. Maybe I'd deal with it someday. Maybe I wouldn't.

It was early on a Sunday evening. We were at the tail end of a barbecue in my back yard. My father was there with his new bride Mary Elizabeth, Elaine and Wayne and their kids, Frampton Washington and his family, now officially including Aricela. Theta was there, but Ronnie'd gone away for the weekend with a hunky actor she met at a screening.

The doorbell rang. Gina got up and went through the

house to get it. She came back and told me to go inside. Mike Lennox was there. His hair poked out in odd directions, bringing memories of the day after his son was killed. His face was pale and the collar of his shirt was tucked under on one side.

I knew why he was there. That low-grade telepathy again. But I waited for him to speak.

"She's dead," he said.

forty-four

When he got off the phone with the embassy in Beijing, he wept, and when he was done with that he decided to kill himself. He got as far as finding the gun he'd bought for "protection" ten years back and never used. Then he decided killing himself would stain Donna's memory, and he knew he needed help. Lu had moved up to live with her kids in San Francisco. None of his Venice crew fit the bill. That left me. He looked up my number, called it five, six, seven times over the course of an hour. Finally he drove over. Later, we found the phone in Gina's office, our old bedroom, off the hook. One of the kids must have knocked it off.

"What'd they say?" I asked. "The embassy people."

"They found her bones."

"Jeez, Mike, I'm sorry."

"Some whack job, hundred miles from where she disappeared. You don't think of serial killers in China, do you?"

"No."

"Had nine or ten of 'em buried in his back yard. They figured out a few so far. All Chinese except Donna."

"Dental records?"

"Yeah. The embassy's had 'em the whole time. They found the bones three, four days ago."

"And they're sure?"

"Yeah."

"Hey, man, I'm sorry."

"Thanks, man. Funny. This happened a few months ago, I wouldn't have had you trying to find—"

Did he really think I didn't know the whole thing with the woman at Staples Center was a sham?

Did it even matter that it was?

"No big deal," I said. "I was happy to do it. What can I do now?"

"Take a ride with me."

His Mustang was parked at the curb. "I'll drive," I said.

"Probably better." He handed over the keys, I adjusted the seat, we took off.

I got us to Pacific Coast Highway, where we could watch the sun setting to our left. Pink light suffused the sky and the ocean turned greenish black. Mike made a cigarette appear, smoked it down, tossed the butt out the window. He talked about Donna. About Dennis too, but mostly about Donna. It was her eulogy.

We drove to Zuma Beach. He dredged up a couple of blankets from the trunk and we trekked out onto the sand. Mike kept talking nonstop; then after an hour, when the sky was black and the stars were shining, he suddenly shut up. I sat there, wishing I had a jacket.

Eventually he said, "Remember at Staples when I went running after—"

"Let's not talk about that."

"But I need you to know. There wasn't—"

"I know. Just shut up about it, all right? I know all about it."

"And you didn't—"

"I said shut up, okay?"

Neither of us said anything for a long time. Down the beach someone had a boombox, and they were playing one of the countless Rolling Stones greatest-hits collections. "She's a Rainbow" came on, and Mike started singing along. I joined in, and we stumbled through to the end. We were laughing at the finish. Something had broken free.

We talked about everything and nothing. Mostly war stories, about music and drugs and insane road trips with birdbrained companions. I recounted that long-ago morning at Pyramid Lake with Sarah and Tony, and when I mentioned mescaline he launched into a story about when he was in college and he and a couple of friends piled into an old Renault and drove two hundred miles to score some, ending up spending the night on the floor of an apartment in New Paltz, New York, with a chick who blew two of them and fell asleep working on the third. I asked his place in the sequence. He said, "A gentleman never tells."

We wrapped our blankets around us and sat there all night, one or the other occasionally wandering away in search of a place to take a leak. Then suddenly, as the sky began to brighten at our backs, he returned to Donna. He said a lot of the same things he'd said the night before. Somewhere along the line I realized he was crying.

I remembered Pyramid Lake, and how good it felt when Sarah put her arm around me. My blanket and I inched over, and I wrapped him up, and we sat like that until the first sliver of sunlight brightened the sand.

acknowledgements

My sincere thanks:

To Jim Pascoe and Tom Fassbender, for letting Joe continue his detective act, and for their excellent comments on the first draft.

To Maryelizabeth Hart, who inspired "But I was purple."

To Olivia Bell, Brian Festerling, Michelle Fitzpatrick, Kristen Isaacson, Annie Thayer Jacquelin, Lisa Manterfield, Latrice McGlothin, Michelle Menna, Clay Norman, Stephanie Rausch, and Tricia Urbano Voltz, my day job colleagues, for all the laughs, and for providing excellent fodder for character names.

To Andrea Cohen, my wife, for everything.

Finally, I want to thank William Relling Jr., to whose memory this book is dedicated. Bill was my first writing teacher, and the one from whom I learned the most, including the greatest of all tips: kill your darlings. Bill's blue pencil struck countless darlings from my early stories and attempts at novels, and my writing is very much the better for it. He was gone much too soon, and I miss him greatly.